undone

USA TODAY BESTSELLING AUTHOR
KARA KENDRICK

Read UNEXPECTED - the Prequel for FREE!
https://karakendrick.com/unexpected/

To the brokenhearted –

May you find peace someday soon.

AUTHOR NOTE

Dear Reader,

This book discusses past pregnancy loss and contains a dream sequence that may be sensitive to some.

ABOUT THIS BOOK

I've only ever loved one woman.

Juliet Capelli.

The one person I can't have. Bad blood has run between our two families for generations—**and she's on the wrong side of the feud.**

Now she's back in town, and I can't seem to stay away. From her sexy curves, her beguiling eyes, that sassy mouth.

But it's going to take more than us sliding back into my sheets to get her to trust me again. Fifteen years ago, I broke her heart to protect her from her toxic brothers.

Can I prove to her that we deserve a second chance?

Everyone is against us. I only hope the sins of the past can be undone.

PROLOGUE

FIFTEEN YEARS AGO . . .

Rose Queen: Call me

King of My Heart: Everything okay?

Rose Queen: I think so. It depends

King of My Heart: ?

Rose Queen: We need to talk

King of My Heart: I'm feeding the horses with Rome. You okay? I can't get away for another hour or so

Rose Queen: I'm fine right now

King of My Heart: Your brothers didn't find anything out, did they? You're safe?

Rose Queen: Yes, babe. All good. But I have news

King of My Heart: Good news? Bad news?

Rose Queen: I think it's good. I hope you will too

King of My Heart: Now I'm nervous

Rose Queen: Me too

King of My Heart: I'll get Rome to finish up here. Meet at our spot in 30?

Rose Queen: Ok

King of My Heart: See you soon

Rose Queen: Love you

King of My Heart: Love you too babe

1

KING

PRESENT DAY

ERRAND DAY.

Twice a month I head into town to get supplies, rain or shine. Today's that day.

I don't much care for errand day. Leaving the wide-open space of the ranch and venturing into Seaglass Beach—where there are bound to be tourists and, let's be honest, other people too—isn't my idea of a good time.

But it must be done. Much as I'd love to be 100 percent self-sufficient, I still need gas, supplies, and the occasional taco.

Although it's not seven a.m. yet, I'm already bumping down the long gravel drive toward the main road. The ranch fades in my rearview as I pick up speed, the ground changing to smooth pavement beneath my tires. At least the sun's peeking out, turning the sky a dusty blue. We've had a ton of rain this past week. Good for the grass, not so great for the mood.

I crank up the radio to Chris Stapleton belting out "White Horse," roll my window down to catch the first scent of the ocean. One of the only redeeming factors of town, really. That and my siblings, I suppose. All three of them live up here. I usually make at least a half day out of the trip, catching up with Roman or Parker for lunch or the occasional beer before heading back home. Sometimes I even swing by the inn to say hi to Poppy, but she's usually bustling about, helping guests. I need to make a freaking appointment to get face time with my sister.

Traffic's light at this time of day, the streets almost empty. People will be stirring soon, heading off to work, school, or the beach, but I'll be knee-deep in horse feed by then.

After glancing down at my gas gauge, I make a quick turn into the only station in town. I still have a quarter of a tank, but might as well fill up while I'm here. Maybe grab a quick coffee to go.

I pull up next to an empty pump and hop out of my truck, going through the familiar motions. I slide my credit card into the reader and am busy selecting the fuel grade when a white blur slams into the open spot directly across from me. I glance up, wondering what the damn hurry is as the driver flies out of the beat-up Toyota SUV and rushes to the pump.

Shit.

My gaze locks on an all-too-familiar pair of hazel eyes, fringed by dark lashes, and my entire body tenses. The pump beeps at me to remove my card—*beep, beep, beep*—

loud and insistent, but I'm frozen in place. Heart pounding double time, palms sweating, my mouth dry as dust.

Juliet squares up, flips her wavy hair over her shoulder, and blinks. Once, twice. A soft pink flush creeps up her neck all the way to her cheeks, and her full lips press into a tight line.

"King."

Her voice is neutral, giving nothing away.

"Juliet." I tip my hat at her, all cool, calm, and cordial, even as my gut churns.

She turns her attention to the task of pumping gas, and I try mightily not to hyperventilate.

I know running into her is a risk I take every time I leave the ranch, but it doesn't make it any easier when it happens.

It's like my worst fears colliding—peopling and *her*—all before eight a.m.

"You gonna take your card out, or are you gonna let it beep in there all morning?" The corner of her lip tips up, and I'm rocketed out of my trance.

"Oh. Yeah. Right." I snatch the card out of the machine, and the word *ERROR* flickers on the screen in front of me. "Shit," I mutter, jamming my card back in.

CARD READ ERROR.

"What the—" I fumble with the card, pulling it back out.

Backward. I put the damn thing in backward.

Trying again, I shove the card back in and wait for the go-ahead to enter my zip code. I try to focus on the pump and not the woman on the other side, a mere foot away from me.

Not on the way that black T-shirt clings to her curves,

not on the smattering of freckles dancing across the bridge of her nose, not on the delicate slope of her neck, the dip of her collarbone, where her skin's so soft and tender. Like a ripe, juicy peach at peak harvest you're dying to sink your teeth into.

The card reader beeps, and this time I manage to pull the plastic out successfully and punch in the right numbers. I lift the gas nozzle, tap the "Regular" fuel button, and start pumping, averting my eyes from Juliet. Instead, I focus on the convenience store, drumming my fingers on the yellow rubber handle to pass the time.

Which crawls, by the way. This must be the slowest gas pump on the whole fucking planet, swear to goodness. Juliet finishes up—the scrape of metal on metal alerts me to the fact—and I breathe a tiny sigh of relief as she opens the door of her vehicle.

But she doesn't climb in and drive off into the sunrise.

Nope. Instead, she grabs her purse and sashays past me into the building, hips swaying side to side.

Damn. I really wanted a coffee too.

At this rate she'll probably be done in there before I finish pumping.

Thump. The lever pops up, signaling the tank is full. I replace the nozzle and shut the gas tank door.

Should I go in there? Stall here until she comes out? Or forget the whole coffee plan altogether?

Taking a deep breath, I weigh my options before deciding to just go for it. I'm a grown-ass man, and I want a coffee, dammit. It'll only take a few seconds—what's the worst that could happen? So I see her again, no biggie.

After locking my truck, I head across the parking lot, shoving a hand in my pocket. All nonchalant.

I push through the door into the small space and shoot a quick wave at Barty, the twentysomething-year-old kid standing at the register.

"Morning, King."

"Morning," I half grunt, rounding the corner and heading back toward the coffee station.

"Aah!" A high-pitched squeal startles me as I collide with an outstretched Styrofoam cup, hot coffee splashing down the front of my flannel shirt. A dark-brown stain blooms over the blue-and-white-checked fabric, now sticking to my skin.

"Well, shit." I pull my shirt away from my body and shake off as much of the hot liquid as I can, then stalk over to the Formica counter, where I pluck white square napkins from the tall pile.

"Oh my gosh, I'm so sorry, King." Juliet trails behind me; then her small hands are dabbing at my shirt, trying to sop up the spill with flimsy gas station napkins. Tiny pulses hit my chest, and my heart's banging so hard I'm certain she can hear it, feel it beneath the wet material.

She's inches from me now, her fresh cotton scent mixing with the strong smell of dark roast and hitting me straight in the nostrils. Every inch of me prickles like I'm on fire as I fight against the sudden hard-on springing to life in my jeans.

Hopefully she stays focused on my chest, because that situation's gonna be pretty damn obvious in a few seconds.

It's her voice that gets to me. Every single time. Soft, seductive, almost a purr deep down in her throat. The vibrations so low only the two of us can hear.

Sexy as hell.

I shouldn't have come in here. This was a big mistake.

"It's fine." I step back, putting space between us. Her hands flutter through the air, suddenly taskless, clutching the soggy napkins.

Against my better judgment, I let my eyes slide to hers, sending a sharp jolt straight through me.

I'll never get over those eyes, the bright ring of green blending into a cocoa center, with gold flecks that sparkle in the sunlight. The way she stares straight at you, all wide-eyed and innocent.

My mom used to say her eyes were *beguiling*. I didn't even know what that meant until I looked it up in the dictionary.

Beguiling /be·guil·ing/ (*adjective*) : charming, enchanting. Highly attractive and tempting.

Tempting is right.

Heat creeps up my chest to my face, and I'm having a hard time getting air into my lungs. A warm cup of joe is no longer important—I need to get out of here right fucking now.

"I can't believe I did that. I'm really sorry." Juliet gnaws at her bottom lip, and damn if I can't stop staring.

Tearing my gaze from her mouth, I somehow force words out, my voice harsher than I mean it to be.

"Whatever, it's fine. I have more shirts."

She swallows hard, and I'm in a weird time vortex where everything's moving fast and slow at the same time. I shove my sweaty palms into my back pockets, try to act casual and downplay the panic attack I'm about to have right here in the gas station.

Taking a step to the right, I attempt to move around

her. Juliet moves to her left, and we're still face-to-face with each other.

"Sorry." She blushes, her cheeks bright-pink splotches, and moves in the other direction at the same moment I slide over to the left. Now we're boot to sneaker, locked in an awkward dance.

"Sorry," I grumble, tipping my hat to her. "Ladies first."

I take a big step to the side, giving her ample space to pass.

"Thanks. I'm just gonna get a refill." She waves her mostly empty cup in the air, her glossy lips screwed up in embarrassment.

"I'll get out of your way then."

Without another moment of hesitation, I hustle out of the gas station, not even bothering to wave goodbye to Barty.

Head pounding, I bolt to my truck, then unlock the door and launch myself into the driver's seat. I slam the door shut, fire up the engine, and peel out of the lot before Juliet exits with her refreshed coffee.

It's been a helluva morning, and it's not even eight a.m. yet.

2

JULIET

Well, that was something. I've been back in Seaglass Beach for a few months, but running into King hasn't gotten any easier.

Luckily it doesn't happen all that often. Total bad luck that I ran into him this morning.

Literally.

He's still the same old grumpy King. Always serious, no sense of humor. To be fair, I did douse him with piping-hot coffee and ruin his shirt, but still. He's the one who's globally in the wrong, not me. You'd think he'd be a little nicer.

No, you wouldn't.

Nice isn't King's style. Politely aloof is more like it. Not cold, exactly. But no one's describing him as warm and fuzzy anytime soon.

He used to be. With you.

But that was a long, long time ago. Before everything happened and my life spiraled out of control.

Stop. Don't go there.

I shake my head, trying to dislodge the unbidden memories flooding my mind.

Our spot at the lake. King's strong arms wrapped around me as I gazed up into his deep-blue eyes. Trusting him fully.

The barn. Our first time together, hiding out with the horses. To this day the warm scent of hay makes my thighs clench.

Lying in the back of his truck at the edge of the woods, cuddling under a fuzzy blanket, and staring up at the thousands of stars in the sky.

With King I always felt safe, protected.

Until I didn't.

I huff out a shaky breath, my head throbbing. At least I have coffee.

Taking a sip, I shut my eyes and focus on the warm liquid sliding down my throat, trying to ground myself in the moment to stop the spinning.

Maybe moving back home was a mistake.

I'm not sure if I can live in the same place as him and be okay. I thought I was over it all—over him—but now I'm not so sure.

Every time I see him, my body reacts. Heart banging, chest flushing, heat unfurling deep in my belly.

Basically the exact opposite of what's going on in my mind. My brain knows it's a bad fucking idea. We'll never be together—too much has happened. Unfortunately, the rest of my system isn't getting the message. Especially from the waist down.

Damn him and his amazing dick.

You still want him.

No, I definitely do not. Sure, his pecs felt pretty damn

spectacular when I was patting him dry. Even bigger and stronger than I remembered. And time only made him more handsome—he actually looks good with the salt-and-pepper stubble, the tiny crinkles around his eyes.

So fucking unfair how men get better looking doing the bare minimum skin care, like fine wines or something, while women spend hundreds of dollars on wrinkle creams and serums and still seem to lose the battle with age.

Well, King's winning, and it's kind of pissing me off.

He broke your heart. Move the fuck on.

Still, my pussy tingles thinking about him, shock waves of desire rippling through me.

Dammit. This isn't supposed to be happening. It's not in the plan.

I grip the Styrofoam cup so tightly it squeaks beneath my fingers, and I shift in my seat, trying to relax. To focus on something—anything—other than King Montgomery.

Buzz, buzz.

The vibration of my cell jolts me back to reality. I grab my phone and stare down at the message.

Cash: You going to see Jagger today?

My older brother is the last thing I want to think about today.

Juliet: Wasn't planning on it

Cash: Come on, sis. It's your turn

Juliet: Can't Damon go? I have to work. And it's not my turn

Cash: He can't. We're collecting rents today

Cash and Damon are the only landlords on the planet who make house calls to get their rent money. Granted, probably half of their clientele don't have bank accounts, being on the wrong side of the law and all. And I don't want to know what goes down when my brothers show up and the tenants can't pay. It's a damn miracle all three of them aren't in jail.

Juliet: Fine. But you two owe me. I'm not going next month

Cash: Thanks, sis. You're the bomb

I roll my eyes at the phone, knowing full well the two of them will try to sucker me into going next month too. But I'm going to stick to my guns. For real this time.

Visiting Jagger in jail isn't my idea of fun. He's never been nice to me, not even when we were younger and still living at home. My brother's an asshole and always has been. I do feel slightly guilty that he's in there in the first place, though. If I hadn't turned over those papers to King, the three of them may have gotten away with the fake documents and won the lawsuit. But I couldn't let them steal the Seaglass Inn from the Montgomerys. It wasn't right.

So now I trudge over to the jail and play the role of the dutiful sister, standing by her brother in his time of need. All to assuage my feelings of guilt over doing the moral thing.

FML.

Which is why King told you to leave Seaglass Beach in the first place. To get away from your family, have a fresh start.

But nothing ever felt right the entire time I was away. I was like a ship tossing on a choppy sea, navigating through unknown waters. No compass, no direction. All I wanted was to come back home.

Totally fucking irrational, I know.

I missed the beach. I missed the town. I even missed my asshole brothers.

You missed King.

Maybe the old King. Not the King I left behind the day I fled from here.

Hard, angry King. His face stony, shoulders square, arms crossed over his chest. I can still see him standing there, scowling at me, telling me to go. Start over somewhere. Somewhere far, far away. From him, from us. From the life we were supposed to have together.

A sharp pain stabs me in the chest, stealing the breath from my lungs.

After all these years, I thought this would be easier.

But it isn't.

Time's healed nothing. I still have a gaping hole inside me, and I can't seem to fill it with anything. Not with a job, a man, friends, food, alcohol, a fucking hobby.

Nothing takes away the pain. I sit with it. Every. Single. Day. Sometimes it's dull, but it's always there. A deep black hole, pulsating with every beat of my heart.

Because I survived.

I'm a survivor.

Honk, honk!

Glancing in my rearview, I toss my hand in the air, signaling I'm leaving, and then turn the key in the ignition.

I wonder how many minutes I've been sitting at this gas pump. Five, ten, fifteen? Time slips away from me now, one of the main reasons I dropped out of school. I couldn't get my shit together, turn in assignments, or make it to class on time.

I look both ways before pulling onto A1A and heading across town toward the jail. Might as well get this over with before work—I'd rather not stress about the visit all damn day. Going into the jail creeps me out, if I'm being honest. It's bad enough I have to see my brother, but the leers from the other inmates are just as bad.

Ten minutes later I'm rolling my window down and identifying myself to the security guard. Thus begins the long, slow check-in process. It's as hard to get in here as any A-list party—not that I've been to any of those, but I imagine it's not easy. There's a visitor list, and you have to apply through the state and everything. A real pain in the ass, all to go see my jerky brother. Now I'm on a verified list I never wanted to be part of, thanks to Jagger and his stupid criminal ways.

"Juliet Capelli, here to see Jagger Capelli." I hand over my ID, tapping my steering wheel nervously. Every time I come here I'm on edge, I swear.

"Thank you, miss. Have a good visit."

As if.

The guard hands my ID back, and I roll into the parking lot, taking the first empty spot I see. Anything to get this over with as quickly as possible.

Clutching my ID, my cell, and my keys, I lock the car, leaving everything else behind. The less I take in with me, the less they have to search and the faster I'll be out of here.

With quick strides I head into the industrial-gray cinder block building. I drop all my belongings in a small plastic bin, then walk through the metal detector. Next I'm ushered into a windowless room where a guard pats me down. Guess they figure lawbreaking runs in families. After that, a different guard leads me down a dim, cold hallway to a brightly lit room with tables, chairs, and glass windows all around, like a fish tank. No funny business goes on here because armed guards lean on the walls, eavesdropping on conversations. Real private and cozy. I especially like the metal chairs and the flickering fluorescent lights specially designed to induce migraines.

I take a seat and wait for Jagger to appear, crossing and uncrossing my legs, trying to get comfortable. Futile effort under the circumstances, but I don't have anything else to do. Finally, he strolls in, acting like I have all day or something.

"Sis, always so great to see you." Jagger sinks into the chair directly across from me, a cocky grin on his bearded face. He's paler than I remember, probably not getting as much outdoor time as he's used to.

"Hey. How're things?" I pick at a hangnail, willing the minutes to tick by.

"Same old, same old. The food sucks, but somebody bought the MMA fight on pay-per-view last week, so that was all right. How's business?"

"At the Tipsy Taco? Swell. Margaritas flowing, especially on Taco Tuesday."

"You know what I mean. Don't be a smart-ass."

"You don't get to tell me how I can and can't be, Jagger. You're currently in jail, remember?"

He leans forward, elbows on the table, and I note that

orange really isn't Jagger's color. Washes him out and emphasizes the dark circles under his eyes.

"I know it was you." Jagger keeps his voice low so the guards can't hear.

Stay calm. There's no way he has any proof of anything.

"What are you talking about, Jagger?" I arch a brow, acting coy.

"You turned the maps over to your little prince. Don't sit here and play all innocent with me, Juliet."

"I did no such thing. Why would I do that, Jags?"

He runs a hand over his chin. "I dunno, Jules. You tell me."

We stare at each other for one minute, two, the wall clock ticking loudly behind me. I fervently wish someone else would walk in and distract him, but we're alone. Morning visits aren't super popular with the criminal crowd.

I shrug. "I told you I didn't do it. Case closed."

Jagger bangs his fist hard, handcuffs clanging on the plastic table, and I jump, my butt flying off the metal chair.

"Bullshit. There's no other way the judge could get those docs. It had to be you. Cash and Damon would never." He glares at me, his dark eyes cold.

Fear pricks at the nape of my neck, but I try to stay calm. He *is* my brother. It's not like he's going to hurt me or anything.

"Believe what you want. I'm telling you I didn't do anything wrong."

He licks his lower lip, slow, like a cat watching a mouse right before he pounces. Every cell in my body tells me to get the hell out of there, but I know that would be way too suspicious.

"Anyway—" I attempt to change the subject.

"Are you screwing him?"

My face burns at the accusation, the guard's attention now piqued.

"What? Who? No!"

"I didn't even answer the *who* yet, Juliet. And here you're already answering the question. Not too convincing."

"Fuck off, Jags. I'm not—and even if I were, it'd be none of your damn business."

He leans across the table, moving in close enough that I catch the faint smell of bleach from his shirt.

"You're my sister. You'll always be my damn business. And I don't like that guy. Never have."

"Good thing you're not screwing him then, huh?"

"Ha. Ha. Ha. Real fucking funny, Jules. So you are screwing him then?"

"I didn't say that. I told you I'm not."

"So you backstabbed me for nothing? It would have felt better if it were over dick."

I blow out a breath, annoyed. "You have anything else to talk about this morning, or are we done here?"

"Jules." Jagger reaches for my hand, but the guard steps forward, tsking at him. He pulls his shackled hands back but keeps his eyes lasered on my face. "You know the Montgomerys are bad news. Stay away from the prince and we'll all be happy."

I hate that my brother's telling me what to do, trying to control me from jail. But I also want him to get off my back, so I cave.

"That's the plan, Jags."

"We're on the same motherfucking page then. How are

Cash and Damon doing?" Jagger easily shifts the conversation to his business dealings, and I go with it, telling him what little I know of their activities. The minutes roll by, and finally time's up.

"Great to see you, Jules." Jagger winks at me, the guard grabbing him by the shoulder and pulling him up and out of the chair.

"Stay safe."

"I will, don't worry about me. I'm running this joint."

Knowing Jagger, he probably is. After his jail stay, he'll likely get into even more trouble, what with all his newfound connections.

"See you next time, sis. And don't forget—I have eyes everywhere. I'll know if you're lying to me about the prince."

I stand up and flick him off. "Keep your eyes on your own paper, Jags. We'll all be happier that way."

"Bye, little sis." He blows me a kiss over his shoulder as he shuffles away with the guard.

Good to know Jagger's still a problem, even behind bars. Super.

Not that anything's going to happen between me and King anyway. I can't risk my heart breaking all over again after I finally pieced it back together.

I just need to peacefully coexist with the man in our hometown. That's it.

Why does that feel like a nearly impossible goal?

3

KING

RUNNING INTO JULIET TANKED MY DAMN MORNING. Besides ruining my shirt, she spoiled my mood. The only thing that could make errand day worse is a full-blown panic attack in the middle of town.

Mission accomplished, Jules. Thanks a fucking lot.

After I finish hyperventilating, I somehow manage to make it to Seaglass Supply and load up on stuff I need for the ranch: horse feed, meds, shampoo. I have a standing order, so it takes less than an hour. Good thing, because my head's still pounding. Missing out on the caffeine fix from the gas station, I guess.

Even though fancy, overpriced coffee's not really my style, I reluctantly hit up Coastal Coffee. I don't think I can make it all the way until lunch without caffeine.

The door jingles as I push into the airy café. They have to overcharge for their brew just to afford the carrying costs here. The location's prime—right in the center of town square—and the furniture's beachy chic. Real designer.

Stalking up to the counter, I wait for the barista to take my order. She's engrossed in her phone—probably some social media bullshit.

I clear my throat and her head pops up.

"Oh, hey, sorry." She shoves her cell into her apron pocket and sidles up to the register.

"I'll have a large coffee. Black, with room for cream."

"Dark roast, light roast, medium roast, or special blend?"

"Uh . . ." I stare up at the menu board, debating. "Medium's fine."

"Regular cream or plant based?"

"Regular."

"And you said *gargantuan*, right?"

"Is that a large?"

"We have mini, midi, grand, and gargantuan."

"Oh. Grand is fine."

"Cool. That'll be five fifty."

"Five fifty. Freaking ridiculous," I mutter, rifling through my wallet and pulling out a ten-dollar bill.

She makes change and then sidles away to grab the coffee.

Jingle, jingle.

"King! Why didn't you tell me you were coming to town today?" My sister rushes over, squeezing my waist in a tight side hug.

"I come to town every two weeks, Pops. Didn't know I needed to get on your calendar."

"I'm surprised to see you here. You don't drink lattes." Her brows raise, and I shake my head.

"Yeah. Prices here are outrageous. But it's a long story."

"Does that story have anything to do with one Juliet

Capelli?" She scrunches up her nose, her eyes locked on mine. I squirm, heat flaming my cheeks.

"What? No, not really. Why?"

Poppy chucks me in the arm. "You're a terrible liar, big brother. I have it on good authority that the two of you had a run-in at the gas station this morning."

"What the—how'd you hear that?"

"Barty's sister's serving in the restaurant at the inn. Plus, you have a big stain on your shirt." She points at the brown bull's-eye marking my flannel.

"Damn. Nothing gets by anyone in this town." *All the more reason to stay away.*

"Word on the street is the two of you looked real cozy together at the gas station."

"No, we did not. She spilled her coffee on me, and then I cleaned up as best I could and left. Period, end of story."

"Not what I heard." Poppy grins, her light-blue eyes practically sparkling at the gossip. "I heard her hands were all over you, and the two of you couldn't stop staring at one another."

"Yeah. She was trying to get the damn coffee off my shirt. Everyone should start minding their own damn business in this town."

"Why so defensive, big brother?" Poppy elbows me, her lips pursed in a teasing smirk.

"I'm not being defensive. Nothing happened. And it aggravates me when people flap their gums about stuff that doesn't need talking about."

"Grand medium roast for King!" The barista shouts out the order even though Poppy and I are the only two customers.

"You have anything else to harass me about, or can I

resume my errands?" I reach around her for the coffee, the pounding in my head louder than ever.

"I guess that's all for now. But are you interested in Juliet? She *is* a Capelli." Poppy scrunches up her nose in distaste.

I press my lips together, gut swirling. For one, it's none of Poppy's business who I'm interested in—or not—and two, I do not need relationship advice from my baby sister.

"Thanks for the reminder of her last name. And no, not interested." I grit my teeth, the words sounding hollow to my ears.

"Oh-kay. Because even though she's cute, the idea of crossing lines is a bit much. Even if she did help with the lawsuit." She flips her hair over her shoulder, reassured that I'm not breaking any unspoken family rules.

"Got it, Pops." I shoot my sister a wave and head for the door, eager to end this conversation.

"You should consider dating someone, though!" Poppy shouts after me, and I shake my head, not bothering to look back.

Yeah, I hate errand day.

Since I'm near the courthouse, I drop Roman a text to check whether he's free. I don't want to hang out until lunch anymore, but it'd be good to see him in person. Since he married Skye, I've barely seen the guy.

King: You busy? I'm in town

Rome: Yeah, I'm working. But I can take a quick break. Where are you?

King: I can meet you at the courthouse

Rome: See you in 5

I tuck my cell into my pocket and head over to the courthouse. It's a short walk across the town square, no big deal. The weather's perfect—spring in Florida is one of the best times of the year. Sunny, low humidity, clear skies. The ocean breeze carries the sound of the waves, and that's enough to calm me, at least a little.

Outside the courthouse, Roman heads down the marble staircase as soon as he catches sight of me.

"Hey." He nods his dark head at me but keeps his hands to himself. Unlike Poppy the hugger, Roman's much more reserved. I like that in a person.

"How's it going? Things good with Skye?"

The corners of Roman's lips tip up in a smile at the mention of his wife.

"Yeah, she's good. She's feeling better, now that she's in the second trimester."

"Good. I hear morning sickness can be rough."

"Brutal, man. It should be called 'all-day sickness.' Glad that part's over. Anyway, what's up? You want to have lunch?"

"Can't. I have to get groceries and head back. Don't want to leave Beau alone too long."

"Too bad. I was hoping for an excuse to go out. Skye packed me a lunch, but I'm pretty sure it's tofu or something really healthy. I could go for a taco—or six."

Chuckling, I shake my head. "Sorry, brother, not this time. Listen—we gonna tell Poppy and Parker about that letter?"

A letter on aqua stationery that came in the mail right after Christmas, shaking me to my core. The swirly cursive handwriting of a woman named Lacey. Someone I've never met—never even heard of—claiming to be our mother's child, given up for adoption before I was born.

Roman exhales hard and tips his head up to the sky, mulling over options. "I guess. I mean, we should, right?"

He cuts his eyes at me, waiting on a response.

"I suppose so. I kinda wanted to get more information before we told them, but with the records sealed, I reckon it's not that easy."

Roman shakes his head. "No, it definitely is not. I wasn't even supposed to access the info that I did. Our best bet is checking her out in person. But I can't exactly leave town right now, what with Skye's condition."

"It's not a great time for me either. I have a new pony coming in later this month and a goat ready to give birth any day now."

"We should tell them, King. Poppy and Parker are grown—they can handle it. As much as we can." Roman folds his arms over his chest, his dress shirt straining at the shoulders.

"Family meeting then? Out at the ranch later this week?"

He sighs, the vein at his temple popping. "Yeah. Family meeting."

"I'll send a group text. You gonna pretend you don't know?"

"Nah. They'll ask too many questions."

Even though the twins will interrogate us, I highly doubt Rome would crack under the pressure. He was Special Ops in the Marines.

"Okay, however you want to play it." I shrug, shoving both hands in my pockets.

"Let's stick with the truth. You got the letter. I saw it and researched. Now we're looping them in. We don't have to tell them it's been over two months."

"That's fine. Works for me. Friday night okay?"

"Sure. Hopefully Parker's not working. But that's enough of a heads-up that he could maybe get someone to cover his shift."

"All right. See you Friday then. Maybe bring a pizza or two."

Roman grins, faint laugh lines crinkling around his eyes. "I'll see what I can do. I have to get back." He gestures to the courthouse, and I nod.

"See ya."

"Bye."

Roman jogs back up the courthouse stairs, and I stand there, getting my bearings. I'm not looking forward to the conversation with our siblings. Probably the reason Roman and I sat on the letter so long in the first place. Poppy's gonna have a total freak-out, and I'm not even sure how Parker will react. Better than Poppy but not as well as Roman, and he took the news pretty hard.

Yeah, Friday night's gonna be a blast.

Might as well get this over with . . .

> King: Family meeting out at the ranch
> Friday night, 7 pm

> Little Sis: What? Why?

Well, shit. I type, delete, retype, delete. I'm not sure what to say here. I can't say it's nothing, because it's family meeting worthy. But I don't want her to freak out and bug me for the next three days.

> King: It's fine. Just come to the ranch.
> We'll talk

Buzz, buzz.

I check my cell. It's Poppy.

"Hey, Pops."

"Don't you hey me, King Montgomery! What's going on? And how come you didn't mention this twenty minutes ago at Coastal Coffee?" She's talking so fast it takes me a minute to process the words.

"Like I said, everything's okay. But there's something we need to talk about. As a family."

"Oh my gosh, are you sick? Are you dying?"

I sigh. My sister's so freaking dramatic.

"No, Poppy. I'm not sick or dying. And neither is Rome or Parker. Or Liv or Skye. And our cousin, Smitty, is fine too. It's just—something came in the mail, and I need you to see it."

"Oh—like treasure?"

"Poppy. This isn't some damn pirate movie. There's no treasure. See you Friday." I disconnect before she asks me any more questions. So, naturally, she takes to text.

> Little Sis: I really want to know what's
> going on. Right now

> Rome: See you Friday

Coward. He doesn't even attempt to field Poppy's question.

> King: Bring pizza

Parker: Did somebody say pizza? Count
me in

Naturally, Parker gets involved at the mention of food,
the subject of the meeting the least of his concerns.

Parker: Should I bring Liv? I think she has
an event

Rome: I'm bringing Skye

Little Sis: Griffin's playing baseball ☹

Parker: Is his team any good this year?

Little Sis: I'm sure. Griffin's on it

Parker: You're biased, sis

Little Sis: Yep, I am

As fun as it is standing on the steps of the courthouse,
texting my family, I have shit to do.

King: Friday, 7 pm. See y'all then

Parker: Cool

Rome: Got it

Little Sis: Fine. But I wish you'd just tell
me now

I leave her hanging and head back to my truck. I've
already been gone longer than I planned due to the gas-
station-coffee explosion, and I hate leaving Beau alone.
He's been my ranch hand for a few years now, but he's a lot

less experienced and doesn't know the ins and outs like I do.

One more quick stop, and then I'll be on my way back to the ranch. I fire up the truck and head north toward the grocery. Traffic's definitely picked up on A1A, people out and about doing their weekday tasks. A Jeep carrying a surfboard cuts me off, sliding straight into my safe-driving distance without so much as a blinker, and I lay on my horn.

"Asshole," I mutter, easing off the gas pedal to avoid rear-ending him.

I make a sharp right into the parking lot of the grocery store and slam my truck into an open spot. After grabbing my shopping bags, I sprint into the overly conditioned air of the grocery, intent on making this the fastest food run ever. I yank a cart out, then head straight to the produce department, reading over my list as I walk.

"Hey, watch it!"

Hot panic surges through me as I stop short, inches away from slamming into Juliet.

4

JULIET

My heart rate had finally returned to a reasonable number of beats per minute, and now here he is again.

King freaking Montgomery.

"Watch where you're going." I scowl at him over the bananas. His face blanches to a shade slightly darker than the skin of a fresh garlic clove, like he's seeing a damn ghost or something.

"Sorry," he mumbles, his deep voice barely audible over the soft, easy-listening hit playing through the loudspeaker. A nice throwback song by Whitney Houston, which I was mercifully not dancing to. That would have been embarrassing.

Not that King would have noticed. Hell, he barely realized I was standing right in front of him. If I would've stayed quiet, he'd have mowed me over with his shopping cart.

We glare at one another, locked in a staring détente, neither of us willing to crack first.

"Are you gonna move? I kinda need to get to the avoca-dos." King tips his head to the right, and my chest tight-ens. Heat prickles beneath my skin, and I'm sure I'm blushing.

I jut out my chin. "You may want to rethink that. They're not in season yet. Been hard as a rock all month. We've had a helluva time making guac at the Tipsy Taco."

"Thanks for the hot produce tip. But I think I can pick out an avocado."

"Yeah?" I pop one hand on my hip and step aside, gesturing to the pile of small green rocks. "Be my guest, Top Chef."

King sweeps past me, our shoulders brushing, and I catch the faint scent of hay mixed with coffee and his alpine cologne. My thighs clench, muscles pulsing, a dull throbbing between my legs.

You should get out of here, Juliet. Nothing good's going to come from baiting him.

He leans over the avocados, his back broad, the fabric of his shirt stretching with the effort. His muscles have always been strong from long days working at the ranch, and it seems nothing's changed in that department. If anything, he's more muscular than before.

A low current of desire hums through my veins, and I'm glad his back is to me, because I'm definitely flushed. He picks up one green rock, then another, squeezing them in his large hands.

Hands that have squeezed more than avocados.

I take a deep breath and exhale, trying to remember where I am and why I'm not going there again.

Ever.

Remember that I want nothing to do with this man.

Even if he did make me—every last inch of me—feel amazing once upon a time.

King sets the first two avocados down and plucks another two from higher up on the pile. Stretching, giving me a nice view of his ass. High and round, perfectly outlined in his worn jeans, the denim sure to be soft from wear.

He turns slightly, a furrow creasing his brow. He's determined to find a ripe avocado, just to prove me wrong. The man's stubborn as an ox—always has been.

"I told ya. Not in season."

He cocks his head at me, bites at his bottom lip that I know would taste faintly of mint ChapStick.

"I'm still looking, Juliet. You can mosey on if you want. No need to stand here and watch me all day."

"Then I won't be able to gloat when I'm right and you're wrong." My voice is a teasing singsong, and King bristles, squaring up straighter.

"You won't be right."

"Mm-hmm."

He turns back to the task at hand, rifling through the avocados, hell-bent on proving me wrong.

I do have to be at work in the next half hour, so I hope he hurries up. I'd hate to miss out on the opportunity to revel in my triumph.

King picks another dark-green avocado off the pile, caressing the dimpled skin with the pads of his fingers, smoothing his thumb over each ridge. My breath hitches as he works the small fruit.

What the hell is wrong with me? Is my love life really this pathetic that I'm getting turned on by a man picking out a damn avocado?

Yes, yes it is, judging by the dampness in my panties right now. I'm glad no one here has X-ray vision, because the last thing King needs to know is the effect he's having on me right here in the produce section under the harsh white fluorescent lights.

"This one's good, I reckon." He holds the avocado out for my inspection, and I gingerly lift it from his warm palm.

The connection with his skin sends an electric shock straight up my arm, tingles spreading through me, and now my panties are soaked.

I focus on the fruit, squeezing the rippled flesh to test the ripeness.

Dammit, he's good.

King managed to find the one freaking ripe avocado in all of Seaglass Beach.

Son of a bitch.

At least I didn't have money on it.

"Maybe. Hard to say. Could be rotten on the inside." I lock eyes with him, my mouth going dry as he stares down at me, unblinking, his pupils wide and dark.

His gaze pierces me for a long second before he lifts the avocado from my hand.

"Could be. You never know."

I flick the tip of my tongue over my lip, not even certain I'm breathing.

"Any more shopping advice for me? Or can I go now?" His voice is gruff, husky, sending more tingles skittering through me.

I shake my head, the whoosh of blood roaring in my ears.

Why do I do this to myself? I should avoid him.

Just stay the fuck away.

He's a blazing fire, and if I keep dancing so close to the flames, I'm definitely going to get burned. King doesn't say another word. He places the lone avocado into his empty cart and wheels away toward the lettuce. I'm rooted to the spot, my heart pounding.

Yes, coming back here was definitely a terrible idea.

5

KING

THE THING ABOUT LIVING OUT AT THE RANCH, AWAY from the crowds and hustle, is the quiet. Space to think. Normally I like it. Crave it, even.

But running into Juliet has me off-kilter. The silence is no longer calming. Just the opposite—it's driving me mad.

All I can think about is her.

With every whisper of the wind, I swear I catch her light floral scent. Wildflowers spring up in the pasture, delicate daisies and lavender thistle, and she's there—dancing in the tall grass, a white flower tucked in the waves of her hair.

Out in the barn a horse neighs, kicking up dust, and we're together again. Sneaking out in the dark of night, hiding among the shadows. Silvery slashes of moonlight filtering through the windows as we lose ourselves in each other.

Pressing up against her, hands sliding over bare skin. Her thigh hitched around my hip, my cock hard, throbbing in my jeans. Sinking into her tight pussy, my fingers threading through her hair, claiming her.

All of her.

Tasting her on my lips, sweet and salty, lapping at her juices. I couldn't get enough, feasting until she bucked beneath me. Wild, out of control.

Crying out, muffling her screams in my chest, nails scratching at my shoulders. The sharp sting reminding me I'm alive.

Every part of me lighting up as she curled her body into mine, my arms wrapped around her narrow shoulders. Holding her to me, our hearts pounding hard and in sync.

She's the only girl I ever loved—or gave myself to.

And she broke me.

The ranch has been my solace all these years, a retreat. Out here, I'm safe.

But now I'm haunted by the memories.

She's here, waiting for me around every corner. I somehow managed to pack all of that away while she was gone. Seeing her cracked something open inside me, something I buried years ago.

All I want to do is forget.

Bedtime comes, and I close my eyes, drifting off to sleep on a prayer that the night will be dreamless.

But she's there.

Tears swimming in those hazel eyes, hurt etched on her face. She cries out, but there's no sound.

Only silence.

Palms outstretched, she reaches for me. I'm beyond her grasp. She stares at me, chest shaking, racked with silent screams.

I want to go to her. Hold her. Comfort her.

But instead I push her away.

She falls to her knees, arms folded across her belly.

Empty.

I wake in a cold sweat, staring up at the light oak planks. Chest heavy with a feeling I've tried to bury for the last fifteen years.

Grief.

The weight sits on my pecs, depressing my lungs, squeezing the air from my body.

With Juliet back in town, I can't hide anymore. Not from her, not from the past. Even all the way out here, I can't get away.

It's always been her.

Buzz, buzz.

My cell rattles against the nightstand, pulling me from my tormented thoughts.

Parker.

> Parker: Tipsy Taco tonight. Liv, Skye, and Poppy are having a girls' night. Come out

I stare down at the message, heart still pounding. I shouldn't go. Juliet might be there, and then what? Seeing her is not going to make things any better. If anything, it'll only stir up more grief.

> King: Don't think I can. Busy

> Parker: Bullshit. Doing what? Crossword puzzles? Watching Wheel of Fortune? C'mon . . .

Dude has a point. That wasn't a very credible lie, especially with my brother. Maybe a night out would be good for me. Get me out of my damn head. If only we weren't going to the Tipsy Taco. But if I say anything about the location, it'll tip Parker off and open up a line of questions I want to avoid.

King: Fine. What time?

Parker: Six work?

King: Sure. See you later

Parker: Cool. Taco time!

I shoot Parker a thumbs-up and head to the shower, determined to wash away the remaining traces of Juliet and start the day fresh.

Somehow I'm going to have to figure out how to live in the same world as her and be all right again. A task proving to be way more difficult than anticipated.

GOING INTO TOWN TWICE IN ONE WEEK ISN'T IDEAL, especially given the circumstances. Yet here I am, shoving through the crowd at the Tipsy Taco, making my way to a booth across from the bar. Parker and Rome are already drinking beers, and Parker's plowing his way through a basket of chips and salsa. He shoots me a wave, and Rome nods as I slide into the booth beside him.

"What's up, fellas?" I roll my shoulders, trying to loosen the tension there. I'd like to blame it on hauling hay bales all afternoon, but that's not the whole story. The fear of running into Juliet again sits heavy on my mind, pressing down on me like a lead blanket. Anxiety hums through me, a low quiver beneath my skin, and I'm jumpy as fuck. I keep my gaze focused on the smooth black tabletop, not daring to let my eyes roam around the crowded restaurant.

"Y'all ready to order?"

My head swivels at the familiar voice, and I'm staring straight into Juliet's hazel eyes.

Holy hell.

She's fucking everywhere. There have to be at least ten servers at the Tipsy Taco. How did we end up sitting in her damn section?

She stands stock-still, staring back at me. The tip of her tongue darts out, licking along the seam of her pretty lips.

Lips that have been all over you.

My cock hardens, muscle memory kicking in.

She's on her knees in the barn, those full pink lips wrapped around my cock. I'm shooting hot cum down her throat, and she swallows every drop.

"King?" Parker waves a hand in front of my face, and I snap out of it, clearing my throat.

"I'll take a beer. Whatever they're having." I gesture at Rome's green glass bottle, my mouth dry.

"Coming right up." She spins and sashays over to the bar.

Damn, she still has a fine ass.

"You okay?" Parker kicks me under the table, and I jump, startled.

Scrubbing a hand over my face, I take a long slug of water from the red plastic cup in front of me.

"Yeah. Fine. Why?"

"Well, every time Juliet comes around, you look like

you might throw up. You have a thing for her or something?" He drops his voice lower, as if someone's listening in on our convo. "After everything that went down with the trial and all, she's not as bad as I thought, you know? Like barely even a Capelli after that move."

"What? No. Get out of here." I shake my head, frowning, my heart pounding so hard I can barely hear over the constant thuds.

"She's pretty. I never noticed before, but she had a glow-up while she was away. I mean—don't tell Liv—but she's got kind of a banging bod."

I grunt, shrugging and dismissing his suggestion. "Hadn't noticed."

"Uh-huh." Rome smirks at me, one brow arched high. "Sure."

"What the hell are you talking about, *sure*? She's all right, I guess." I fiddle with the paper napkin beneath the plastic cup, wishing desperately for that beer. Preferably delivered by a different waitress.

"You guess?" Rome lifts his drink, taking a sip. "You act all weird every time she's around is all. Seems like you might have a thing for her." Fixing his eyes on me, he's gauging my response like the trained military operative he is.

"No, I don't. You're full of shit."

"Okay," he snickers, the corner of his lip tipping up.

"What?" I scrub a hand over my neck, the skin burning. "What are you talking about?"

"Nothing." Rome mercifully drops the subject as Juliet sidles back to the table with the beer.

She plunks it down in front of me, and I nod, murmuring a *thanks*. I face forward—otherwise I'll be eye level with her tits, and I'm already having a tough time in the hard-on department.

"You boys know what you want to eat?" Her pen's poised above a pink notepad, ready to take our order, and now all I can think about are her full, round breasts. The delicate skin, the way her nipples turn a deep, dusky pink when she's aroused, a sharp contrast to her fair skin.

Rome steps in, interrupting my daydream. "Sure, I'll have the burrito bowl, extra beans and sour cream. No onions."

"No onions? Since when?" Parker tips his head at Roman, one brow raised.

"Since two months ago. The smell gets to Skye now that she's pregnant."

Beside me, Juliet flinches, her knuckles turning white because she's gripping the pen so tight. I swallow hard, beer churning in my gut. I'm torn between catching her eye and avoiding contact altogether.

I focus on the menu, black and white swimming in front of me, a sea of meaningless letters.

"Weird. Did she puke a lot?"

Parker won't let the damn thing go.

"In the beginning. She's over that phase now, thank god. But her sense of smell is better than a drug dog. If she catches one whiff of something that bothers her stomach, she gets triggered."

"Bro, I had no idea." Parker shakes his head, his blond hair flopping over his forehead. I love the guy, but sometimes my brother is clueless.

Juliet clears her throat. "Parker? What's it gonna be?"

"Taco trio, with a side of guac." He taps the menu, pointing to the trio.

"Pass on the guac," I say without thinking.

"What? Why? I love the guac here."

Juliet's lips quirk, and she almost smiles. Almost.

"Trust me. I have it on good authority that avocados aren't in season."

"Is that so?" Rome rubs his hand along his jaw, peering over his shoulder at me.

"Yeah. I had a heck of a time finding a ripe one at the store."

"All right, that's good enough for me. How about queso then? Is cheese in season?" Parker grins at his stupid joke, and Juliet scrawls the order down, not bothering to respond to my idiot brother.

"What about you, King?" She bites at her bottom lip, and I have no idea what she's thinking, how she's feeling.

My mind whirs, running on overdrive, my knee bouncing up and down beneath the table. Itching to move, get away from the tension.

"Uh—I'll have the same thing as Parker. No queso. And hold the avocado."

I finally glance up at her, a smile teasing at her lips. "Solid choice."

She holds out her hand, and I almost reach for it, run my fingertips across her smooth palm. Then I realize she's waiting for me to give her my menu.

"Oh, here." I pry the sticky plastic off the table, gathering my brothers' menus as well, and hand them all to her.

We lock eyes—one quick second—and I can't breathe, can't think. All I can do is get lost in Juliet's beguiling eyes, falling under her spell.

A spell I'm not sure I'll ever be able to break.

A spell I maybe don't want to break at all.

6
───────

JULIET

MENUS IN HAND, I SPIN AROUND AND BOLT FROM THE Montgomerys' table as fast as I can.

After dodging through customers, I toss the menus on the messy pile at the bar and duck into the kitchen.

Away from the crowded dining room.

Away from King and his stupid handsome face.

Away from that deep-navy gaze I still can't read.

What's he thinking? How does he feel about Roman having a baby?

The air evaporates from my lungs, and a sharp pain stabs me in the chest.

It should have been us.

I rip the order from the pad and hand the paper to the line cook, then duck into the alley for a quick breath of fresh air. Evening humidity envelops me, and I breathe in and out, in and out, salt stinging my nostrils.

Leaning against the building, I squeeze my eyes shut and try to block out the pain washing over me.

The pain of that horrible day. I still have nightmares about it, waking up with a tear-streaked face.

That was the worst day of my entire life.

And I've had some awful days, growing up with an abusive father and a drug-addled mother. So that's saying something.

The blood. So much blood, a deep crimson. Gushing everywhere, soaking through my panties, my jeans. Warm and sticky, the strong metallic scent.

I couldn't get it to stop. I wanted to make it stop, squeezing my thighs together, trying to keep it all in until I could make it to the doctor.

King found me on the bathroom floor, half-delirious, on the verge of passing out.

Juliet! Panic in his voice, his face, as he carried me to his truck and drove me to the hospital. Clutching my hand all the way, speeding through town, blowing through every stoplight.

But by then it's already too late.

I'm sorry, but there's no heartbeat.

My wail bounces off the cold, sterile tile, echoing down the hall. Searing pain in my belly, then I'm numb.

Dead inside.

Just like the baby.

Our baby.

I wake up hours later, my mind fuzzy from anesthesia, mouth dry as cotton. A thin, scratchy bedsheet's draped over me, and I'm cold all over.

King's sitting next to the bed, head in his hands, staring at the floor. Monitors beep all around me, but otherwise the room is quiet.

I can't breathe. I'm gulping at the air, and it burns my nose. Sharp and antiseptic.

He glances up, his gaze flat. He doesn't move from the chair, doesn't reach out to touch me, hold me, reassure me.

A pang in my chest, a tiny voice whispering it's over, but I shove it away, try to drown it out.

It can't be over.

A large fibroid decreased the blood supply to the baby.

I'm sorry, but the baby's gone.

We did a D&C, cleared everything out. You lost a lot of blood, so we gave you a transfusion. You can always try again later.

A hot tear rolls down my cheek, and I sweep it away, open my eyes to ground myself back in the present.

The sound of the ocean waves rolls over me, soft and soothing to my soul. One of the reasons I came back here in the first place.

"Hey."

A deep, low voice, so quiet I barely hear it. I glance over my shoulder as King walks toward me, a hand shoved deep in his pocket.

My stomach flip-flops as he closes the gap between us.

"Are you okay?" His lips press together, a deep V etched between his brows.

I swallow hard over the lump in my throat, swipe at my face to erase any evidence of pain.

"Sure." I kick at the asphalt, heat flooding my system.

His leather boots appear next to my white Converse, the sharp scent of his cologne winding around me. Twinges of something I thought died a long time ago flutter low in my belly, and I ball my fists.

Don't go there.

"Sorry about that." His soft tone sends a shiver straight through me.

I clear my throat, try to force out sound.

"Not your fault. It's fine."

He steps closer to me, and my breath hitches in my throat, heat from his body tickling my skin. I should get away, go back inside, but I'm glued to the spot. Locked in his force field.

I lift my head, and our eyes meet. Instantly I know it's a mistake.

I cannot—will not—fall for this man again.

His hand flexes; then he reaches out, touching my forearm. Lightning zings through me, burning all the way up my arm, my skin on fire.

"Don't." I pull my arm away, banging my elbow against the wall. Which really freaking hurts, but not as badly as the vise grip squeezing my chest. "You don't get to come out here and act like a hero, like you give a shit. Not after all this time."

I lock eyes with him, a quick flash of pain dancing across his face before he goes neutral.

He swallows hard, Adam's apple bobbing.

The silence is filled with so many things unspoken between us. Things I fervently wish to leave buried. Nothing good's going to come from unpacking all this baggage.

"I'm no hero, Juliet. Never claimed to be."

Truer words have never been spoken. He's definitely not a hero.

He used to be. To you, at least.

I don't know what to say back, so I smash my lips together and stay quiet. The silence stretches between us, long as the years that have passed, and I'm so fucking confused. My head's telling me to run, but my body's frozen in place. I'm all twisted up inside, and I hate it.

I want him to say he's sorry. To say he made a mistake when he pushed me away. That he wishes he held me in his arms as I cried myself to sleep night after night all those years ago.

That he wanted to be together—be a family—just as much as I did.

That he fucked up and he'll do anything to earn my forgiveness.

But I don't say anything at all.

I keep all my emotions, all my words, buried.

Another minute passes, and then King walks away.

Like he always does.

I watch as he retreats, getting smaller and smaller until he fades from sight.

Gone.

I'm alone.

A sharp breeze blows in from the ocean, and I shudder, goose bumps rising on my skin.

This is hard.

I thought I was over it, over him.

Turns out I'm not. I only managed to tape the pieces of my heart together. And every time I see him, the tape loosens—a piece here, another piece there—threatening to come completely undone.

I don't know if I can live like this.

It hurt living without him, but being here—orbiting around each other like this—hurts more.

$$7$$

KING

Back inside, I make an excuse to my brothers about a horse emergency at the ranch and grab my taco order to go. After my exchange with Juliet, there's no way in hell I can sit here and behave like it's another normal boys' night.

I'm not that good of an actor.

And I'm certainly no fucking hero.

Never claimed to be. Never wanted to be.

I didn't sign up for this shit.

Seeing Juliet crying out in the alley hurt.

It's your fault.

Those tears are on me, and deep down I know it.

You should have been there for her. But you pushed her away because you couldn't handle her pain.

No. I pushed her away because it was a sign from God. Our baby died so Juliet could be free.

Free from her family.

Free from this town and her place in it.

Free from me.

I blow out a shuddery breath and ease up on the gas

pedal when I realize I'm pushing seventy in a fifty-five. Last fucking thing I need is a speeding ticket.

The town fades behind me, disappearing in the rearview as I put miles between me and Juliet. Me and everyone else.

I wanted her to save herself.

No, you wanted to save yourself.

Slamming my hand down on the steering wheel, I fight against all the emotions tumbling back: the anger, sadness, fear.

But the worst one's the grief. Heavy, unrelenting, always with me.

Still with me.

She's right and I know it—I did push her away. Because every time I saw her, all I could think about was our baby, our future.

And it was gone in minutes.

I wanted to be there for her. To hold her, tell her everything was going to be okay.

But it wasn't. In that instant our entire future changed. The world tipped on its axis, topsy-turvy, and I was off balance. Nothing was the same again.

Selfishly, I wanted to keep her for myself. Hide out here in the country, away from everyone, everything. Stick to the plan and be together.

The two of us against the entire fucking world.

But being with Juliet was complicated. Beautiful, but complicated.

Just like her.

And we were so young, only in our twenties. What did we know about life back then? Having a kid, being parents? We were practically babies ourselves.

It was a sign.

She was throwing away her entire future to be with me, and it wasn't right.

Juliet deserved better. More than I could give her.

I pull down the dark driveway, gravel crunching beneath the truck tires. I made record time, arriving back home early enough to feed the horses. Shooting Beau a quick text, I let him know I don't need him to come back tonight.

I've got this.

I swing into the house, dropping the tacos on the kitchen island, then head out to the barn. The air's chilly, the temperature falling as soon as the sun set. The sound of the horses neighing gets louder as I near the barn.

"Hey, boys and girls." I flip the light switch, wall sconces illuminating the space.

My dad renovated this barn a few years before he died, upgrading the light fixtures and feeding stations, adding a guesthouse where I lived before my parents died in the car accident three years ago. This space in the barn, though, is one of my favorites, mainly because of all the memories I have out here with him. We used to spend hours in this barn, working and talking. My dad was one of the best men I've ever known, and I wanted to be just like him with my kid.

My chest aches, and I move faster, racing around the barn, adding fresh water to the trough and hay to the feed buckets.

That's the trouble with silence. There's nothing to distract you from the ghosts.

I finish up the chores, winding up the hose and cutting the lights before making my way back to the main house. By now my food's cold—and I'm not hungry anyway.

Stepping into the kitchen, I'm struck by the quiet. Usually I like it. Love it, even. But tonight it feels empty, magnifying the sadness inside me.

Throbbing in my chest, in my gut, banging around in my head.

I cross over to the bar, pour myself a healthy shot of bourbon, and drink it straight up. The amber liquid burns as it slides down my throat, stinging my nose. I wait a few seconds, then pour myself another. This time I sip at it, taking it slow and tasting the light notes of vanilla.

I remember the first time Juliet had bourbon. She wasn't even old enough to drink. I snuck it from my parents' liquor cabinet, brought it out to the guesthouse. We sat in front of the fire—she wore only my T-shirt—and I couldn't keep my eyes off her. The way the flames danced over her face, highlighting the round apples of her cheeks, the long slope of her neck. Laughing as she scrunched up her nose at the sharp burn of the alcohol.

Winding my fingers through the silky waves of her hair, laying her down on the rug, and covering her body with mine. She fit perfectly beneath me, her curves pressed against my chest, nipples diamond sharp through the thin cotton. Her skin soft under the rough, calloused pads of my fingers, already hardened from working at the ranch. The way she shivered at my touch, goose bumps rising on her skin, the pink flush of her arousal.

Sinking into her wet pussy, her muscles clenching around my rock-hard cock as she quivered and cried out.

I shut my eyes against the memory, dick swelling in my jeans. Aching for her.

Topping off my drink, I wander outside, the glass heavy in my palm. The night's clear and cool as I cut across the lawn, each blade of grass bathed in the white glow of the moon. Somewhere in the distance an owl hoots, the leaves of the oaks rustling overhead.

Walking around the paddock, I bypass the barn, heading over to the guesthouse. The space has been vacant for a few years now, and I can't remember the last time I've been out here.

Fumbling in my pocket, I find the key, twist the metal in the lock. It clicks open, and I shove through the door. A shiver races down my spine as I stare into the darkness, letting my eyes adjust to the dim light.

I half expect to see Juliet there, sitting on the couch in an oversize T-shirt, waiting for me.

But the room's empty, the furniture covered with white sheets.

Abandoned.

With an outstretched hand, I move through the room, shuffling my feet to avoid bumping into any furniture. I pass the fireplace, the shaggy rug long gone. Ducking into the narrow hallway, the bathroom glows from the moonlight slanting through the window.

Now I'm standing just outside the bedroom, heart hammering. I take a deep breath, and stale, dusty air fills my lungs.

The room's small, with space for a queen-size bed, a dresser, and not much else. Curtains cover the window, shafts of light peeking through and pooling on the bedsheet. The bed's still here—I didn't have anywhere to put it when I moved up to the main house, so I just left it.

I sink down onto the mattress, lean back against the

hard wooden headboard. There aren't any pillows to cushion my back, and I'm sure every vertebra's going to be screaming at me in a second. I'm not twenty-five anymore, able to be comfortable no matter where I am. No, this body's worked long, hard hours, and I feel every second of it deep down in my bones.

Closing my eyes, I surrender to the waves of grief I've been pushing away all night. My chest cracks open, and a sob escapes my lungs. Long and low, racking my body. My throat burns, tears pricking behind my eyelids. I take shallow, shuddery breaths, let everything out.

I still want Juliet.

My fingertips tingle as I think about touching her, running my hands over her shoulders, down the bare skin of her arms. Tiny bumps rising on her flesh, a slow shiver of pleasure telling me everything I need to know.

Reaching beneath her shirt, realizing she's wearing nothing beneath the flimsy fabric. Caressing her breasts as they swell in my palms, rolling and pinching her nipples as she gasps with pleasure. The only sound in the room a low moan quivering deep in her throat.

Dropping my mouth to the source of the noise, the vibration humming against my lips. Licking at her, tasting her, nipping as I slide my palm over her belly. A slight bump there, and only she and I know why.

I glance up at her face, a smile dancing at the corners of her full, pink lips.

We're happy.

So damn happy.

My gut clenches with pain, and I throw back the rest of my drink. A sharp sting, burning all the way down my throat. Tears spill onto my cheeks, and I wipe them away, ashamed.

I should have manned up tonight, out in the alley. Told her I'm sorry, at least.

Instead, I walked away like a fucking coward.

She hitches her legs around my hips, and I lower her down onto the bed, tugging her shirt off as she props a hand behind her head. Smiling down at me as she spreads her thighs, beckoning to me.

Come inside.

Cock hard, I press into her heat, our bodies perfect for one another. Me giving, her taking. Pistoning in and out, her fingers squeezing my shoulders, her legs wrapped around me, urging me to go deeper, harder.

Never stop.

Setting my glass on the floor, I unbutton my jeans, springing my cock free from the tight cotton prison. Fisting myself, running my hand up and down the shaft, I grow bigger, longer, harder. Moving faster, pumping up and down and squeezing. Shutting my eyes and floating away, I can feel her all around me. Her tight pussy muscles clenching my dick, contracting as she bucks against me. Our bodies slap together, and I'm nervous about the baby, but she giggles and tells me not to be ridiculous. Everything's fine with the baby. She's so warm and responsive, the scent of her arousal stronger now that she's pregnant. I slide in and out, her clit swollen and greedy. Wanting more.

My balls tighten, the base of my spine tingling. I fist myself tighter, jerking and squeezing, wishing it was Juliet's wet pussy instead of my damn hand.

"Fu-uck," I hiss into the empty room, hot cum spraying from my dick. Muscles tight, I pulse in my hand, and I'm warm all over. Too warm—from the bourbon and the lack of air circulation in the stuffy room.

I slump back against the headboard, my release sticky on my shirt, dick limp. Breathing hard, a light sheen of sweat beading at my hairline.

Eventually my pulse and breath return to normal, and I tuck my dick back into my pants, then zip up. I slide my cell out of my pocket, tap the screen, and the glass lights up. I hold my finger down on the contacts, my throat tight.

I should do it.

Dragging my finger down to "R."

Tap.

Moving down, down, until I get to "Rose Queen."

Click.

Hovering over the message button.

Press.

Typing out the words I should have written long ago.

> King: I'm sorry

Pausing, hand shaking as I stare down at the phone, a lump lodged in my throat.

Do it.

I hit send, then toss the cell to the end of the bed. It's well past midnight, and Juliet's tucked up in her bed, sound asleep, I'm sure.

Shutting my eyes, I drift off, knowing full well I'll dream of Juliet all damn night.

8

JULIET

I'm brushing my teeth, finally getting ready for bed after this absolute trash day, when I hear my cell ding from the other room.

Shit.

Nothing good comes after midnight. That's something my mama used to say. Admittedly, she slurred the words, drunk or high off her ass. But the truth still holds.

The only calls that come this late are from my brothers, looking for a damn bailout.

Well, forget it. I'm not going back out there. I don't care if they're all snuggled up in a jail cell together, keeping each other warm.

Good riddance, honestly.

Trudging out to the den, I pluck my phone from the side table and stare down at the message. My heart pounds, and the metal shakes in my quivering palm.

The message isn't from my brothers. Nor is it a collect call from the jail or a group text from the servers at the Tipsy Taco.

Air seeps from my lungs, my eyes burning as I gaze at the screen. I'm not sure what to think, what to do.

Fifteen years later, I finally get an apology, and it's over motherfucking text.

Adrenaline spills into my veins, pumping through me, and I'm fully awake now. I bang out an angry reply.

Thumb hovering over the send button, heart hammering in my chest, I hesitate. The strong, set jawline, the pain flashing in his navy eyes, has me pausing.

Thinking.

Like I've thought of anything else this past decade and a half.

But this was never the scenario. It was always a face-to-face talk. Heartfelt, with a good, hard sob on his part.

This is too soft, too easy.

Probably not worth a **Go fuck yourself**, though.

I delete the words, collapse down on the sofa with a shuddery exhale.

What in the actual fuck should I say?

"Yeah, me too" seems weak. Even if it's true.

I *am* sorry.

Sorry I failed.

Him. Us. Our baby.

The doctors said it wasn't my fault, that I did nothing wrong. But I'm still racked with guilt, haunted by the thought that I did something to cause the miscarriage.

Fresh pain springs up inside me, sharp, pressing against my ribs. Sucking all the oxygen from my lungs until dark spots dance at the corners of my eyes, my head pounding.

Damn him.

I'm exhausted, every inch of my body heavy, and now the idea of sleep is so absurd it's laughable.

Out of habit I flick on the TV, eyes glazing as Ross and Rachel have yet another predictable, avoidable fight on *Friends*. The canned laugh track cuts through the silence of the room, and I tuck my legs up beneath me. Still holding my cell, glancing back down at the message in disbelief.

> King of My Heart: I'm sorry

Yeah, well, you should be.

I bite down on my lip, pick my head up, and stare at the bright television screen. Heat unfurls low in my belly, and King's here, sitting beside me. His fingers grazing my arm, shooting a ripple of excitement through me, straight to my core. My skin hot beneath his touch, the muscles in my thighs squeezing, pussy throbbing.

I want you.

Sliding his hand up my thigh, cupping me, feeling the heat between my legs. His fingers dip inside my panties, trailing through the wetness, sinking into me.

Ride my hand. I want to feel you come.

Jerking against his palm, his thumb circling my clit, my breath coming in quick pants. I'm so hot for him, his eyes hooded with lust. My muscles tense, and I know I'm about to unravel beneath his touch.

All for him.

Always for him.

Come for me, Juliet.

His voice, a growly command, sends me spiraling over the edge into a blissful abyss, floating away. Every inch of me tingling.

You're so beautiful. I love to watch you come.

Tears prick at my eyes. More laughter from the television, but I have no idea what's funny. I'm not watching it, my hand between my legs. Hot and wet, wishing for more. I grind and grind, sinking my fingers inside, trying to find my release.

Over and over again until I'm hot and sweaty from the exertion.

But it's not there.

I can't find it. It's teasing me, just beyond my reach.

King of My Heart: I'm sorry

Aggravated, I give up and slump back against the sofa cushions. The furniture's a hand-me-down from another waitress at the Tipsy Taco, and the fabric is both ugly and scratchy. Not a winning combination. It's probably seen a lot of action, too, judging by the wear and tear on the light-green brocade.

The price was right, though, and beggars can't be choosers.

But they can rise off the sofa and go the hell to bed.

I mash the off button on the remote, and the television goes dark. I cut the light and stand, cell in hand. I take a quick pee, then plug my phone into the charger, leaving King on "Read" with no response.

Not out of spite. I just don't know what the hell to say.

I WAKE EARLY. TOO EARLY, THE ROOM STILL GRAY, untouched by the first bright rays of sunlight.

I roll over and check the time on my phone.

Five a.m. What the hell am I doing up at five in the morning? Jagger's not even awake at this ungodly hour. I stretch in my bed, lengthening my spine, arms above my head. Sucking my stomach in, hollowing out as I stare up at the ceiling.

I should go back to sleep. I'll be exhausted by the end of my shift tonight, but the memories from yesterday keep coming back. Playing over and over in my mind like a bad pop song.

King of My Heart: I'm sorry

Swinging out of bed, I pull on a pair of cutoff shorts and a white *Good Vibes Only* T-shirt, then scrounge around for my sneakers. After a quick splash of cool water to my face, I snatch my keys from the side table and head out.

The sky's moving from jet blue to a more subtle azure, a dark-rinse denim. A few wispy clouds hang low on the horizon, and a seagull cries, warning one of his bird buddies off his fish. I skip down the steps, hop into the SUV, and crank the engine. Mercifully, it roars to life, and I reverse out of the parking spot.

Maybe if I go there, I'll know what to say.

Our spot.

Out by the lake, ringed by woods. No one could find us all the way out there. Not back then, anyway.

Maybe they just weren't looking. Who knows.

I scoot through town, never hitting a red light, the streets deserted at this hour. Windows down, the humid salt air fills my car, and I hum absently to the music. Some sad country singer crooning about a breakup.

#relatable

Ten minutes later I park my SUV on the edge of the dirt road, tucking it out of the way as best as I can. Not that there's traffic out here, but just in case. Then I hike the short distance through the woods until I come to a clearing.

The sun's up now, the sky streaky with pink and orange. A fine white mist sits over the still lake, the soft chirping of crickets breaking the quiet. Some animal or large insect hits the smooth, glassy water, sending out a ripple of concentric circles. The skin on my arms puckers, a chill racing through me. Early-morning dew's wet on my shoes, soaking through the white canvas as I cross through the tall grass to the edge of the lake.

Our spot.

King and I used to spend hours out here, kissing and talking. Touching and laughing, hiding away from the world. Our families, my problems.

Some of the best moments of my life happened out here, beneath this very sky.

It's entirely possible we conceived our baby in this grass, naked on a blanket from his truck, our bodies twined together.

A shudder rolls through me, flutters of desire twinging in my belly.

What am I doing back here? I'm playing with fire, and I know it.

I slide my cell out of my pocket, click on the message again. For the hundredth time.

King of My Heart: I'm sorry

Chest tight, the skin beneath my shirt flushes. A slight sheen of sweat breaks out between my shoulder blades, and now I'm chilly.

With a shuddery breath, I walk along the edge of the lake until I come to an old, sprawling oak. The tree's massive, shading the water even though it sits well off the shoreline. Making my way over, I reach out and touch the rough bark. Run my fingers along the smooth indentation.

K & J, enclosed in a heart.

King carved our initials in the trunk over fifteen years ago now. Seeing the sharp lines of our letters takes my breath away. Together forever.

"Juliet."

I freeze, my fingers still touching the tree. My stomach swoops at the deep voice.

Slowly, so slowly, I glance over my shoulder. King's standing behind me, and my heart lodges in my throat.

I still don't know what to say, so I say nothing. Only nod at him, the waves of my hair rustling against my shirt.

He scrubs a hand over the back of his neck, rolls his head like he's trying to work out a crick.

"You look like shit. You sleep at all last night?" I ask.

"Gee, thanks. Good morning to you too, sunshine." He drops his hand from the back of his neck, shoves it in the pocket of his jeans. My eyes follow the movement, dropping down to his crotch. Realizing I'm staring somewhere I have no business looking, I pop my gaze back up to his face.

"You never texted me back." He presses his lips together, the corners of his mouth turning down.

I shrug, acting way more casual than I feel.

"Not much to say."

He pins his navy eyes on mine, and I'm a butterfly trapped under glass in biology class, getting scrutinized. He's watching, observing, wondering.

He clears his throat, and the sound bounces off the water. I kick at the grass with the toe of my sneaker. Mainly for something to do, somewhere to look.

Anywhere but at him.

I've dreamed of this moment for so long—so many years. Now that it's here, I'm bobbling it badly.

"Really? Nothing?"

"Fine. You want to know what I have to say, say the words. Out loud this time. Face-to-face. Like a man." I force my chin up, stare straight at him. His jaw's tense, and he bristles at my insinuation.

Like I just kicked him straight in the balls.

Instead of apologizing, he takes two long, quick strides toward me, gripping me by the hips and pulling me close to him. We're inches apart now, closer even than we were at the gas station. Every hair of his scruff visible, a few strands of gray mixing with the dark stubble peppering his jaw. Tanned skin, fine lines around his eyes, evidence that he does laugh every once in a while. He smells of mint and hay, and I want to get lost in that scent again. Like I used to.

He's so close, I'm half-afraid he can hear the pounding

of my heart, sniff the perspiration beneath my shirt. Sense the flutters between my thighs, the heat in my belly.

"I'm. Sorry." Serious eyes locked on mine, his tone's flat, the words clipped. "Does that work for you?"

I try to wriggle out of his grasp, but his fingers flex at my waist, gripping me tight. I know I'm going nowhere until King's good and ready to let me go.

Thrusting out my chest, I plant my feet deeper into the grass, the earth firm beneath me.

"No. That doesn't work for me, King."

"And why not?"

"It didn't sound real heartfelt."

"I'm not a damn actor, Juliet."

"Exactly. I need a sincere apology. Not just some words you think you're supposed to say."

"Dammit, woman." He shakes his head, the vein in his neck throbbing.

"Try again. This time with feeling."

King glares at me, swallows hard as he struggles with his words.

With a low, quiet voice, he says, "Juliet. I'm sorry for hurting you."

"Good start—"

"You need more?" He raises a brow.

"Yes. You've had fifteen years to work on this apology. I expect it to be good."

Clearing his throat, his eyes slide up to meet mine. "I'm sorry I wasn't there for you. That things got messy."

Hot tears surface, heat flooding my system. I've waited so long to hear these words, to have this conversation.

But it's still not enough.

"You hurt me, King."

"I know. And for that, I'm sorry. But I did it for you."

I jerk away from him, and he's so surprised he releases his grip.

"No! You don't get to be the hero here. You did it for yourself, to save *you*. You shut me out because you were in pain. Sure, I failed you, and the baby—" My voice breaks, a sob stealing my breath as I choke back my tears.

King reaches out and wraps his arms around me, pulling me to his chest. "No. You didn't fail me, or our baby. It wasn't your fault."

I let the tears fall onto his shirt, the soft flannel absorbing my liquid pain. His strong hand rubs my back, calming me.

Like he should have done before.

"I wanted you to go, be free of this place. Of your family." He murmurs the words, his face close to my ear, breath warm on my cheek. "To save yourself."

Inching away from him, I meet his gaze. "That wasn't your choice. It was my decision to stay or go. But you forced it on me."

We stare at each other for a long minute as he absorbs my words.

"I tried to do the right thing, Juliet."

"And then you stand here and pretend you're not a hero."

9

KING

Right, but aggravating. Her sharp words sting, cutting me to the quick.

Maybe I was trying to be a hero back then.

I wanted to save her, protect her, rescue her from her horrible family. I was so wrapped up in my own pain that I didn't bother stepping back and taking into account her perspective.

I blow out a shaky breath, my insides churning rougher than the ocean on a stormy day. I'm not big on apologies, and this one's particularly tough. Given the fact that I sat on it for fifteen years and all.

"I needed you, King. And you threw me away—threw us away. Like we were nothing."

Her eyes fill with tears, lower lip trembling, and I haven't felt this awful in a long time. Probably since my parents died.

"Juliet—" I brush a hot tear from her cheek with my thumb, the skin as soft and smooth as I remember.

She's so damn beautiful it's almost painful to look at her. Like staring at the sun, the golden rays blinding.

I cup her face, and she tips her head into my palm, the flecks in her eyes sparkling in the light. My body aches from wanting.

Wanting her forgiveness. Wanting her body.

Wanting her.

"You always meant something to me. Always." I run my fingers over her cheek, my chest tight. Barely breathing as I wait for her to say something.

She only sighs, whisper-soft, shoulders relaxing.

"I never meant to hurt you. Swear on my life. I only wanted the best for you. And that wasn't me."

To my horror, my voice breaks, cracking from pain and sadness. All the self-doubt crashes back, rolling over me in a tidal wave. I push down the burning in my chest, my gut, stare out at the lake and try to get a fucking hold of myself.

"King—" Juliet waits for me to meet her gaze.

I slide my eyes back to hers, and everything around me fades away as I fall back under her spell.

Beguiling.

"You were the best for me. Why can't you believe that? All I ever wanted was you, King."

I take her face in my hands, crash my mouth down onto hers. A tiny gasp of surprise escapes her lips, but I swallow the sound. Her fingers curl in my shirt, holding on to me, and it's as if time stood still for us. None of the last fifteen years matter.

Nothing matters except me and Juliet, right here, right now.

I lick at the seam of her lips, tasting her. So sweet, the

same cherry lip gloss she always wore bright on my tongue as I slide into her warm mouth.

I love this woman.

Her hand winds around the back of my neck, twining in my hair, and my body floods with heat. Dick rock hard in my jeans. Our tongues tangle, dancing together, and I wrap my arms around her. Bringing her in close to me, no space left between us anymore.

Erasing at least some of the hurt.

Moving from her hips down to her ass, I palm the round globes. *Such a fine ass.* I squeeze her cheeks lightly, and she shimmies against me. My erection presses against her flat stomach, and I'm certain she can feel the effect she's having on me.

Her nails scrape against the tender skin at the nape of my neck, sending a shiver of pleasure down my spine, balls tightening. Lower torso taut, ready to spring into action.

I want Juliet. All of her.

I need her to be mine.

She pulls away, breaking the kiss. Her cheeks flushed a pretty shade of pink, lips swollen, she's never been more gorgeous than she is right now.

"King . . ."

Holding my breath, body aching, I wait. A light breeze blows, the waves of her hair feathering over her shoulders.

"I don't know if I can do this again."

My chest contracts so hard I think I might crack a damn rib. I need to convince her to take another chance on me. On us.

But the words catch in my throat. A frog croaks somewhere nearby as I search for the right thing to say.

All I manage to get out is one syllable.

"Please."

Something flashes across her face, but it's so quick I can't quite read the reaction. She turns her face toward the water, away from me.

I silently pray to God she reconsiders, blood whooshing loud in my ears.

"How do I know I can trust you? That you're not going to shatter my heart into a million pieces again?" She locks wide eyes on mine, gazing up at me through thick lashes.

Something twists hard and tight inside me.

Shatter my heart again.

I lace my fingers through hers. Her hands so small in mine.

"You just have to trust me, Juliet."

Her lower lip trembles as she takes a shuddery breath.

"I don't know if I can." The words a whisper, so quiet I barely catch them.

I have to make her believe in me.

"What do you want from me? You want me to beg? Throw myself at your feet? What?"

She shakes her head. "No. Well, maybe . . ."

"Oh, c'mon," I grumble, frowning.

"I mean, I do like bringing you to your knees."

Reflexively, I drop to the ground. The grass still dewy, soaking through my jeans as I glance up at her. A smile breaks over her face, and it's the prettiest thing I've seen in my whole damn life.

I grip her hips and pull her to me, pressing my mouth to the zipper of her shorts. I kiss her through the denim, and she relaxes into me, swaying a little. I slip my hand under the hem of her shirt, caress her warm, smooth skin, goose bumps rising on her belly beneath my touch.

"So beautiful," I murmur as her fingers wind in my hair, pulling me closer to her body. Pliant and willing, just like before.

"King . . ." She moans my name as I unbutton her shorts, slide the zipper down with one hand. Tug at the fabric until it pools at her feet. Black satin floods my vision, and I run my hand over the thin, silky material. She's already wet, a dark spot evidence of her arousal.

She blushes a brighter shade of pink as I press my lips to the wetness, her sweet scent filling my nose. My cock throbs, and I want nothing more than to lay Juliet down on this grass and make love to her. Hear her cry out, scream my name.

A soft mewl of pleasure rises from deep in her throat as I suck her clit through her panties. Teasing the tight bud, yanking the satin down her thighs, and diving into her pussy like a starving man. Licking and lapping at her, her juices coating my tongue. She spreads her legs wider, allowing me better access to her most sensitive spot. Flattening my tongue, I feast on her, her thighs quivering. Her hands move from my head to my shoulders, gripping me tight and holding on for support.

"Oh!" She bucks, coming on my tongue, unraveling for me.

I hold her by the thighs, watch as pleasure dances across her face.

So damn beautiful.

Her body sags against me, and I cradle her legs, her hot core still at eye level.

"I fucking love your pussy."

After wiping my mouth with the back of my hand, I

slide her panties back up her legs and rise, keeping a tight grip on her so she doesn't topple over.

"Mmm," she murmurs, eyes glazed with lust. "That was a good start."

She lifts up on tiptoe, pressing her lips to mine. I slip my tongue into her mouth, tangle with hers. After a long minute, she breaks away.

"It can't be this easy." Her voice is soft, barely above a whisper.

I skate my thumb across her heated cheek, tracing over her brown sugar freckles.

"Why not?"

"Everything between us is complicated."

"It doesn't have to be."

She closes her eyes, chest rising, falling. Coming back down to earth.

After a few long seconds, she answers.

"You broke me, King. It's going to take more than a little sex to fix that."

"How about a lot of sex?" I tease, smacking her ass lightly.

She rolls her eyes. "More than sex."

"Fine. More than sex. I get it."

"And I don't want to sneak around this time. If we're going to be together, it needs to be out in the open. With your family. And with mine."

These words hit me straight in the solar plexus, knocking the wind out of me. I'm sure I'm pale as she stares up at me, waits for a response.

Licking my lips, I flex my fingers before answering.

"Okay."

"Okay? Really? You're going to cross that line? For the first time in history, a Capelli and a Montgomery will be together? No more hiding, no more lies? Everything on the up-and-up?"

I nod. "Yes. No more hiding out."

"And I need real time with you. Not just stolen moments."

"You're driving a hard bargain here."

She tosses her hair over her shoulder, standing up taller, straighter. More confident than I've ever seen her.

"I'm worth it."

I drop my lips to hers, breathing her in. Wishing we could stay here forever, this moment suspended in time.

"More than worth it. Trust me on that at least, Juliet."

10

KING

I HAVEN'T FELT THIS GOOD IN YEARS. LIGHT, LIKE A heavy load's been lifted from my shoulders. A load I didn't realize I was holding on to until it was gone.

I've been a damn fool.

I should have gone after her when I realized how bad it hurt to let her go. But it wasn't the right thing to do. What's that old saying?

If you love someone, let them go. If they come back to you, they're yours. If they don't, they never were.

Guess Juliet's mine. Because she flew back. Back to Seaglass Beach, back home.

Back to me.

I'm pretty sure she meant what she said out at the lake, though. Things between us can't be like last time. All the sneaking around, hiding from everyone.

Sure, she's a Capelli and I'm a Montgomery. But we're not fucking ten years old anymore. We're grown-ass adults who can date anyone we choose.

No matter which side of the feud they fall on.

I wonder if Rome, Parker, and Poppy will see it that way. They've ribbed me about Juliet for a while now, so I doubt they'll be too shocked. But that doesn't mean I'm looking forward to talking about my love life with my siblings.

And Juliet's brothers? That's likely to be a whole different ball game. The one thing we've got going for us right now is Jagger being behind bars. He can't cause too many problems from the inside. Cash and Damon are thugs, sure, but Jagger's the mastermind of that crew. Without him around, those two don't know which way's the damn ocean. Juliet may even be able to bring them around without Jagger's influence.

I top off the water in the trough for the horses, then head out to the pen to check on the goats. We have babies now, the mama giving birth yesterday afternoon. Triplet kids, born under the warm afternoon sun.

Luckily Beau was still here. He was just getting ready to run into town when the mama went into full-on labor. A few hours later, she birthed three kids in quick succession. Beau helped clean up the kids, snipping umbilical cords and dipping them in iodine to prevent infection, while I gave antibiotics and caught the placenta on a tarp for the mama.

Now we have to watch her real close, make sure she's getting enough food to produce milk for the kids. The last twenty-four hours have gone fine, but I need to be vigilant.

"Hey, babies." I open the gate, entering the pen as two of the kids wobble over to check me out. Bending down, I stroke the soft black fur of the nearest one, the other nudging his brother out of the way to move closer to me.

Chuckling, I pet the head of the other kid.

"There's enough attention to go around, little buddy." I wander over to the mama doe, patting her on the back.

"Hey there, Sophie. How you doing?"

She stares up at me with large black eyes, then bleats.

"I hope that means good, since I don't speak goat. Not yet, anyway."

I head over to the feed bowl and drop in the ration. She sniffs at the air, then wanders over to forage.

"Eat up, Sophie. Lots of kids to feed now. I don't want to be out here bottle-feeding your babies. Don't have the time for that."

Satisfied with Sophie and her kids, I leave them to their supper. Tonight's the family meeting, and I doubt anyone will appreciate me smelling like a farm animal at the dinner table. I should have just enough time for a quick shower before the gang shows up. Hopefully bringing food, because with all the excitement of yesterday, I didn't have time to smoke the ribs, like I'd planned.

Stomach growling, I take the offensive and shoot Poppy a quick text. She's the most likely to pull through on the food. Parker'd probably forget, and Rome's leaving straight from the courthouse.

> King: Sophie had kids last night. Didn't get a chance to make dinner. Can you bring something?

> Little Sis: Sophie had babies? Aww! Pics!

Shaking my head, I scroll through my recent photos, sending a few over to her.

> Little Sis: Oh my gosh, they're precious!
> You should put them on Insta. You could
> prob make goat milk soap or something
> now

> King: Sure. Dinner?

An eye-roll emoji comes through, followed by a goat milk soap blog post complete with step-by-step instructions on making soap.

Uh-huh. In my spare time.

A second later, another text.

> Little Sis: What do you want to eat? Still
> want pizza?

> King: That works

> Little Sis: See you soon!

Poppy sends a GIF of a newborn kid stumbling around a pasture, and I laugh at my screen. Sometimes she's pretty funny.

I hope she and Parker take the news about Mom and our secret half sister well tonight. Maybe Rome and I should have told them sooner, but a good time never presented itself. Not that there's ever a great time to find something like that out.

They'll have to settle for better late than never, I guess.

My cell buzzes again, and I'm just getting ready to remind Poppy to order extra pepperoni when I realize the message isn't from her. My stomach swoops as I stare down at my screen.

Rose Queen: Yesterday was unexpected

Muscles coil in my lower torso, remembering kissing Juliet out at the lake.

I need to see her again.

Fingers tingling, I text:

King: Want to get together tonight after you're done with your shift?

Squinting down at the phone, I pray she says yes. My cock's already twitching at the thought of seeing her again. Touching her, kissing her, tasting every inch of her.

But I have no idea how long this stupid family meeting thing's gonna last. Could be thirty minutes, could go for an hour or two. Worst case, I figure they'll be gone by ten. Leaves me plenty of time to meet up with her.

Rose Queen: Your place or mine?

King: Yes

Straightforward, honest. Because I don't care where I kiss Juliet again as long as it happens.

Rose Queen: Your text game is strong

Snorting at the phone, I tap back a response:

King: We both know that's not where my skills lie

Rose Queen: You're going to have to
prove it tonight

King: Challenge accepted

I'm 1,000 percent down for that challenge, judging by
my rock-hard, aching cock. My balls are so full right now, I
may have to jack off in the shower to get some relief from
the stiffy situation. Can't be sitting at the head of the table,
holding a family meeting with a raging boner.

Rose Queen: So—your place or mine?

King: Hate to ask, but could you come to
the ranch? Our doe had kids yesterday
and I have to keep an eye on them

Rose Queen: You have baby goats and
didn't send me any pics?

What the hell's up with all the women in my life
wanting baby goat pics? Never even crossed my mind to
share photos, and both of them seem pissed about it.

Just like I did with Poppy, I fire off a few of the pics.
This time I include one of me holding the smallest kid, the
one Beau and I named "Oreo" since he's black with white
patches.

Rose Queen: Adorable. The baby goat's
pretty cute too

Rose Queen: 😊

Cheeks heating, I grin down at the phone like a total
dope.

Fuck me.

I'm happy.

And the feeling's so unfamiliar, so raw, it scares me shitless.

Because I know better than anyone that happiness never lasts. It's as fleeting as a perfect sunset sinking down over the field, or a wave crashing against the shore.

Blink and you miss it.

Worse, the tighter you hold on, the faster it seems to slip away.

My cell vibrates again with another text.

> Rose Queen: I'll see you around ten

Shoving the doubt away, I take a deep breath and text Juliet back.

> King: I'll be waiting

Deep down, I've been waiting for her to come back for years. This time I can't screw it up.

I TAKE A FEW EXTRA MINUTES GETTING READY, ON account of my meetup with Juliet later tonight. I slap on aftershave, the cool liquid making my skin tingle. I dry my hands, then pull on a navy T-shirt and jeans. The weather's warming up, and I anticipate the conversation getting heated too.

"King?" Poppy's voice echoes down the hallway.

"Be out in a sec." I finish tucking in my shirt and grab my cell off the nightstand on my way out.

"Hey. You look nice." She scrunches up her nose at me, and I can practically see the wheels turning in her head as I walk down the stairs.

Oh geez.

I brace myself for the game of twenty questions I know is coming.

"Did you get a haircut or something?" She tilts her head to the side, squinting.

"No."

"New shirt?"

"Nope."

"You shaved."

"Yes."

"Wow. Saving up your words for the family meeting?" She pops her hip out, nudging against mine.

"Funny. Thanks for bringing the food." I lift the boxes from her hands, easing her load.

Heading toward the kitchen island, she follows behind me. The change in direction effectively cut the interrogation short, and for that, at least, I'm grateful.

I set the pizza boxes down on the granite counter, then head to the bar to fix Poppy and myself a drink.

"What do you want?" I ask, snagging a rocks glass for myself.

"I'll take wine, if you have any."

"White?"

"Sure."

I pour her drink, then mine. I'm going to need more than one drink to get through this night, I think.

"Parker's on his way, and Rome was stopping home to change."

"Okay."

"Think they'll care if we eat? I'm starving. Worked through lunch because we had a glitch in the computer system, and two guests were booked in the same villa. Total nightmare trying to figure out the rooms."

I shrug. "I'm sure they won't care, long as you leave them some food."

"Cool."

Poppy takes her wine, and I grab plates from the cabinet, setting them on the island next to the pizza. She opens the box, and the scent of baked dough and fresh garlic hits my nostrils.

"Seaglass Slice has the best pizza, I swear." Poppy takes a bite, nibbling at a string of cheese dangling from the triangle.

I nod and sip at my drink, the burn of the bourbon a sharp contrast to the icy temp of the liquid.

"They do."

"Aren't you going to eat?" She narrows her eyes at me again. Why does Poppy always make me feel like she's taking notes?

"In a minute. I'm not that hungry."

"Hey!" The screen door bangs open, and Parker saunters into the kitchen. "Y'all started without me?"

He doesn't bother with niceties, instead beelining for the pizza.

"Seaglass Slice never disappoints," Parker mumbles, his mouth already stuffed full of pizza.

"Do you two share a brain or something? Poppy just

said the same damn thing not two seconds ago." I stare at the both of them, marveling at their similarities. Uncanny, really, how they're so interconnected.

"I have most of the brain, I think. I let Parker have, like, a quarter."

I snort, and Parker chucks Poppy in the arm. "Not funny, sis. At all. I have at least half, and you know it."

"Well, at least you're not claiming a full brain." Poppy grins at Parker and takes another bite of pizza as Rome strolls in.

"Hey." Unlike Parker, he bypasses the pizza, instead heading to the fridge and helping himself to a beer.

"Where's Skye? Thought she was coming?" Poppy peers down the hallway toward the front door, but Skye doesn't appear.

"She's wiped from work. Said she wanted to lie down and rest. I made her some scrambled eggs and toast before I left—that's why I'm late."

"Such a doting husband." Poppy beams over at Roman, a wide smile on her face.

"She's doing all the work. Least I can do is make her some food. I did promise I won't be gone too long."

"Understood," I say, secretly glad it's just the four of us for the family meeting. Not that I don't like Skye. This just feels like family business.

"Now that we're all here, spill the beans, King. What's this meeting about?" Poppy spins and faces me, one brow raised.

I've thought long and hard about how to deliver the news about our mom. Practiced it, even. In the end, I decide straightforward is the best way. Rip the freaking Band-Aid off and deal with the pain.

I take a deep breath, exhale, Poppy and Parker both staring at me.

"Our mom had another baby."

11

KING

"Wʜᴀᴛ?" Pᴏᴘᴘʏ's ᴠᴏɪᴄᴇ ɢᴏᴇs ᴀʟʟ ʜɪɢʜ ᴀɴᴅ sʜʀɪᴇᴋʏ, cheeks flushing pink. "What are you talking about?"

Rome shoots me a sideways glance, and I begin to second-guess the straightforward approach.

Maybe not the best tactic here.

"A letter came. Here, addressed to Mom." I pull the aqua stationery from my back pocket, toss it onto the table. Parker stares at the letter, brow furrowed. Poppy doesn't hesitate, lunging forward, snatching the paper up and reading.

Her lips move as she silently reads, then rereads, the letter. A letter I've read dozens of times now. Not that I'm about to admit that fact.

Shaking her head, Poppy tosses the note down on the table.

"No. I refuse to believe this." She folds her arms over her chest, frowning. "No way could Mom have another child all this time that nobody knew about."

Rome chimes in. "It's true, Poppy. I looked into it and

found the birth record for Lacey with a little bit of digging."

Poppy spins to face Rome, whirling so fast her hair creates a wind I feel from my chair.

"You knew about this and didn't tell us?" She gestures between her and Parker. "After promising no more secrets? How could you do this, Rome? I expect it from him—" She jabs a finger through the air, pointing at me. "But you? I thought we were all on the same team."

Her lower lip quivers, voice shaky, and I silently will her not to cry. I'd much rather deal with an angry Poppy than a sad Poppy.

"I was here when the letter came. That's the only reason I know about it, Pops," Rome lies smoothly.

"And you're certain this is legit?" Parker scowls at the letter, still not touching the aqua square.

"Pretty sure, yeah. Looks like the baby was born five years before King." Rome sits back, propping one ankle over his knee.

"You think Dad knew?" Parker asks, his hands gripping the table.

"Not sure." I rattle the ice in my glass and watch as the liquid swirls round and round, an amber whirlpool.

Parker blows out a breath. "Guess we'll never know."

A heavy silence falls over the table as we all retreat into ourselves, processing the stark reality of this statement.

Poppy interrupts the quiet. "I think we need to see this Lacey woman with our own eyes."

"It's true, Pops." Rome's voice is quiet yet firm.

"I hear what you're saying, Rome. But I still think we should meet her, vet her, before we do anything else. I mean, are you planning on calling her? Writing her back?

Or did you already do that?" She glares first at me, then at Rome, her aquamarine eyes flashing.

"No, Poppy. We didn't do anything." I work hard to keep my voice neutral, even as hot aggravation builds in my gut. This is exactly why we put off having this conversation in the first freaking place.

"Parks? What do you think?" Rome cuts his gaze to Parker.

Parker shrugs, fingers drumming on the table to a beat only he can hear. "I don't know, guys. I'll do whatever y'all think is best."

Parker the peacemaker, going with the flow.

"So—who's going to Peachtree Grove? Rome?" Poppy turns to face Rome, one eyebrow lifted high.

"I really can't go right now, Pops. Not with Skye being pregnant. Plus work. I don't have that much time off yet and need to save it up for when the baby comes."

Poppy huffs out an aggravated breath, then swivels to face me. "King? You going?"

"Umm . . ." I bite at the corner of my lip, stare down at the wood grain of the table. Anywhere but at my sister, who's royally pissed off.

"Since you apparently know the right thing to do all the damn time now."

Her tone's snippy, the words biting. Even if I maybe earned the wrath a little.

"I'll go, I guess. Y'all want me to send you photos? Do a formal interview? What?" I look at each of them in turn. First Poppy, then Parker, then Rome.

Parker shrugs. "Sure. All of the above, I guess. I mean —she deserves a response to her letter, don't you think? If it were me, I'd at least want to know why no one wrote back."

Parker pointing out the obvious is a sharp punch straight to the gut, the remaining air sucked right out of the room. Sadness hangs over the table as we all sit with our grief.

Eventually I clear my throat, force words out. "Fine. I'll go. Long as Beau can pick up the slack. Maybe y'all can take turns checking on things while I'm gone."

Rome leans back in his chair. "We can do that, King. You probably won't be gone long, right? A few days?"

"I reckon at least three. It's a day's drive to Peachtree Grove."

Poppy rolls her eyes. "Of course you already know that."

The comment pisses me off, but I let the jab slide. No use getting into a fight with my sister right now. She'll cool off eventually; she always does.

"You gonna tell her you're coming? Or is it gonna be a sneak attack?" Parker asks, grabbing for another slice of pizza. Good to see this conversation hasn't dampened his appetite any.

"Sneak attack, I guess." Because what would I say on the phone? *Hey, bad news. Your birth mom's dead.*

Not that it's going to be any better in person, I suppose. But I'll have more time to figure it out, get the lay of the land, and check her out.

"I want a full report this time, King. And I'm serious. No. More. Secrets." Poppy punches each word, leaning forward and locking her narrowed eyes on mine.

I nod. "Understood, Pops. Promise. I'll get you a full report and try to get photos."

"Fine." She pushes away from the table, standing. Clearly pissed. "See y'all later."

She stalks out of the kitchen, heading down the hallway. The screen door creaks open, and I wait for the inevitable bang as she storms out.

But the door never slams. Instead, I hear Poppy's voice pitch up in shock.

"Juliet! What are you doing here?"

Shit.

I glance at my watch, heat blazing my face. It's not even eight p.m. yet. I wasn't expecting Juliet for at least another hour or two.

Poppy and Juliet appear in the doorway of the kitchen, Juliet's cheeks stained a bright pink as her gaze flies around the table. First at me, then at my brothers.

A hand on Juliet's shoulder, Poppy thrusts her in my direction.

"King's just full of surprises tonight."

12

JULIET

Well, this is awkward.

Hadn't planned on seeing the whole Montgomery gang tonight. But I guess it's time for King to put his money where his mouth is and fess up.

My eyes meet his across the room, his navy gaze filled with panic. None too inspiring.

He clears his throat, breaking the silence.

"Y'all know Juliet."

Poppy shakes her head, her blonde ponytail swishing through the air. "You're unbelievable, King Montgomery. Honestly—"

She tightens her grip on my arm, pushing me across the kitchen as my mind whirs with all the wild thoughts and possibilities of what could happen right now. Kinda feels like walking into the lions' den, complete with the baring of sharp teeth.

"Don't act dumb in front of us, King. Tell us what's going on here. Right the fuck now."

Poppy shoves me toward him, and I stumble forward, feeling like an intruder, a captive who crossed over into enemy territory and was caught. My hip hits the edge of the table, and King stands, catching me before I fall into his lap. His large hands grip my biceps, and I take a deep breath, inhaling his spicy scent.

"Calm down, Poppy. And not that it's any of your concern, but I invited Juliet over. Because this is my house and all." He looks past me, his stare flinty. Clearly not interested in answering questions.

"So you're, like, dating? Hooking up?"

"Geez, Poppy. Nosy much?" Parker cuts in, chiding his twin sister. "King and Juliet are grown-ups. They don't have to answer to you, me, or anyone else."

"Exactly," King growls, thrusting out his chin, and I'm not sure how I feel about his response. Kinda lukewarm, to be honest.

"I'm tired of all the damn lies, guys. Sure, he can hook up with whomever he pleases. But since when did honesty fly out the window with all of you? First you, Parker—" She whirls to face him, pointing her index finger accusatorily. "Sneaking around with my bestie, no less. Then Rome and Skye." She glares across the table at Roman. "So many secrets, I can't even keep track of them all. And now King. What the hell?" She pivots to face me and King, her lower lip trembling. I'm not sure with anger or sadness, or maybe a combo of both.

"We were never like this. Not when Mom and Dad were alive. And it needs to stop. Right now." Poppy crosses her arms over her chest, frowning.

King lets out a long, low sigh. I'm fully regretting cutting my shift short.

"Fine. You want to know the truth? We're, uh, kind of seeing each other." King stumbles over the words, and my gut roils with anxiety. I'm not sure what I expected him to say. Because what are we doing? Getting reacquainted? And how much do I want him to tell his family?

The whole truth.

That's what. The realization bubbles up inside me, but I keep my lips sealed tight. This is King's deal, his kin, and he needs to handle them how he sees fit. We can fight about it later.

"Since when?" Poppy keeps on keeping on, not letting anything go, mining for details.

"Recently." King shuts her down with a terse one-word response.

"You're not on trial, you know. You can answer in more detail. I probably won't use it against you." Her wide eyes flash as she goads her big brother.

"Well, it sure the hell feels like I am."

"Poppy," Roman cuts in, his tone warning her to back down.

Big mistake. She spins around on him, glaring across the table.

"You knew about this, didn't you?"

"Nope." Roman takes a slow swig of his beer, totally calm.

She purses her lips, cocking her head to the side. Probably trying to work out if she believes him.

"I'm gonna need a minute to think about this." Poppy glances over at me, then at King, then back at me again. Sizing us both up, gnawing her lower lip. "I don't know—"

"Well, the great thing is this has nothing to do with

you. So you don't actually have to know." King snarls at his sister, the vein at his temple throbbing.

"See, that's where you're wrong. We're family, King. And what you do affects all of us, whether you like it or not. Family is fun like that. You dating a Capelli is the kind of thing we should discuss."

King slams his fist down so hard on the table, both Parker and Roman jump.

"Enough! I'm not going to discuss my love life with you. It's not actually open for discussion. Who I do or don't date is none of your damn business. Period." He glowers at Poppy, but she doesn't back down, not even a little bit. Instead, she stands taller, pushing her chest out.

"It is, King. If that person is a Capelli." She spits my last name out of her mouth like battery acid, and for the millionth time in my life, I curse my family name, our collective reputation.

"Still none of your business, Pops," Roman says, glancing over at his sister and shrugging.

"Gawd, y'all just don't get it. This is going to have repercussions. On all of us." Poppy sweeps her arm out before turning her aquamarine eyes on me. "I mean, no offense, Juliet, but your family's reputation is crappy."

"Gee, thanks. Like I didn't already know that."

"Shut your damn mouth, Poppy. Leave it alone already."

"I can't, King. Word's gonna get out that you're with *her*, and there could be blowback. On me, the inn. It's bad for business."

Even after years of this sort of thing, hearing the words spoken out loud still stings. My stomach clenches, hands clammy, and I just want to get out of here.

"I'm gonna go . . ." I step back, ready to bolt across the kitchen.

"No. This ends now," says King. "Poppy, I hear what you're saying. Rude as hell, but I get it. And I'm sorry about any blowback you might have to deal with. Tell anyone and everyone who dares to utter a word to come see me about their issues. Not your problem."

Poppy opens her mouth, then shuts it again, unsure of what to say, I guess.

My chest loosens a little as his words sink in. *King's finally standing up for me.*

Tension hangs heavy in the air between the siblings, and I can feel three sets of eyes boring into me. I squash down the urge to squirm, like I used to back in elementary school when kids would chant *Crooked Capelli* at me as I ran off the bus.

King's hand finds mine, interlacing our fingers right there in front of everyone, and hot tears spring to my eyes.

Do not cry, Juliet. Do. Not. Cry.

My heart bangs wildly, and a lump lodges in my throat as relief and happiness surge through me.

We're really doing this.

"Hmph." Poppy juts out her bottom lip, her brow furrowing. Clearly not happy about this turn of events. It's gonna take more than King's say-so to gain her approval.

"Anyone else have something to say about my love life, or can we move on?" King glances at each of his siblings, but wisely no one else opens their mouth.

"Good. That's settled then. Meeting adjourned."

Parker and Roman both take the hint, pushing away from the table and muttering their goodbyes. Poppy clearly has a death wish, because she stands frozen in her spot, even as her brothers shuffle by.

"C'mon, Pops. Let's leave these two alone, 'kay?" Parker grabs her elbow, dragging her out of the kitchen in a trance. She follows along, shooting one last withering look my way before heading out.

The screen door slams, and King exhales.

"Sorry about Poppy. She can be—a lot."

I screw up my lips and shrug. "It's fine. I know my family sucks."

"It's not fine for her to speak to you like that. And I won't stand for it again. She got a pass today because of the shock. But that's the last time." He spins and faces me, his expression serious, and my chest loosens.

"Well, thanks. I appreciate that. Next time I'll call before I stop by."

"Next time?" King tips his head, cocking a brow high.

Heat floods my cheeks, and I'm so far out of my depth right now, I'm not certain what to say. We've never been in a legitimate situation, in front of people—family—before. My heart's still hammering from the confrontation—and how King handled it.

I swallow hard before answering.

"Yeah, I'm kind of assuming there'll be a next time, since you just declared your feelings to your entire family."

"Come here." King pulls me to him, hands tight on my hips as he drops his lips to mine. Applying just the right amount of pressure, telling me he's in charge here. And I love it.

"You know I'm teasing," he murmurs, and a ripple of desire flutters through me.

"Mmm" is all I manage to say, our tongues sliding

together. The anxious tension fades away, quickly replaced with a much better kind of tension. My lower belly tingles, a familiar throbbing pulsing between my thighs as King deepens the kiss. His hands glide from my hips to my rear, his large palms squeezing, eliciting a moan from me.

"I love your ass."

I smile, one hand finding the back pocket of his jeans and sliding in. "I love yours too. I missed it."

"Only my ass?" He pulls away slightly, the right side of his lip quirking up.

"There might be another part of you I missed too."

"Besides my charming personality?"

I chuckle. "Yeah, definitely besides that."

"I'll try not to be offended."

"Don't be," I say, my fingers tiptoeing to the button of his jeans. Tracing around the metal circle, his abs flex beneath my hand. Everything about this moment feels surreal. I've dreamed of this reunion so many times but didn't think it would ever happen.

Yet here we are, standing in King's kitchen, and I almost can't believe this is real.

"Juliet . . ."

King's deep voice startles me out of my thoughts.

"You okay?" He runs his thumb along my jawline, tipping my face up to meet his gaze. I nod.

"Yes. It's just—" My voice wavers, breath hitching. I take a quick, shuddery inhale. "I've thought about being here, like this, with you—"

"So have I."

"You have?"

"Yeah." He licks his lower lip. "Of course. I thought

about you from the moment you left town. I never stopped thinking about you."

"King . . ." I reach up, resting my hand on his broad chest, his heart thudding beneath my palm. "Why didn't you reach out, all this time?"

"I couldn't." His eyes flick to the ground, deep lines etched between his brows.

"Yes, you could. I never changed my number."

Lifting his chin, he locks his eyes on mine. "No. I knew if I called you, wrote you, I wouldn't be strong enough to stay away."

"I didn't want you to stay away."

Taking my face in his hands, King kisses me with the heat of a thousand suns. As if he's been waiting for this day —for me—all this time. I melt into him, letting go of a little bit of pain, the hurt. Letting him kiss it away and accepting his apology.

"I'm so sorry," he murmurs. "So, so sorry. I just wanted you to be happy."

My fingers curl into his T-shirt, my throat and chest tight with regret. For all the time we've lost. Time we should have spent together.

"I wasn't happy without you," I whisper, hot tears pricking behind my eyes.

"Neither was I. I was actually a miserable son of a bitch. Rome can attest to that for me."

He tucks a stray lock of hair behind my ear, sending a shiver of pleasure racing down my spine.

"I wish I could undo the past, Jules. But I can't. All we can do now is try to move forward."

I blink, trying to push the tears down. Every inch of my

body screams at me to say yes, get naked right here, right now. But the pang in my chest has me hesitating.

"I want to, I really do. But I'm scared, King." A hot tear splashes onto my cheek, and he bends down, lips brushing my skin, kissing the drop away.

"I know, baby. I know. Things will be different this time, though. I promise."

13

JULIET

I want to believe King so bad it hurts. All the way down to my core, a constant, dull, throbbing ache.

Desire.

Hot, pulsating want.

Still there after all this time.

Fuck it.

The only way I'll ever know if I can trust him is to put my heart back out on the line.

Fragile, bruised, broken, and taped back together.

Just do it.

My brain's shouting at me to ask more questions, pull out the exact words needed to earn my trust, get it all in writing, for fuck's sake.

But the rest of me? The rest of me is in a full-blown hormonal surge, with King's body pressing up against mine. All muscle and power and sex.

Yeah, not turning that down.

Rising on tiptoe, I press my lips lightly to his, offering up a tentative yes.

He doesn't hesitate, sweeping me off my feet and into his arms, not straining the least bit as he carries me up the stairs. Moving down the dim hallway toward what I assume to be his bedroom. I'm not positive, though, because I've never actually been in the main house, only the guesthouse in back.

King angles us through a doorway, careful not to knock my ankles or knees against anything. He lays me gently on the bed, in the center of a pool of soft moonlight shining through the window. I remind myself to breathe, taking a full inhale instead of short, staccato puffs. The room smells like him, clean and a little bit earthy.

"You're so damn beautiful, Jules." He stares down at me, runs a hand up the inside of my thigh. Warmth carries straight through the denim, and pleasure ripples through me. Familiar yet different.

He's older, stronger, tougher. Thick veins pop from his forearms, every muscle in his body toned from working the ranch.

I want this man. On me, over me, buried so deep inside me I don't even know where I stop and he begins.

Reaching down, I undo my jeans, shimmy out of them as sexily as I can while lying on the bed. Not the easiest feat. King helps me out, his palms spreading over my thighs and pulling the pants all the way down to my ankles. I kick my shoes off, the denim hitting the ground with a soft thud. Cool air hits my bare skin, and I inhale, a quick, sharp breath. Sucking in oxygen and sheer masculinity, a force so strong I can almost see it, hear it humming around us.

Just like I remembered.

King always taking the lead. Leaving me to sit back and enjoy the ride.

He lifts his shirt over his head, then tosses the blue cotton to the ground. The sight of him shirtless still takes my breath away. Broad shoulders, tanned skin, hard planes of chiseled muscle. Not gym-bro 'roid muscles either. Real man muscles, earned through years of backbreaking, honest work.

His expression's serious as he bends over me, his face hovering just above mine.

"I want you, Jules. Do you still want this? Because once we start, I don't know if I can stop."

I nod. The words won't come right now, but I've never wanted anything—or anyone—more in my life.

My hands flutter to his shoulders, fingertips stroking the warm, smooth skin. Tracing over the sharp lines of his triceps, around to his biceps. Instinctively, he flexes beneath my touch, and heat unfurls in my belly. He drops his lips to my neck, kissing the flesh, nipping lightly. I shudder, pleasure washing over me, thrumming through my veins with every wild beat of my heart.

Gliding my hands across his pecs and wrapping around to his back, kneading the tight muscles. The bulge in his jeans presses against my center, and I scissor my legs around his hips, pulling him in closer to me. Heat shimmers between us, the air charged with delicious anticipation.

Of what's about to happen and what comes after that.

For the first time in forever, a vision of a happy future dances in front of me. I only need to be brave enough to take the first step.

"Fuck me, King. Please."

"I planned on it."

"Good. We're on the same page then." I smile up at him in the dark, a lone moonbeam glimmering in his navy eyes.

Everything about this feels right.

I wind my hand around his neck, and my thumb runs along the sharp edge of his hairline. I lift my head, kissing him, hard and possessive. Mint and bourbon mix on my tongue as I sweep into his mouth. His tongue twines with mine, and wetness floods my panties.

He grazes the skin of my belly with his hand, and then he's lifting me up, peeling my shirt off. Unclasping my bra, easing the satin from my body until it falls to the bed. He nuzzles into my cleavage. Breathing me in, the warm exhale a whisper over me. Chill bumps rise on my skin, nipples peaking. His tongue circles one sharp point, sucking soft, then hard, and my pussy clenches. He rolls the other nipple between his thumb and his finger, his skin rough, increasing the friction. I buck, grinding against his hardness.

Fumbling with the button of his jeans, panting with need.

I've been with only two other guys in all this time, and neither of them came close to King. In the bedroom—or anywhere else, for that matter.

His pants are off, and now he's ripping my panties down my legs. Fast and hungry, pupils dilated. We're both naked as he spreads my thighs, licking through my wetness. Finding my clit and sucking greedily on the tight bud. A sharp bolt of pleasure rips through me, a soft moan vibrating low in my throat.

"You taste so good." He mumbles the words, each syllable tickling my sensitive flesh.

I arch up, trying to get more contact, and he sucks harder before dipping two fingers into me. My pussy clenches around him, and it feels so damn wonderful. He adds another, moving in and out of my wetness, and every inch of me's on fire right now. He moves back up my body, licking and sucking, until we're face-to-face. His cock twitches against my thigh, demanding attention, and I happily give it.

Running my fingers over the sensitive tip, already damp with pre-cum. I rub it into his skin, then encircle his cock, slide up and down his thick shaft. He lets out a moan, hardening even more in my hand.

"God, I missed you." King brushes the hair from my eyes, and my chest swells with emotion. Too many feelings to identify, so I latch on to desire.

"Me too."

The question hovers on my tongue, but I'm afraid to ask.

I shouldn't ask.

"How many?"

"What?" King frowns.

"How many others?"

"What are you talking about?"

"How many girls—women—have you been with since I've been gone?"

He blinks, once, twice, and I hold my breath, my stomach sinking.

I shouldn't have asked.

"None."

"What?"

"No one."

"For real?" My voice tips up with incredulity.

"Yes. For real. I told you—it's always been you."

My heart twists so hard it aches.

All this time, he waited for me. Waited for me to come back and be his again.

"What if I never came back?"

"Guess I'd die a lonely, horny old man."

"King—"

He presses his lips to mine, effectively shutting me up. He always did say talking was overrated.

That kiss tells me everything I need to know.

King loves me, and always has.

14

KING

"Should I even ask? Do I want to know?" I stare into Juliet's eyes, focus on the golden ring circling her dark pupils.

Hold my breath, because obviously the answer's not zero. Otherwise she wouldn't have asked. Not that I expected her to live like a nun, but still. I'm not sure I want to know the answer.

"Two." She whispers the number, like she's at confession. As if I can absolve her of her sins.

My gut twists, thinking of anyone being with her. Any other man touching her skin, feeling her lips on his, tasting her sweetness.

I shouldn't have asked. But, perversely, I need to know.

"Okay."

"Okay?" She squints up at me, one brow arched.

"I mean—if I ever meet the fuckers, I will kill them. But what's done is done."

I cup her cheek with my palm, reassuring her. Even as my gut churns with jealousy. No need to make her feel worse about the past. There's plenty of regret swimming between us right now—I sure as hell don't need to pile on.

She presses her lips to mine in a soft, slow kiss, melting against me, and I haven't felt this good, this at peace, in a long while.

I nudge at her opening with my cock, teasing her, and she smiles up at me.

"We should probably use protection," I murmur, pulling away.

She grips my shoulder, stopping me.

"No, it's fine. I'm on the pill."

I don't fool around with second guesses, lining up and easing into her wet heat. Sinking in deep, so deep I'm not sure where she ends and I begin.

"God, you feel amazing." I gaze down into her wide, hazel eyes. Fully involved and in the moment.

"I love you."

All the breath leaves my body, my heart squeezing so hard I'm not sure I'll make it through the next minute.

Juliet still loves me. Even after all this time.

I stroke her face, her eyes fluttering closed beneath my soft touch. So fucking beautiful, a shimmering butterfly, back after a long flight.

With me.

I kiss her, softly, gently. On the mouth, her cheeks, her eyelids. Brushing my lips against the long column of her neck, the graceful swoop of her collarbone. Nipping at the freckle I've always loved, watching her squirm as I caress her breasts. I run my hand down over her ribs, then ease my cock in and out, back in again. Her pussy clenches around me, and she sighs, content.

Like she's home.

"Look at me, Juliet."

Her eyes pop open, locking on mine as I sink back into her. She clamps around me tighter, and my cock responds, growing harder still.

"King," she murmurs as I pick up speed, thrust faster.

I lace my fingers through hers, and her chest flushes a bright pink, nipples sharp. I know she's close. She lifts up her hips, seeking more, and I deliver, grinding down.

Now she's breathing heavy. I thrust deeper, and she gasps, nails digging into my skin.

"You're so . . . fucking . . . beautiful . . . ," I murmur, pounding into her tight pussy. She bites on her lip, and I drill down. Matching my rhythm, she rides me. Not skipping a beat, like no time has passed at all.

"Such a good fuck."

That pushes her over the edge, and she unravels beneath me, shuddering and crying out.

"King . . ."

"That's good, baby. Let go. Let it all go."

I keep moving, in and out, as she crests. Seeking my own release, finally exploding deep inside, spilling my hot cum into her.

"Fuck," I hiss, pulling out and collapsing. Scooping her up and onto my chest, still heaving with the exertion. I stroke her hair, the silky strands tickling my bare chest as our breathing syncs. Everything's quiet, the only sound the thudding of our hearts.

Warm liquid hits my pec, dripping onto my heated skin, trailing down over my ribs before falling to the sheets. Juliet's chest rises and falls, a soft sniffle filling the air.

I keep stroking her hair, my hand wandering down her

back, the smooth skin of her ass. Pulling her in close to me, trying to erase any distance, any doubt that still exists.

Juliet's mine and always has been.

And I am hers.

There's never been anyone else.

"I'm sorry." Her voice is the quietest whisper, floating up to the ceiling's wooden beams.

"Baby," I murmur, pressing my lips to the crown of her head.

"They meant nothing to me."

My chest squeezes, and I'm not sure what to say, so I say nothing. Just keep stroking her soft, smooth skin. Willing her to know how I feel.

She lifts her head, gazes up at me.

"Do you forgive me?"

Her eyes wide, regretful.

How can I say anything but yes?

I kiss her, soft and slow, licking at the seam of her full lips. I'd be lying if I said it was all good. But it's unfair to have expected more.

"I had no claim on you."

I swallow hard over the lump in my throat, pushing down the thick heat—jealousy, anger, regret swirling around. Knowing the truth to my words but still hating that any other man ever touched her.

"What's done is done."

She laces her fingers in mine, sighing against my chest.

"I have to check on the goats."

Juliet wraps her leg around my calf, her foot sliding up and down.

"Right now?"

"Yeah." My voice comes out gruffer than I expect.

"I'll go with you."

"It'll be cold out there."

"I'll be fine."

Lifting her head from my chest, she unwinds her body from mine, stands. Bathed in moonlight from the window, she glows, all soft curves and perfect lines.

Mine from now on.

The thought helps calm the storm of anger and jealousy brewing inside me, a cool balm to the fire. I follow Juliet's lead, climbing out of bed and throwing my clothes back on. She does the same and starts toward the door.

"Wait."

I hustle over to my dresser, pull a long-sleeved shirt out of my drawer.

"Here." I thrust the shirt at her, and she smiles at me. Our fingers brush as she takes the garment, an electric current running between us. She tosses the shirt on, and then we head out to the barn together, me leading the way.

True to my word, the air's cold now, and despite the extra shirt, Juliet shivers. I wrap my arm around her, bringing her in close as we walk across the dewy grass toward the barn. An owl hoots somewhere in the distance, a cool breeze rustling the leaves of the trees overhead.

Unlocking the gate, I usher Juliet through, then check to make sure it latches closed behind us. Bleats cut through the quiet of the night as we tread to the barn. I flick the lights on, and the mama goat stares at us with her dark eyes. All three kids are snuggled up against her, fast asleep.

"Aww, they're so cute." Juliet's lips tip into a smile, tiny laugh lines crinkling around her eyes. "Can I pet them?"

I shrug. "Sure. If the mama will let you."

She crosses over to the goats, and I follow right behind.

Bending down, she offers her hand to the mama. The goat sniffs at her; then Juliet strokes her head, scratching behind her ears. Having gained her trust, Juliet reaches down and strokes the back of Oreo, then the tiny heads of the other two kids.

"They're so soft." Her voice is a reverent whisper as she pets each of the kids in turn.

"They're real soft right now. The coat gets tougher over time as it grows in."

"I can't believe how tiny they are."

"You should have seen them wobbling around. It was pretty funny, just learning how to walk. Now they're running all over."

"They're precious." She keeps stroking and petting the babies, cooing at them one by one.

"I'm gonna feed the mama."

"You need help?"

"Nope. Keep hanging with the babies; then we'll be done."

Moving around the barn, I refresh the water and the feed pellets, handling the horses while I'm out here too. I finish within fifteen minutes, but Juliet's in no rush to leave. She's cross-legged on the barn floor, bare legs and all, two of the kids snuggled up in her lap. Mama goat has her eyes closed, resting, not at all concerned about her babies.

"You have a real good feel for this." I run a palm over Juliet's hair, the glow from the lights catching the blonde highlights in her waves.

"I love animals. I always wanted a puppy, but we could never afford one. Daddy said even stray dogs need to eat, and we barely had enough money to feed ourselves. Then I went to school, and after that I moved around so much.

Always in a rental, and I worked long hours. No time for a dog. Plus, a puppy needs space to run and play. A teeny-tiny apartment's not fair to an animal."

She strokes Oreo, scratching behind his ears, and my chest aches for her. All she wanted was a dog, and her asshole family couldn't even give her that.

"Plenty of animals to take care of out here." I gesture at the horses, the goats.

"Keeps you busy, huh?"

"Yep. Supposed to be getting a new pony soon too."

She tips her face up, eyes shiny with excitement. "Really? A pony?"

"In the next few weeks. Keeping him for a while until the owner decides what to do. He's not sure if he wants to train him or not. Depends on how sturdy he is, how good he is with people."

"Wow. That's exciting."

"It'll be a lot of hours. But we can always use the work."

"You ever think about giving riding lessons? Or selling goat milk or soap?"

What is it with her and Poppy, coming up with all these wild business ideas?

"Not really. I got plenty to keep me busy. Don't need more things to do, more people in the mix."

"Just a thought." She lifts the kid off her lap, scooting him close to his mama before brushing her hands off. I extend my palm, helping her up to standing. "Thanks for showing me the babies."

She presses her lips to mine, kissing me soft and slow. Reminding me of the stolen moments we used to have out here back in the day.

"Welcome. C'mon, let's get some sleep."

I flick the lights off; then we walk back to the house hand in hand, neither of us speaking.

A lot happened today—most of it good—and I don't want to spoil anything with empty, hollow words. For now I'm content to live in this moment, the outside world at a safe distance.

15

JULIET

SOMETIME IN THE MIDDLE OF THE NIGHT, I WAKE. Blinking into the darkness, I'm out of sorts, the room unfamiliar. A warm, quiet breath tickles my ear, and I remember where I am.

Nestled in King's cozy bed, safe and sound. His arm wrapped around my torso, heavy with sleep. Spooning me, his body pressed to mine. All hard muscle, his cock still semi-erect. Every inhale, every exhale, we move together. His chest rising and falling behind me. I rock against him, snuggling in. Relishing the closeness, the stillness of this moment.

His fingers flex, cupping my naked breast, the rough pad of his thumb sending a shiver of want racing over my skin. Desire thrums through my veins as my nipple peaks beneath his touch. Closing my eyes, I inhale his scent. Spicy and masculine, thoroughly intoxicating. I stifle a moan, biting down on my lip. I rub my ass against him, his cock lengthening along my back. Hot and hard, he pulsates against my skin.

Teeth nip at my earlobe, and a bolt of pleasure zips through me. I'm wet, heated, thighs clenching as King sucks on my ear. Chill bumps rise on my neck, nipples puckering to sharp points, and now I'm fully awake and aroused.

He doesn't speak, instead running his tongue from my ear down my neck. Sucking at my collarbone, kissing up and down my shoulder as he rolls my nipple between his fingers. I undulate my hips, seeking relief from the throbbing ache between my legs. Wanting—needing—to fill the emptiness.

King responds, thrusting his cock deep inside me. So quick, so decisive, it takes my breath away. Pleasure blooms in my chest as he drives into me, tight balls smacking against my ass. Burying himself deep inside me. Pinching at my breasts, tweaking them, dancing along the thin line between bliss and pain. The blood racing to my skin when he abruptly releases. I cry out, biting down hard on my tongue, tasting the metallic tang of blood.

One hand keeps stroking my breasts while the other seeks my wet heat. Circling the tight bud, the nerve endings swollen and sensitive. I gasp as he applies pressure, shock waves rolling through me. Working my body like only he knows how, my flesh trained to respond to his touch. Every flick, every swirl stirs excitement deep within. A feeling I've pushed down for so long it almost hurts now, all of it rushing to the surface and threatening to explode.

"Do you like that, baby girl?" King's deep rasp tickles my ear, an electric shock zapping me at my core.

"Mm-hmm," I murmur, black and white dots shimmering in my peripheral vision. I grind against his hand, and he smacks my pussy lightly. More shocks of bliss shoot through me, and I'm panting as he drives into me. Hitting my most sensitive spots, every inch of me flushing with heat and carnal want.

"Tell me." He nips hard at my earlobe, his words a growly command.

I love this side of King. Rough, but fully in control. Of me, my body, my sex.

"Tell me how you want it, baby. Harder? Softer?"

"Harder. Please, harder."

He pistons against me, ramming so hard it hurts in the best way possible. I know I'll be sore tomorrow, a subtle reminder of his possession of me.

Chest heaving, the wave of my orgasm crests as he drives into me, over and over again. Shimmery ecstasy as the dam breaks and I cry out.

"King!" My voice shrill, almost a shriek.

He doesn't stop, doesn't even slow down, drilling into me again and again. Using my body to seek his release, my pussy clenching around his hard cock. He kneads and squeezes my breasts, fucking me until he comes.

"You're amazing." The words staccato, breathy grunts as he spills his release inside me.

Raining kisses across my shoulders, down my neck, my back. Finally softening and slipping out of me. He keeps me wrapped in a tight embrace, holding me as I slide back into sleep.

THE NEXT TIME I WAKE, BRIGHT SUNLIGHT FLOODS THE room, warming my face. I roll over, expecting to see King, but he's gone.

Of course he is. Gone to tend to the morning chores, no doubt. Unlike me, King rises and retires early. His shift work is on an entirely different schedule from mine.

I raise my arms overhead, my body deliciously tender in places that haven't been stretched in ages.

And never like that, if I'm being honest.

King is the best fuck I've ever had, and he knows it.

He's never been shy in the bedroom—or in the barn, in the field, at the lake, in his truck. And now that he's older, he apparently exercises even less restraint.

And I don't mind at all.

The way he takes charge of the situation, dominant, milking every last ounce of pleasure from my body.

I love it.

Dampness pools between my thighs as I think about him. His rippling abs, the tightness in his jaw right before he comes.

Slipping out of bed, I throw on yesterday's clothes and lace up my shoes. Judging by the height of the sun in the sky, I need to be getting home soon to get ready for my early-afternoon shift. But I can't leave without saying goodbye.

I creep down the stairs, tiptoeing through the kitchen as quietly as possible. Why, I have no idea. King lives alone, so it's not like I'm disturbing anyone. But the air's so still, so silent, it doesn't feel right to be loud in the space.

Grabbing my keys off the granite island, I head out the screen door, making my way to the barn. The temperature's warmed up quite a bit from last night, the sun's rays heating my bare arms and legs. Wind carries the neighing of horses across the yard, and I'm certain King's out here.

I move through the gate and cross the dusty paddock, lighter on my feet than I've been in ages. Good sex will do that for a girl, I guess. Entering the barn, I blink once, twice, my eyes adjusting to the lower light.

King's at the far end of the barn, fussing with the horses' hay net.

"I thought you didn't like to use the hay net."

He lifts his head, peering at me from beneath the rim of his hat.

"I don't, normally. But I'm going to be gone for a few days, and I'm not sure Beau's gonna want to stay the night."

My stomach sinks, hot panic flooding my system. Which is absolutely ridiculous, because we haven't even said what we are, and I have no claim on him or his time.

Still, the words sting, a sharp blow to my already-tender heart.

I tuck a stray lock of hair behind my ear, kick my toe against the dusty ground.

"Oh?"

The word comes out a question, my throat bone-dry, pulse fluttery with nerves.

"Yeah. Family business."

I have no idea what that means or how I fit into the equation. I don't, I suppose.

"Hey."

He's standing in front of me, the smell of fresh hay mingling with his spicy cologne. Reaching out, he lifts my chin with one finger, forcing me to meet his navy gaze.

"What's wrong, Juliet?"

His eyes crinkle with concern, and the ache in my chest lessens a touch. At least he cares.

"Nothing." I shrug, try to play it off. I don't want him to think I'm a needy ball of anxiety, scared to be left alone.

"Bullshit. Talk to me."

I swallow, willing my voice to come out this time. Preferably in something louder than a whisper.

Huffing out a quick exhale, I force myself to speak.

"I know I have no rights to you—we haven't even said what we're doing here . . ." I wave my hand in the small pocket of air between us, careful not to make contact with King's strong abdominal muscles.

"Do we have to put a name to it?" King frowns, and I can't figure out his expression, whether he's mad or not.

"I mean, not yet. But eventually, I suppose . . ."

"Fine." He reaches for my hand, gripping my fingers up to the knuckle, and stares deep into my eyes. "Juliet, will you be my girlfriend?"

Heat flames my cheeks, and a startled giggle bubbles up inside me, spilling from my lips.

"Yes, King, I'll be your girlfriend."

He raises my hand to his mouth, grazing my knuckles with his lips.

"Well, that's settled then."

I shuffle my feet, uncertainty still nagging at me, pinching low in my gut.

"But . . ." King gazes at me over our intertwined hands.

"Where are you going? How long will you be gone?"

Can I come with you? hangs on the tip of my tongue, but I somehow manage to bite the words back, holding them inside.

He huffs out a quick breath, licks at his lower lip. His thinking face.

"Normally I wouldn't speak of this outside the family. But since we're official as of one minute ago, I suppose I can tell you. Swear you won't breathe a word of it to anyone."

I mark an X across my chest with my free hand.

"Swear on all things holy."

"I'm making a trip up to Peachtree Grove, Georgia. Turns out we may have some kin up there we never knew about."

"Really?" Shock rattles around deep inside me, but I try to stay cool.

There might be more Montgomerys?

"Maybe. I need to head up there and see for myself."

"Oh. Okay."

"Okay? Or Oh-kay?" He teases me, tracing my jawline with his thumb.

"Okay. I mean, I'll miss you a ton."

He presses his lips together, his nose scrunching up a teensy bit. A horse neighs from the stall behind him, the thick, dark tail swishing through the air. Swish-swish, swish-swish.

"Come with me."

"What?" Shock tips my voice up an octave, and my chest is light and fizzy. "You want me to go on a road trip with you?"

"Sure, why not? Seeing as how we're boyfriend and girl-friend now." His eyes glitter with amusement at the phrase, which sounded funny rolling off his tongue. "Think you can get someone to cover your shifts at the Tipsy Taco? We'll probably be gone a few days."

I rack my brain, trying to calculate who owes me a favor at the restaurant.

"I think I can get them covered, yeah."

"It's settled then. Can you leave tomorrow?"

Slipping my cell from my pocket, I tap on my calendar. Empty of all engagements, save for work.

"Yes."

"Let's do it then."

King grips me by my hips and pulls me to him, his mouth smashing against mine, and I feel like I'm floating on air.

A few whole days together, just me and King. Free from the stigma of our names, our personal reputations, the stupid family feud that's kept Montgomerys and Capellis separate for generations.

Just the two of us, out in the big, wide, judgment-free world.

16

JULIET

KING PUTS ME INTO MY CAR AND SEES ME OFF WITH A long, sweet kiss, promising he'll call me later tonight. I drive all the way back to Seaglass Beach with my head in the clouds, barely registering time, distance, or the song playing on the radio.

I'm still in love with King Montgomery.

Even though deep down I knew it, the words hit me smack-dab in the chest. A perfect bull's-eye, straight to the center of my pounding heart.

I never stopped loving him, no matter how hard I tried.

Turns out, slipping back into loving him was way easier than trying to get over him.

Like we were meant to be.

Whistling, I make a sharp right into the apartment complex, then park my car and grab my stuff from the passenger seat.

"Where ya been, little sis?"

Cash's nasally voice sends a cold shiver of fear racing

down my spine. I take a quick sip of air and prepare to lie through my teeth.

Spinning around to face him, I press my lips into a tight line, arching one brow.

"None of your damn business, Cash." I fold my arms, standing up as tall and straight as possible. Tough when he towers over me, but worth a shot.

He lumbers forward, closing the gap between us in two long strides, the stench of motor oil and stale cigarettes clinging to his black T-shirt.

"Course it's my business. You're my baby sister. I've got to watch out for you, especially now that Jags is in jail. So . . ." He stretches his arm over my shoulder and leans against the side of my SUV, effectively boxing me in. "Where've ya been? I've been waiting out here for at least an hour. And I know you weren't at work, because the Tipsy's not even open yet."

Wheels spin frantically in my head, but my mind is totally and completely blank. Not one plausible-sounding lie pops up.

"Out."

Cash huffs a disbelieving breath, an acrid puff of air blowing my hair over my shoulder.

"Do I need to bring in reinforcements to get the truth out of you?"

"What—you don't think you can do the job?" I jut my chin out, goading him.

Big mistake.

In one quick move, he's gripping my shoulders so tight my muscles crunch beneath his fingers. Pain radiates down both my arms, and a cold clutch of fear claws at my chest.

"Don't be such a bitch, Juliet. Tell me where you were.

Were you out fucking around last night? Who's the not-so-lucky guy?"

His eyes bore into me, hard and beady, his upper lip curling into a sneer. It's still morning, yet the distinct scent of cheap beer hits my nostrils, making my eyes water.

"Get your fucking hands off me right the fuck now, Cash." I spit the words out, but he doubles down, squeezing harder.

"I'll let go when you tell me who you were with." He digs his thumbs into my shoulder sockets, and I yelp in pain.

"No one, you son of a bitch. Get the fuck off me." I kick at his feet, knocking him off center, and he stumbles, releasing his grip.

"You're such a fucking cunt. I can't believe we're related."

"Yeah, me neither."

I pull my T-shirt down and step out of his reach, my car key extended between my fingers in case he tries to manhandle me again.

"What do you want, Cash? I have to get ready for work. Because—unlike you—I have an honest job."

"If you call whoring yourself out for tips honest, sure." He runs a hand through his dark, greasy hair, tries to act cool.

"I'm a waitress, not a stripper."

"Same diff."

I roll my eyes and back away, heading toward the stairs. Half-tempted to make a run for it but scared he'll grab my ankles and pull me down.

"I saw Jags yesterday. Word around town is you're hot for the prince."

The juvenile nickname my brothers have for King irks me, crawling under my skin and making me queasy.

"Who are you talking about?" I tip my head to the side and pretend I don't know what he's talking about.

"You know who I'm talking about, Juliet. Jags asked me to deliver a message."

I stare at Cash. *How the hell did Jagger find out what happened between me and King already?*

"He says stay away from him. Or else." Cash makes a fist, cracking his knuckles, the sound echoing around the lot.

I make a *pshaw* sound and try not to dwell on the implied threat.

"Okay, sure. Whatever." I shrug before turning and sprinting up the stairs as fast as my legs will carry me. I twist the key in the door lock, slamming it shut hard behind me—turning first the lock, then the dead bolt before leaning back against the wall in my dark apartment.

I stand still for one minute, then another, waiting for my pulse to return to a reasonable number of beats per minute.

My brothers are such assholes, every single one of them. Thank god I'm getting out of town with King. I know I'll be safe with him.

THE TIPSY TACO LOT IS PRETTY EMPTY, SINCE I'M covering the early lunch shift. Not too many people stop in for tacos before noon, even in a beach town. The tips suck at lunch, making this the least desirable shift. Could work in my favor, since I have several dinner shifts in a row I need to get covered.

Shoving through the door, I wave to my friend Sabby—short for Sabrina, the given name she hates—standing behind the bar. She's counting liquor bottles, taking inventory before our next five-dollar-margarita night.

"Hey, babe. What's good?" She reaches up, tightening her high, dark ponytail, the tips dyed a bright blue. Extremely bold hairstyle for this sleepy beach town. She probably had to color it herself at home.

"Not much." I slide behind the bar, grabbing the shift calendar we keep there for handy reference. "Listen—"

"Uh-oh. I hear an ask coming . . ." Sabby chomps hard on her bubblegum.

"Could you cover my shift tomorrow? And the next two days too?" I clasp my hands together, pleading.

Sabby peers over my arm at the schedule. "I don't know, I kinda have plans."

"'Kinda' doesn't sound too solid."

"Whatcha gonna do for me?" *Smack, smack, blow.* A bright-pink bubble breaks through her full, puffy lips, almost entirely covering her face.

"I'll spot you next time. Promise."

"Fine." She flutters her long, dark eyelashes. "I'll take all your shifts. I could use the money anyway. I'm trying to go to Cancun for spring break."

"Can't get enough margaritas here?" I tease, popping her hip with mine.

"Exactly. Thought maybe I could pick up a few tips from the locals, bring the recipes back with me to Seaglass Beach."

"I'm sure Candy would appreciate it."

Sabby leans closer to me, her bargain-drugstore perfume potent, making my eyes water.

"Listen—your brother was in here last night, after you left. He was asking around. Lots of questions about where you were."

A yawning pit opens in my stomach, dread flooding through me.

"Which brother?"

"Cash."

"What'd you say?"

"Nothing, babe. You know I've got your back. Besides —I wasn't positive about where you went anyway. And my mama always taught me not to spread rumors."

She stares at me with kohl-rimmed eyes, waiting for me to spill the deets. I toss my options around quickly, straightening the bottles behind the bar as a distraction.

"It's best you don't know the details, Sab. Safer that way. Do me a favor, though, will ya?"

"Geez, another one? You're really racking up a tab today."

I shoot her a half-hearted smile. "If either of those bozos come in here asking after me, tell them I have a highly contagious stomach bug, and you're covering my shift for me."

"Got it. Toxic vomit spewing from nostrils. She's home tucked up in bed, quarantined."

"Perfect."

Sabby's lips slide into a knowing grin. "Who's the guy?"

"You don't know him."

"Literally no chance of that, unless he's an out-of-towner. And you don't seem like the type to drop your panties for a tourist."

My cheeks flame at her crassness—and her spot-on assessment. Sabby's smarter than she lets on.

"Better if you don't know. Trust me. My brothers are sniffing around. The less you know, the better."

"Fine. But I'll be expecting some X-rated details when you get back. Least you can do for all my troubles."

I giggle in spite of myself. "Names and places will be changed to protect the innocent. But we'll have a girls' night when I get back from 'quarantine.'" I put the last word in air quotes. "Promise."

The first lunch customer sidles up to the bar, slamming his hand down to get our attention and breaking up our little chat. Sabby scurries over to take his drink order, and I hustle to the back to grab my apron and get ready for my shift. Staying busy will keep my mind off my brothers until I can be with King again. I'm already counting down the minutes.

KING

I DON'T KNOW WHAT THE HELL I'M THINKING, INVITING Juliet on a road trip with me. To potentially meet my half sister no less.

Like why in the actual fuck did I do that?

Because you don't want to spend another second without her, that's why.

Her soft, supple body next to yours, sharing the same air, the same space. And maybe, just maybe, having someone to lean on when things get tough.

The realization hits me like a sucker punch to the gut.

I'm King Montgomery.

I don't *need* people. They need me. That's how things have always worked, how we operate.

Needing people is a sign of weakness. And no way in hell am I weak.

Maybe I should call her and cancel. Tell her to stay home and I'll see her in a few days.

Those wide eyes flash before me, filled with so much sadness that my heart aches for her.

No. No way am I canceling.

Buzz, buzz.

> Little Sis: Heard you're going to Peachtree Grove tmrw

Damn. How'd she already hear that?

> King: Word travels quick around here

> Little Sis: It does. You going alone?

I lick along my lower lip, consider the best way to answer.

Poppy said she was tired of the lies. The only other option is the truth.

> King: Juliet's going with me

I hurry and hit send before I can change my mind.

> Little Sis: You're kidding me

> King: You said you wanted the truth. There it is

> Little Sis: Wow

Because she's Poppy, she doesn't ask after specifics like Parker would. Maybe even Rome, although he uses a little more tact. But I know she won't just drop it. That'd be too easy.

Little Sis: Do you even know this girl?
Now you're going on a road trip with her?

Well, shit.

I'm not diving into history via text. No one has that kinda time.

King: Enough

Nice vague answer.

Little Sis: I think you should go slow. You don't know if you can trust her

Oh, the irony. Juliet's not sure she can trust me, yet Poppy believes it's the other way around.

King: She's not like her brothers, Pops

King: She's a good person

Little Sis: How do you know? Because she helped with the trial stuff?

King: Yes

I leave it at that, hopeful it's a juicy enough bone for her.

Not a chance.

Little Sis: Feels like that's not enough, to have just helped out that one time. What about all the bad blood between our families? They tried to steal from us, King. She's one of THEM

Now I'm riled up, anger bubbling inside me. I hate how everyone lumps Juliet in with her family just because her last name's Capelli. She's not like them, and I know it. I've seen it time and time again.

King: Only by blood. She can't help her family ties, Pops. You know that

Little Sis: Damn, you must have it bad for her

Heat rushes to my face, but I ignore the jab. Nothing good will come from responding.

Little Sis: She must be really good in bed

Okay. Now Poppy's crossing the line.

King: Shut the hell up

Little Sis: So you're admitting you're sleeping with her. Fabulous

Little Sis: Seriously, King. You could have any girl in town. Why her?

Because she's cute, and sweet, and sassy. She fits beneath the crook of my arm perfectly, and I love the way her face lights up when she laughs. Her scent's intoxicating, and she's the most free-spirited person I know besides Poppy.

Also, my mother loved her. She was the only person who knew about the baby, wrapping her arms around Juliet after the miscarriage, drying her tears and murmuring everything was going to be okay.

But I'm not telling my little sister any of this. It's none of her damn business.

> King: Thanks for the vote of confidence. Also very doubtful I could have any girl in town, judging from my past dating record

> Little Sis: So you're settling for a Capelli?

Ouch. That one stings. And is unfair—and untrue.

If anyone's settling here, it's definitely Juliet.

I growl down at my phone, tapping out several responses before going with:

> King: Stay out of it, Poppy

Mercifully, she doesn't respond. She's either super pissed or super busy. Either way, I'm off the hook. For now.

But tough conversations need to be had, and I better figure out what I'm going to say.

My cell vibrates again, and I squint at the screen in aggravation. If Poppy keeps coming after me, I'm going to end up saying something I regret. I know it because it happens every damn time.

Push. Push. Push. Until she shoves me right over the edge.

But it's not from Poppy.

Rose Queen: Can I come over again
tonight? That way we can get an early
start in the morning

I feel my frown relax, turning into a grin as I stare down at the phone, my gut unclenching.

King: Of course. When will you get here?
I'll wait up

Rose Queen: I finish my shift at 10, then I
have to swing by my apartment and grab
my stuff. So probably won't be there
until 11

King: Okay. Want me to pick you up?

Rose Queen: Sure. That'd be nice

King: I'll be there

Shoving my phone into my pocket, I break into a whistle as I move on to my next chore. The road trip to Peachtree Grove just got a whole lot better.

I FINISH ALL THE CHORES, GET EVERYTHING READY FOR Beau, and pack my stuff for the trip, including snacks. The clock ticks by so slowly I wonder whether it's broken.

Fuck it. I'll head into town early, grab a beer at the

Tipsy Taco, and wait for Juliet to finish her shift. Better than sitting around here twiddling my thumbs.

I slap on some extra cologne, grab the keys to my truck, and head into town, nerves humming with the anticipation of seeing Juliet again. After all this time, I'm still like a damn teenager around her. My cock perks up just thinking about her, and I have half a hard-on already, my jeans getting tight. Everything about her turns me on, from her slow smile to her tight, perky ass.

Twenty minutes later, I pull into the Tipsy Taco. The lot's crowded, music thumping so loud I hear it through the closed windows of my truck. I park and take a deep breath, preparing myself to people.

I push into the busy restaurant and survey the scene. A cover band's banging away, the singer wailing about the highway to hell while the drummer closes his eyes and taps out the rhythm. A crowd of college kids forms a tight circle in front of the band, arms thrown around each other, swaying to the beat. Several servers are busing tables, eager to get off work. The bar's still packed, but there's one empty seat at the end. I head over, snagging the wooden stool for myself. I don't see Juliet, but she may be back in the kitchen.

"Hey, handsome, what'll it be?" A dark-haired bartender with heavy eye makeup presses against the counter, waiting for my order. I vaguely recognize her, mainly because she has blue streaks in her hair. Not something you see every day in Seaglass Beach.

"A beer. Whatever you have on tap's fine."

"Coming right up." She winks at me, and I nod, careful to avert my eyes from her ample breasts outlined in a very tight Tipsy Taco T-shirt.

I sit back, glancing around, trying to spot Juliet. A few seconds later, the bartender slides the beer across the bar to me.

"Here ya go. Want to start a tab?"

"Nah. I'm good."

"Okay." She scribbles the order on her notepad, then hands the check to me.

I pull out my wallet and hand her the cash to settle my bill. She takes the money, keeping her eyes fixed on me the whole time.

"Keep the change."

"Thanks." She stuffs the cash into her apron pocket but doesn't move away.

I break eye contact with her, wishing Juliet would magically appear and cut the awkward tension. Glancing around, I try to find her.

"You looking for someone, handsome? Blind date?"

Aggravation rumbles in my gut at her questions, but I squash it down and try my best to be polite.

"Not here on a date. Is Juliet here?"

Her eyes widen, lips forming a scarlet O. She nods.

"Yeah. She's here."

Saying nothing else, she gives me no further information. The band finishes up their set, making a bumpy transition to DJ tunes. I take a long slug of the beer and vaguely wonder whether coming here was a bad decision. Time's not moving any quicker at the bar than it did back at the ranch.

"Hey."

A light squeeze of my shoulder from behind startles me, the sultry voice sending all the blood rushing straight to my cock.

"Hey." I peer over my shoulder at Juliet, a slow smile creeping over my face. She's beautiful, her cheeks flushed a soft shade of pink, hair pulled away from her face, highlighting her high cheekbones. Fucking stunning.

"You didn't have to come pick me up here." The tip of her tongue darts out, licking at her full bottom lip.

"I know." I shrug, leaning back in my seat to relieve some of the pressure in my pants. I'd love to pull her into my lap and grind against her, feel her warm curves on my body. There'd be time enough for that, I suppose.

"You almost done?"

"Almost. We're closing in a few minutes; then I have to help bus tables. Probably less than twenty minutes."

"Cool. Take your time. I'll wait."

She smiles at me, her eyes sparkling beneath the glow of the Tipsy Taco's overhead lights.

"Thanks for coming."

She sidles off, my eyes following the slow sway of her hips as she moves around the restaurant. The crowd thins out, the lights coming up, the volume of the music lowering. Juliet cleans tables, leaning over and swiping at the black surface—the round globes of her ass on full display. Vivid images of me driving hard and deep into her warm pussy play in my mind as I watch the show.

Finally, she's finished, untying her apron and tossing it on the bar.

"Ready?" Juliet slides her hand into the pocket of her jeans and walks toward me.

"Yep."

I tip the stool up until it rests against the bar and sling my arm around her narrow shoulders. She winces at my touch, and I pause, frowning.

"What's wrong?"

She bites on her lip, eyes cast down toward the floor.

"Nothing. Just a bruise."

My gut twists. "From me last night?"

She shakes her head.

"No."

"From what then?"

She shifts from foot to foot, clearly uncomfortable.

"And don't bullshit me, Juliet, with some dumbass story about running into the wall. What the hell happened?"

She blows out a shaky breath. "Cash was waiting for me at my apartment when I got home this morning."

I drop my voice, trying to control the rage storming through my veins.

"And that fucker put his hands on you? Did he hit you?"

"No. Nothing like that. He just—squeezed is all. It's fine. It's nothing."

"My ass," I growl. "If that dickhead ever puts his hands on you again, I will break every one of his fucking fingers. Swear to god."

Juliet sighs, her ponytail swishing behind her. "See. This is why I didn't want to mention it. I don't need you defending me. I've got it."

"The hell you do—"

"King." She reaches out, placing a hand on my chest. I'm certain she can feel my heart, pounding hard with rage.

"I mean it, Juliet. No man should put his hands on a woman. Family or not."

"Thank you. I appreciate the sentiment. And if my brothers bother me again, I'll pass along the message." She rises on tiptoe, pressing her warm lips to mine. "C'mon.

Let's go get my stuff. I'll leave my car at the apartment. I gave Sabby the story to tell my jerk-off brothers. Should keep them off my tail for a few days."

Saying nothing, I grip her hand, keeping her close. No one's going to hurt Juliet again. I'll make damn sure of that.

18

JULIET

King tails behind me all the way to my apartment, so close I'm worried he may rear-end me. And I sure as hell can't afford any car repairs, so I'm careful to avoid any abrupt stops. In the parking lot, his eyes flick from one end of the asphalt to the other, searching for Cash or Damon. Mercifully, they aren't waiting for me. Lucky for them. Looks like they'll live another day with intact knuckles.

I hustle into my apartment, grab my stuff. I don't bother changing out of my uniform. I just want to get the hell out of town before either of my knucklehead brothers shows up.

"Ready to go." I wheel out my suitcase and toss my bag over my shoulder, wincing as the strap digs into the bruised skin.

Damn Cash.

"I've got it." King takes my suitcase and lifts the bag from my shoulder so tenderly tears well in my eyes.

How did I get so lucky? Having a handsome, considerate

man looking after me, loving me, is a dream I gave up long ago.

"What's wrong?" His brows scrunch together as he tries to read my emotions.

"Nothing." I swipe at my face, pretend I have a stray eyelash making my eyes water.

"You still want to go, right?"

"Definitely."

"Okay."

I cut the lights, locking the door behind us. We head down the stairs, and King opens the truck door for me, sliding the luggage behind my seat before helping me in. The perfect Southern gentleman. His mama raised him right—unlike my bozo brothers, who think beating up on women is a form of sport.

King fires up the truck, and then we take off into the night, heading out of town to the ranch. He rests his large, strong hand on my thigh, stroking my leg with his thumb every once in a while, and I've never felt safer. We don't talk the whole way out to the ranch, a comfortable silence filling the cab. The low twang of classic country hums on the radio, and I close my eyes, sleep beckoning.

The next thing I know, we're outside King's house, and he's shaking me awake.

"Baby, we're here." He brushes his lips against mine, the sweetest wake-up call I've had in a long while.

I rub my eyes, blinking in the darkness. Everything's so quiet, so still out here. A nice change of pace from the deafening hustle of the Tipsy Taco.

"Come on." He hops out, coming around and opening the door for me, extending his hand.

A light breeze blows, the distinct stench of beer,

tequila, and tacos wafting around me. I definitely need to clean up before I crawl into King's bed.

"You mind if I take a shower?" I glance over at him as we walk up the porch stairs.

"Not at all."

We head directly upstairs, my muscles tired and achy from standing all night. Dropping my bags on the wood floor, he shuffles away to the bathroom. A golden rectangle glows on the dark planks, and I head into the bathroom, toiletries in hand.

The bathroom's large, with an oval tub sitting beneath a window overlooking the wide lawn. A walk-in shower takes up the far-left corner of the room, and a long marble countertop with double sinks runs the length of the wall.

King opens the glass door, turning the shower on.

"There you go."

He grabs a white towel from a nearby basket and sets it on the sink.

Wild butterflies wing around my stomach, and suddenly I'm shy. Which is stupid, seeing as how he saw me naked less than twelve hours ago.

Steam rises from the shower, the glass already fogging. King starts to leave as I pull my T-shirt over my head and drop it to the ground.

He freezes. Reaching out, he traces the reddish-purple circles marking both my shoulders.

"That fucker."

I try not to wince under his touch, although the spot's sensitive.

"I'll be fine."

The rough pads of his thumbs send a shiver rippling through me, a dull ache throbbing between my thighs.

Chill bumps rise on my arms, my belly, as he runs his fingers over my skin.

Bending down, he kisses the bruises. So softly, so gently, just a slight whisper of breath. Wetness pools in my panties, and I wind my arms around his neck, bringing my lips to his.

"Stay," I murmur, my fingers tracing the sharp hairline at his nape.

He says nothing, his hands cupping my ass and squeezing before he steps back and begins unbuttoning his shirt.

I help him, fingers flying over the plastic buttons. Warm, humid air fills the bathroom, and steam swirls around us. He sheds his shirt, then steps back to take off his pants. I do the same, the denim clinging to my skin. Struggling, I finally manage to peel off the jeans.

Glancing up, I notice the clear outline of his cock in his boxer briefs, and I try not to stare at the large bulge.

"Like what you see?" he teases.

I nod. "Very much."

He pulls at the waistband of his briefs and his cock springs out. Now he's fully naked, magnificent, every inch of him solid, rippling muscle. I lick at my lips, fluttery excitement vibrating through me.

Running my hand over his broad chest, I trace the sharp lines of his muscles, the outline of his pecs. Tiptoe my fingers down his abs, counting as I go. One. Two. Three. A perfect six-pack, followed by the sexiest V pointing straight to his dick. I take a quick sip of air, try to remember how to breathe.

King dips down, claiming my mouth. His tongue slips in, exploring. He unclasps my bra, the satin falling away and exposing my breasts. Nipples already sharp peaks, begging to be caressed. He wastes no time, tweaking both of them, pain and pleasure colliding. Wetness gushes into my panties, and I yank them down, eager for his touch.

Cupping my sex, he thumbs at my clit. Hot, swollen, ready for him.

"So wet already. Such an eager girl." He murmurs into my open mouth, and I sigh into him, leaning against his hard body.

"Come on, baby, let's clean you up."

Linking his fingers with mine, he leads me to the shower. Steam billows out when the glass door opens, and I breathe in the hot, humid air. I step in and King follows, closing the door behind him. Now we're cocooned together, the scent of eucalyptus and tea tree oil rising and tickling my nose.

The warm spray of water hits my shoulders, spilling over my breasts, and my muscles begin to relax and unwind. Everywhere but between my legs, my pussy clenching and releasing, waiting to be filled.

King squirts dark-blue shower gel in his hands, then lathers me up, white bubbles clinging to my arms. Marking me with his scent, claiming me. His fingers move up and down my body—slowly, gently—and he's especially careful around the bruises. I close my eyes and give in to the sensations. Heat and nerves and desire, water and excitement, mixing together into a tight ball of want.

He keeps washing my body, hands running up and down my sides, over my breasts. Palming the flesh, his thumbs tracing circles round and round, finally homing in on my nipples. A low moan falls from my lips, the sound muffled by his mouth meeting mine. I push my tongue in, droplets of water dripping down my face and into our mouths.

I'm drowning—in this man, this moment—and I don't even care. This would be a wonderful way to die, truth be told.

King wraps his arms around me, large palms splaying over my ass cheeks. The flesh burns beneath his touch, and I press up against him, his cock dancing on my belly.

"You know how many times I've dreamed about fucking you here?" He gazes down at me, water droplets beading in his dark hair.

"No."

"Too many to count."

"How'd you do it?" My hand finds his cock, slides up and down the thick shaft. He twitches in my fingers, pulsing.

"Lots of ways."

"Show me your favorite."

"You want the rated-R version?"

"Are you implying there's a dirtier version than that?" I tease, moving my finger back and forth over the tip of his cock.

"Definitely."

"Give me the dirtiest one then."

His pupils dilate, a deep growl sounding low in his throat. Without hesitation, he spins me around, raising my hands above my head and pressing them against the slippery tile. Then he grips my hips and spreads my legs apart, nudging me farther open with his thigh. I widen my stance, following his direction, and he smooths his palm over my right ass cheek.

"Such a sweet, tender ass." He playfully smacks the

skin, leaving a light sting on my behind. I wiggle against his hand, urging him to keep going.

He leans over me, his mouth hovering at the shell of my ear.

"You like that?"

I nod, biting down on my lip.

"You're a dirty, dirty girl." He slaps my left cheek, then my right, then my left again, the water streaming over my heated flesh.

If any other man hit me, I'd knee them in their dick. But when King does it, I'm beyond turned on, horny as hell. Pussy dripping, nipples so hard they hurt as he spanks my ass.

"Ohh!"

His hand moves from my ass to my pussy, snaking around and stroking, front to back. He sinks two fingers into me, and I gasp as he scissors inside me, stretching me. Another finger slides in, and I'm contracting around him, hips rocking, seeking more.

More friction, more fullness, more relief from the desperate ache between my thighs.

A King-size ache only he can fill.

"Such a dirty girl, grinding on me." He thrusts harder, hitting my G-spot, and the first waves of an orgasm start to build.

He feels it, too, easing his hand from between my legs.

"Not so soon, baby girl. I need to feel you come all over my cock."

The words sink in as he nips at my earlobe, a sharp bolt of pain zipping straight to my clit.

"Spread your legs wider for me—that's a good girl. Let me fuck you from behind."

Eyes closed, I nod. I'll do anything he wants right now, as long as he relieves this painful ache.

Cool gel hits my ass; then King's rubbing on me, sliding over my tingling skin. The spicy scent fills my lungs, and I relax against him, sticking my cheeks up higher into the air.

Hands gripping both my hips, he anchors me in place before driving into me. Hard and fast, forcing me forward. Up against the tile, my eyes fly open as he thrusts deeper. I push against him, the spray of water misting us, our bodies slipping and sliding together.

"So fucking tight." His voice is tense, words clipped from his efforts.

One hand moves from my hip around to my clit, flicking at the tight bud, and I almost unravel right then and there. But he backs off, stroking long and slow, leaving me frantic for more, and he knows it.

His hand creeps higher still, over my belly, up to my breast. Pinching the nipple until I cry out, throwing my head back. He sucks at the exposed column of my neck, licking droplets of water from my skin, and I'm light-headed, giddy. Release taunts me, dancing just out of reach as King alternates his thrusts. Hard, then slow and lazy, then hard again. Keeping me on edge.

"Do you want to come, dirty girl?" he murmurs in my ear, sucking the tender lobe between his teeth.

"Mmm" is all I can murmur, my voice high pitched and needy.

"Tell me. Tell me how badly you want to get off."

"So. Fucking. Bad." I grind the words out, panting.

He pinches my nipples, one then the other, and my

pussy spasms, tightening around him. I'm so close I can taste the release, strong waves rolling through me.

His hips stop moving, and he wraps his arms around my torso, pinning me to him. Our bodies are still joined together, but the waves are slow, and I feel my release ebbing. A strangled cry rises from my throat.

"Are you close, baby?" His voice is teasing, fingers tickling my belly. A shiver of anticipation runs through me, and I nod.

"Tell me. How close are you?"

"I'm right there. So close," I moan, frustrated, as he strokes me. Everywhere but my sex, the burning spot begging to be sated.

"What do you want me to do about it?" His warm breath skates over my cheek, and I'm desperate for him.

"Fuck me."

"Good girls say please," he chides, biting down on my neck. Not hard enough to leave a mark, but the sensation still surprises me.

"Please."

He undulates, rocking and hitting all my most sensitive spots, and I almost cry it feels so good. Then he slows.

"Oh no, don't stop," I whimper, pushing back against him. Willing him to move.

"What did I just say about good girls?" He swivels his hips, hitting me in all the right places, and black dots swim in my peripheral vision.

"Please. Please."

Ramming up into me, he buries himself so deep inside me I scream.

"Yes, that feels so good . . ."

Pounding into me, hard and fast, my breasts bouncing

with every thrust. Skin tingling, the warm water dripping from his shoulders down my back. My fingers flex, hands stretched wide on the smooth tile. Trying to hold on to something, anything. His hands grip both of my hips as he drives into me again and again until I finally explode, crying out and shaking. He follows right behind, hot cum shooting deep inside me. King thrusts into me a few more times as I milk his cock, wringing every last bit of energy from him.

"Juliet . . ." His hands loosen on my hips, trailing over my shoulders, up and down my spine. My pussy tingles, finally relieved of the ache that plagued me all day.

Spinning me around, he smooths my hair away from my face, kissing my eyelids, my cheeks, the tip of my nose. Claiming my mouth with his.

"You're amazing," he murmurs, fingertips trailing up and down my side.

The water temperature cools as we kiss under the spray, now warm instead of hot. I'm not sure how long we stand beneath the water. Finally, there's no heat left, and King shuts the water off, then bundles me in a soft, fluffy towel. As if I'm something fragile, precious.

I could definitely get used to this.

We get ready for bed, climbing naked into the cool sheets. King wraps his arm around me, spooning me and pulling me up against him. A few minutes later, he's snoring softly near my ear, warm breath feathering my hair with each exhale.

Everything about this moment is perfect.

So why can't I shake the nagging feeling that we could implode at any second?

19

____

KING

Waking at dawn, I slink out of the house as quietly as possible. Don't want to wake Juliet up this early for nothing. She had a rough day yesterday, and I'm sure she could use the extra rest.

I hustle through the chores, feeding and watering the horses and goats as fast as I can. Beau will be here later today, so I leave the mucking for him. Every once in a while it pays to be the boss.

"All right, Mama. I'm gonna be gone for a few days. Look out for Oreo, Nilla Wafer, and Chip while I'm away." I scratch behind her ears, the soft bleat an acknowledgment between us. Like she understands what I'm saying.

I'm spending way too much time with goats.

Heading back up to the house, I brew a pot of coffee, pouring the extra into a thermos for the road. I listen for any sounds coming from upstairs, but there's only silence.

Buzz, buzz.

My cell vibrates against my thigh, chest tightening reflexively. I do not want to start my day off arguing with

Poppy, and she's the person who texts me the most. Especially since Juliet's here, sleeping.

I'm relieved when I see the message is from Roman.

> Roman: Poppy called me all upset about Juliet going with you

> Roman: IDGAF what you do. Just wanted to give you the heads-up that she's freaking out

> King: I know. We had words yesterday

Great. Poppy's running her mouth to Rome now, and probably Parker too. Not helping the Juliet cause at all, I'm sure.

> Roman: I probably shouldn't ask—and you can tell me to fuck off if you want

> Roman: But how serious are you two?

I grip the phone tight, staring down at the words. Not sure what to say, really. From the outside, Juliet and I don't make any sense at all.

I'm a Montgomery. She's a Capelli.

Out of context, it looks like we're just having sex, hooking up out of the blue.

I never told Roman about me and Juliet, the baby.

The only person who knew the truth all those years ago was our mom, and she never breathed a word of it to anyone. Not even Dad.

Instead, I kept it all buried deep inside. Tried to hide from the pain, the ghosts that haunted me ever since Juliet left.

Now that she's back, all of this is a surprise to my family. I get it, and I should probably explain everything to them.

But it's too damn painful. Why rehash the past?

King: Serious enough

Roman: That's vague as hell. Your polite way of telling me to mind my own business?

I frown down at my cell, shoulders creeping up toward my ears. I roll them back down, try to reduce the tension sitting between the blades.

King: No. Not really. Just the truth

Roman: Any chance I can get a gauge on "serious enough"?

Well, hell. I don't have a great answer to that.

King: She's my girlfriend. Which makes me sound about 12

Roman: LOL. King has a girlfriend. Y'all exchange promise rings too?

King: STFU. This is exactly why I don't go spreading my business around

Roman: I know she helped us with the trial and I appreciate that. You at all worried about the Capelli thing?

King: Wish she had a different last name, but it's out of her control. She's not like her brothers

Roman: If you like her, that's good enough for me

King: Thanks. I appreciate that. May need you to back me up with Poppy. She lost her shit on me

Roman: Buy her something nice and tell her she's pretty. Haha

King: If only she were that easy . . .

Roman: I'll work on her, but you know how she is

King: Yeah, I do. That's why I'm worried

Roman: Sorry, man. Skye's calling me, gotta bolt. Safe trip. Keep me posted on what you find out

King: Will do

"Everything okay?"

Juliet's voice startles me, and I almost drop my phone. She's standing at the foot of the stairs in one of my T-shirts, the fabric skimming her upper thigh. Sexy as hell.

"Yeah, all good. Why?"

"You're scowling." She crosses the kitchen, winding her arms around my neck and pressing her warm lips to mine. I relax into her, minty toothpaste tingling as I slide my tongue over her teeth.

"Not anymore," I murmur, palming her bare ass. My fingers itch to dive into her wet heat, drive her wild right here in the kitchen. But we need to get going. Figure there'll be plenty of time for that later.

Pulling away before I change my mind, I brush a lock of hair from her face. "You want coffee? Breakfast? I can scramble some eggs before we head out."

"Coffee sounds good. I don't usually eat a big breakfast."

"Okay. We can always stop for an early lunch on the road. But we should head out soon. It's a solid drive. Don't want to pull into Peachtree Grove too late."

"Agreed. I'll throw on my clothes, and then we can hit the road." She flashes a bright smile at me, and my anxiety slides away.

Half an hour later, I'm easing onto I-75, heading north toward Atlanta. Windows rolled down, music cranked up, Juliet singing along to Every. Single. Song. Like, word for word.

"You know every song on the radio?" I cut my eyes at her, marvel at her full pink lips as she belts out the chorus to Garth Brooks's "The Thunder Rolls."

She laughs, throwing her head back, the waves of her hair brushing over her narrow shoulders.

"Not every song. But most of them. I used to want to be a singer. Back before I realized that only about one in a million make it in Nashville."

She tucks a leg up under her, twirls a strand of hair in her fingers.

"You have a great voice. You ever try to sing, like with a band or something?"

Juliet guffaws. "Sure. With all that spare time I have."

"For what it's worth, I love listening to you sing." I squeeze her thigh, and she shoots me a wide smile.

"Thanks, King. But you may be a touch biased."

"Why? Because you're my girlfriend?"

The word feels weird coming out of my mouth. Strange, different. But not bad.

Her cheeks turn a bright shade of pink, and she glances over at me.

"Yeah. Because you're my boyfriend. And that's something a boyfriend would say."

"Well, I'm just speaking the truth."

"Thanks. If *American Idol* ever comes to town, I'll be sure to audition."

"I'll hold you to it."

The radio cuts to a commercial, and Juliet gnaws on her lip, silence stretching between us. She folds and unfolds her hands, fidgets with a hangnail.

"What kind of kin are you searching for in Peachtree Grove? A cousin or something?"

She tips her head, peering over at me. My stomach squeezes, acid from the coffee churning round and round, as I debate what to say.

"Not exactly. Not a cousin. More like a half sister."

Gasping, her hand flies to her mouth.

"What? How?"

I focus on the road, grateful for the distraction of driving.

"What do you mean *how*? Same way all babies are made, Juliet." My voice is gruff, the words terse. I'm not mad with her, and I know it's unfair to be short. It's my natural reaction to this entire mess, though.

"You know what I mean, King. Your dad?"

I shake my head.

"No. My mom."

Juliet inhales sharply, and I hate that I'm making this damn trip at all.

"Wow. I don't know what to say."

"I know. It's a shock to us all."

One hand on the wheel, I pull my wallet from my pocket, hand it to her.

"Open it up. There's a letter in there. From her. My half sister."

Juliet rifles through my wallet, then pulls out the now-worn aqua paper. She reads it, her eyes flying over the paper.

"You sure this is legit?" She waves the note through the air.

"Rome checked into it. It's true. I want to lay eyes on this woman, see for myself who this Lacey McCauliffe is. I suppose she deserves to know why no one's written her back."

I swallow hard over the lump in my throat, the reaction the same every time I realize my mom's really gone.

"Well, in that case—I'm glad I came with you. This is a lot to deal with on your own."

I reach over and squeeze her hand. Find comfort in the warmth there, the inherent strength coursing through her small body.

"Me too."

Morgan Wallen comes on the radio, crooning about whiskey shots, and Juliet joins in. A nice shot of whiskey sounds good right about now, but that'll have to wait until later tonight, once we're in Peachtree Grove.

The gas gauge dings, the truck chirping at me that it's

thirsty. I take the next exit, pulling into the nearest gas station. Juliet heads in to use the ladies' room while I pump the gas. Effectively this time. A few minutes later, she walks out with a plastic bag bursting with stuff.

She waves the bag at me.

"I got us snacks. Chips, soda, and those sweet-and-salty nuts you like."

Warmth spreads through my chest. I can't believe she remembers that.

"Thanks. I appreciate it. Gimme a sec to use the restroom; then we'll get back on the road."

"Okay."

She climbs into the truck, and I jog inside, hustling so we can get back on the road.

A few minutes later, I slide behind the wheel, ready to get going again. Juliet's quiet, shoulders hunched, brows squished together.

"What's wrong?"

She thrusts my cell at me.

"I didn't mean to snoop. The message popped up and caught my eye. Sorry."

I glance down at the text marching across my screen. From Poppy, in all caps.

> Little Sis: ARE YOU IN LOVE WITH HER?
> YOU CAN'T BE WITH HER FOREVER,
> YOU KNOW. IT WILL RUIN US

With an angry huff, I toss my cell into the cup holder and pinch the bridge of my nose. My sister can be a real pill sometimes. Why does she care about my love life so damn much?

Juliet doesn't say anything, just sits still, waiting.

Finally, I lift my head and look at her. Cheeks splotchy, her chest flushing with anger and indignation, hurt swimming in those wide hazel eyes. Gone's the carefree attitude, replaced with all the same old bullshit. We can't escape the multigenerational feud, no matter how many miles we put between us and our families.

A feud that has nothing to do with me or Juliet.

"Sorry about that. I didn't tell her anything. She's working off rumors."

"Solid strategy." Juliet bites out the words, bitterness lacing every syllable.

I press my lips together, anger rolling through me. Swirling around in my gut, bubbling up into my chest.

"Do you believe what she said, King? That us being together will ruin y'all?" She stares at me, unblinking.

Waiting for a good response, one that will quell her doubts.

"What? No, of course not. What I do—we do—is none of anyone else's damn business."

I scrub a hand over the back of my neck, wishing I'd taken my cell in with me to the bathroom. Then none of this shit would have been stirred up, and she'd still be singing, happy.

"I don't want to come between you and your family." She worries at her bottom lip, and I hate that she's this upset. I desperately want to make everything better, wipe away all the hate and bad blood.

Taking her hand in mine, I lock my gaze on hers. Willing her to trust me, believe me.

"You won't. Poppy'll come around. She always does."

Juliet keeps biting at her lip, tiny red indentations marking the delicate skin around her mouth.

"Hey." I drag my thumb across her lip, cup her jaw in my hand. "It'll be okay."

She closes her eyes, leaning into my palm. "I hope so, King."

I lean over, dropping my mouth to hers.

"I promise."

After a few minutes, I pull out of the gas station. Juliet's quiet, the fun vibe gone like the golden streaks of sunrise.

Damn Poppy and her stupid text. Why couldn't she stay the hell out of it?

Despite what I promised Juliet, I know it's not going to be that easy to win Poppy over. Of all my siblings, she'll be the toughest to convince. Guess she has the most to lose, being in charge of the inn and all.

But still.

She's going to have to get past Juliet being a Capelli. Because this time I'm not letting her go. For Poppy or anyone.

THE SUN'S STARTING TO SINK LOW IN THE SKY WHEN WE finally pull into Peachtree Grove. One road runs straight through town: Main Street. This place is tiny, small-town USA, complete with one stoplight.

"You have a game plan?" Juliet glances over at me, a brow arched high.

"Not really. Rome printed out some documents and legal info, plus a photo of Lacey McCauliffe. Seems like she has a bunch of relatives in town from her adoptive family, so probably won't be too hard to track her down. Figured we'd find someplace to stay the next few nights, then go from there."

"Doesn't seem like there's gonna be a Marriott in town."

She has a point as I scour both sides of the road, searching for anything that resembles a hotel or motel. Any place with a flashing "Vacancy" sign.

"Maybe I should have done a little more research." I slow the truck to a crawl, noting a diner, a few shops, a mom-and-pop grocery. But not a motel in sight.

"Looks like there's a bed-and-breakfast nearby. We could try there." She holds the phone out for me to see, then punches the address into the GPS. "Turn right."

I follow her directions, pulling up to a white two-story clapboard house with a wide wraparound porch.

"Cute. Hopefully they have a room."

"Yeah. Because the next town's about thirty minutes away. And I'm too damn old to sleep in the truck."

20

KING

We make our way up the steps, and I open the door for Juliet. The clean scent of lemon hits me as soon as we step inside. There's an old-fashioned-looking desk shoved up against the wooden staircase. A gray-haired woman's sitting in a chair next to the desk, knitting. She glances up at us when we walk in.

"Welcome to the Grove, y'all! What can I do ya for?" She pauses her knitting, needles poised.

I stride across the room toward her, nod a hello.

"We're in town for a few nights and need a place to stay. Do you have any rooms available?"

"You're in luck. The Magnolia Room's ready to go. Y'all in town for something special?" Her eyes flick from me to Juliet, taking us in. I shove a hand in my pocket, not sure what to say.

Juliet pipes up. "We're on a little vacation. Just a quick getaway."

"Oh, how nice for you. Romantic!" She claps her hands, her face breaking into a wide smile. "Murphy! Guests!" she hollers over her shoulder, and an older man shuffles in. He's wearing a long-sleeved white button-down tucked into pressed khakis, the pants held up with black suspenders.

"Murphy, please take these kids upstairs to the Magnolia Room." She waves toward the staircase, and he grunts in her direction.

"Fine, fine." Without saying a word to either me or Juliet, he pivots and marches up the stairs, not worrying if we're following behind.

"Right quick, before I forget. Continental breakfast is set out at eight every morning. If you want something heartier, I highly suggest the diner down the road. After you're settled, come back down and I'll get you the keys. One for the front door, the other for your room. Me and Murphy usually retire around nine, but you kids are welcome to stay out as late as you want. Not that there's a whole lot of nightlife around here." She shrugs, shoulders rising halfway up her neck.

"Thank you, ma'am. We appreciate the hospitality." I tip my hat at her; then Juliet and I trot up the stairs.

As we make our way up, Juliet reaches for my hand, her fingers sliding through mine. My heart does a weird stutter thing, and I vaguely wonder if I should get that checked out back home.

Murphy's already all the way up the stairs, standing in the airy hallway outside the last door on the right. There's one other bedroom up here, along with a small hall bath. A picture window lets light in at the end of the hall and over-looks a small but tidy backyard.

"This is the Magnolia Room." Murphy turns the brass knob. The door groans and creaks, not budging. "Well, fiddlesticks. I thought I fixed this up," he mutters, shaking his head. He presses his shoulder to the door.

The tall white door still doesn't move.

"Mind if I try?" I ask.

"Sure."

Murphy steps aside, and I lower my shoulder, leaning against the solid wood. I push hard, but the casing around the door is old and swollen with years of dampness and Southern humidity. The door doesn't crack, not even a quarter of an inch.

"Well, hell feathers," Murphy curses under his breath.

"Let me give it a go." Juliet taps my arm. "Lots of experience with tricky doors. My last apartment was a real pain."

I arch a brow at her, doubtful she's going to be able to unstick the door, but I move aside anyway.

She twists the brass in her hand and pulls it toward her. Then she pops her hip in the center of the wood, giving the middle panel a hard thrust. The door springs open with a loud creak.

She glances over her shoulder at me. "It's all about finesse."

"Alrighty. Glad we got that worked out." Murphy dusts his palms together, brushing off invisible dirt. "I'm going to grab the WD-40 for ya, just in case."

"Sounds good. Thank you." I nod at the older man, but he's already shuffling back down the hall.

"Okay." I step aside, letting Juliet enter the room first.

The Magnolia Room is spacious, complete with an en suite bathroom, and I'm grateful we don't have to share the hall bath.

A king-size poster bed stands in the center of the room,

covered with a white duvet. A mountain of pillows is piled high against the dark headboard, and the bed looks mighty comfortable. The floors are wide-plank wood, the walls painted a light blue. A television hangs on the far wall across from the bed, and there's a chest of drawers. A window seat flanks the wall, the last rays of daylight spilling into the room.

"I'll grab your bag and the key; then we can figure out where to get dinner."

Juliet nods, and I head outside to the truck to get our stuff. The air's cooler here, and a lot less damp without the ocean nearby. A dog barks next door, but otherwise the street's quiet. A few porch lights flicker on, families settling in for the night. Getting ready for work and school the next day, I suppose.

We better hurry, or we may not find anywhere to eat tonight. I have no idea if the diner's open past lunchtime, and I didn't see a single restaurant on the way into town.

Bags in hand, I stop back at the desk to retrieve the keys.

"Here ya go. I'm Liz, by the way. Liz Moss."

"King Montgomery. Nice to meet you."

"I suppose you two will be needing to get some supper. The diner I told ya about stays open the latest around here. It's called the Five-to-Niner. But you best hurry, since it's Sunday. Milly's taken to closing early on Sundays."

"Thank you, ma'am." I tip my hat and head back upstairs to fetch Juliet.

Ten minutes later we're sitting in a booth at the diner, and I swear I'm back in the 1950s. Everything about this place screams vintage, from the long Formica counter at the back to the pleather booths and the white linoleum tile floors.

"What are y'all drinking tonight?" Our waitress stares down at us, pen poised over her pad.

"I'll have a tea, please," Juliet says, still scanning the menu.

"You want the peach tea? Sweet or unsweet?"

"Peach sounds great. And I'll take it sweet, thanks."

"And you?" The waitress stares at me, waiting.

"I'll have a water."

"It's tap. Nothing fancy."

"That's fine."

The waitress scurries away with our drink orders, and Juliet peers at the menu, her finger running up and down the sticky plastic.

"Anything sound good?"

"Think the meat loaf's decent here?"

"I'd bet my life on it," I say, taking in the other patrons. A few older couples, a family with three young kids, two cops sitting at the counter. Everyone seems local, chatting with each other across the tables.

The waitress returns with our drinks, setting the clear plastic cups down on the table.

"Y'all ready to order?" She fixes her gaze on Juliet.

"I'll take the meat loaf, please."

"Okay. You?"

"The roasted chicken with mashed potatoes and beans, please."

"Alrighty. I'll get that in for ya." She spins on her heel and heads back to the kitchen.

The door tinkles, and another couple walks in, snagging

menus and moving straight to a table in the back. I scan the woman's face as she walks by—not Lacey.

"King, you have a plan yet?" Juliet drops her voice so the customers in the nearby booth won't overhear. "You going to ask around about her?"

I spin my drink, watch as the ice bangs against the plastic wall of the cup.

"I dunno. Maybe?"

Even though I had six hours of driving to think about this, I still have no good plan.

"Do you know where she works?"

"Yeah. She's a teacher, so I imagine the local elementary school."

"Well, we can't be loitering around a school. We'd probably get arrested. But we could do some searching and try to dig up her home address."

"Rome looked and couldn't find it. The letter said she's divorced, so maybe she's listed under her married name still."

"Hmm . . ." Juliet bites at her lip, thinking.

"Here y'all go." The waitress sets down two heaping plates of food. "One meat loaf, one chicken. Y'all need anything else?"

"No, we're good. Thanks." I shake my head, unrolling the silverware from the paper napkin.

"Quick question," Juliet says, plastering on her brightest smile. "We're visiting and may be looking to move here. The town's so cute and all . . ."

I stare at Juliet, my mouth dry. *Where's she going with this?*

"And I was just wondering if you have any recommendations on places to see? You know—to really get a feel for the town."

The waitress slides her notepad and pen into her apron pocket and holds up a finger.

"One sec."

A moment later she's back, a thin newspaper in hand. She drops the paper on the table in front of Juliet.

"Here you go. Local news, plus a list of restaurants—although you're in one of the few in town—shops, the grocery. That'll be closed up for the night, but Liam'll have it open again tomorrow morning, in case y'all need any essentials. There should be some real estate listings in there, too, if you're in the market for a house. If you see something you like, you should scoop it up quick, though. There's not a ton of available real estate in town. Y'all have kids?"

She asks the innocent question, but Juliet bristles. Shifting in her seat, she keeps her eyes glued to the table.

"No. No kids."

"Well, we have decent schools here, and our peewee football team is coached by a former pro football star."

"Wow." Juliet feigns interest, although I know she is zero percent interested in sports. "That's great."

"Yeah, he's kind of the hometown hero around here. Ryder McCauliffe."

My ears perk up at the last name *McCauliffe*, and so do Juliet's, our eyes locking across the table.

"Very cool. Not every town can say that, I bet." Juliet smiles up at her, folding and unfolding her napkin, trying to keep her talking.

"Nope, I reckon they can't. He took us all the way to

the state championship. The whole town showed up to support the team. Really fun time for everyone."

"Sounds like. He grew up here then?" I ask, flipping through the paper and pretending to scope out the real estate.

"Sure did. His parents used to run the general store before his cousin, Liam, took over. Real nice family, the McCauliffes. Ryder's brother, Quinn, went to school with me. He works for the fire department now."

"Nice. Seems like a great place to grow up."

"It is—if you like small towns. I never minded it, but my younger sister couldn't wait to get out. Moved to Arizona the day after graduation and hardly ever comes back. Says it's stifling here."

Juliet shrugs. "Small towns aren't for everyone. But I like them."

"All right, I better let y'all eat before your food gets cold. You need anything else, just holler."

"Thanks." I nod in appreciation, and the waitress waves before heading over to the next table to refresh drinks.

"Nice work." I raise my chin at Juliet in appreciation. "You'd make a pretty decent detective."

"Thanks. I watched a lot of *Law & Order* growing up. Just in case I had to bail my family out, ya know. I wanted to know how the legal system worked and all."

The vision of a young Juliet, sitting and taking notes in front of the television, makes me tense up, a hard pit settling low in my stomach. I hate that she had such a rough childhood—and that what happened between us didn't make her life any easier.

But nothing can be done about that now. Just have to press on and try to make it up to her now, a day at a time.

I cut into the chicken, taking a bite and mulling over a plan.

"So tomorrow we'll pop into the general store, scope it out, and see what we can learn. Then, in the afternoon, around dismissal time, we can do a drive-by of the school. Maybe we'll be able to spot her."

Juliet chews thoughtfully, her nose scrunching up as she stares out the picture window.

"Okay. Seems like a decent plan. Long as we move through the school zone real quick. Don't want to raise too much suspicion."

"Agreed. At least we have a solid lead now. Hopefully we can get more info in the morning."

"You think she's related to the football star and the firefighter?"

I shrug, taking another bite of chicken. "No idea. I don't even know if she's a McCauliffe by marriage or not. But I suppose we'll find out more tomorrow."

21

JULIET

I SLEEP GREAT, WRAPPED UP IN KING'S STRONG ARMS. Safe from my brothers and a world away from all the drama back home.

"Hey, sleepyhead." King's warm breath tickles the shell of my ear as he brushes a stray lock of hair from my face, still spooning me.

"Hey." I snuggle back against him. "What time is it?"

"Seven thirty."

"So early." I yawn, blinking. "Do you ever sleep in?"

"No. Can't. I've got horses and goats to feed. Even on the weekends. You wanna keep sleeping? We can hit the diner again for breakfast instead of going downstairs."

I spin to face him, twining my legs with his. Unlike me, he's wide awake, and I wonder if he slept at all. The lines on his face seem deeper, salt-and-pepper stubble stippling his tense jaw. Even stressed he's hot as hell.

"No, I'll get up. We're on a mission, and I'm here to help you, not lounge around all day."

"Okay. Thanks." He presses his mouth to mine in a long, slow kiss.

"Mmm, I like starting the day like this." I stroke his stubble, his jaw relaxing beneath my touch.

"Me too." He kisses me one more time for good measure, then rolls out of bed.

We take a few minutes to get ready, brushing teeth and dressing for the day. King grabs his keys and hat; then we make our way down for breakfast.

The sounds of clinking silverware float up the stairs, and we head in the direction of the noise. A dining room sits beyond the front parlor, a long farmhouse table in the center of the room. Against the wall is a matching wooden buffet covered with a long white runner, a stack of dishes, and napkins and silverware in a basket. Liz stands next to the buffet, working on the neat rolls of cutlery.

"Morning, y'all! I hope the Magnolia Room was to your liking." She bobs her gray head at us, a wide smile lighting up her face.

"Yes, ma'am, thank you," King says politely.

"Help yourself to some juice and fruit. I just saw the delivery van pulling up with the pastries."

We do as she says, shuffling up to the buffet and pouring juice into recycled jelly jars. A cute touch, along with the fresh wildflowers in a vase. The plates are also clearly a family heirloom, fine china laced with roses and golden swirls along the rim.

"Morning, Liz! Sorry I'm a few minutes late." A petite brunette pops into the dining room, carrying an oversize platter of assorted pastries.

"No problem at all, Delaney." Liz motions for her to set

the plate down on the buffet, and she does so with ease. Clearly this isn't her first rodeo.

"Delaney, these are our guests for the next few days. The Montgomerys, visiting from out of town. Folks, this here's Delaney Miller. Oh—it's McCauliffe now, isn't it?"

Delaney grins at Liz, holding up her left hand to show off a sparkly diamond wedding ring set. King stands up taller beside me, now on high alert at the mention of the McCauliffe name.

"Yes, ma'am."

"Sorry, I'm taking a few minutes to adjust. You'll always be a Miller to me!"

Delaney laughs, leaning forward and hugging Liz. "I know, it's all right. You can call me whatever you like, honest. And nice to meet you. I'm Delaney." She turns to us, thrusting her hand out, first to me, then to King. "I own Laney's, the local bakery. Where are y'all visiting from?"

"Seaglass Beach, Florida," I say, flipping my hair over my shoulder.

"Oh nice. It must be amazing to live at the beach."

"It doesn't suck." I smile and Delaney chuckles.

"I doubt Peachtree Grove can compare to the beach, but I hope y'all have a nice trip here. You should stop by the bakery later—I have a new tart I'm working on for Peach Fest."

"Sounds yummy," Liz says. "Peach Fest is the town's biggest event of the year. It's held at the park, and everyone comes out for the food, fun, and games. Too bad y'all aren't here a little later or you would have hit it."

"Too bad," King deadpans. I'm certain he's being sarcastic, but Liz doesn't pick up on it.

"And if you're looking for something to do once the sun goes down, you should definitely check out the Rowdy Tractor. It's pretty much the only spot in town that has any sort of nightlife. Tonight's karaoke night too."

"Tonight?" King nudges me with his elbow, and my face heats. No way is he dragging me up on the stage to sing in front of a crowd of strangers.

"Yes. It's always a good time."

"Thanks for the suggestion. Maybe we'll stop in." I shoot Delaney a friendly smile, even as my throat goes dry at the whole concept of karaoke night.

"Gotta run for now. Those peach tarts aren't going to bake themselves!" Delaney waves, then jogs out the door.

"Such a nice girl, that Delaney," Liz says, staring after her.

A grandfather clock chimes loudly from the corner of the room, alerting us to the eight-o'clock hour.

"I'll leave you two alone to enjoy your breakfast. Feel free to eat here at the table or enjoy it in the backyard, wherever you might like."

"Thanks, Mrs. Moss. We appreciate it." King tips his head at the woman, and she blushes.

"Please, call me Liz. Once you stay here, we're practically family. If you need anything else, give me a shout. I'll be in the kitchen." She hitches her thumb over her shoulder, then sidles off.

"Another McCauliffe. That's at least four mentioned in the last day," I whisper as soon as Liz is safely out of earshot.

"Yeah, but still no Lacey. So far we've got a football player, a firefighter, a baker, and the general store manager, plus the parents. But not her." King plucks a peach danish from the tray of goodies and sinks down onto the bench.

"Don't worry. In a town this small, someone's bound to know her. Especially with the same last name."

"I think after breakfast we head over to the general store and see what we can find out. Then we explore the town, making sure we're near the school around dismissal."

"Okay, sounds like a plan."

We eat quickly, stacking our dirty dishes and setting them at the end of the table before hitting the road.

"Let's drive over to Main Street and park near the general store. Then we'll walk around from there." King opens the door for me and helps me up into the cab.

"Roman didn't find any information about her adopted parents?" I ask as King starts the truck and eases out of the driveway, heading toward the center of town.

"Nothing. It wasn't an open adoption. We're lucky we have as much intel as we do."

"Crap. Not much to go on."

"I know." His fingers thrum the steering wheel twice as fast as the beat of the music. I slide my hand over, resting my palm against his strong thigh. He relaxes a little, but the line of his jaw is still set, clearly anxious about the situation.

Playing detective is *not* high on his bucket list.

"Relax, it's going to work out."

King huffs out a quick breath, pulling into a spot near the general store. After cutting the engine, he sits back and observes the quiet street, eyes darting from the canopied storefronts to the cobblestone street, and back again.

"I bet the park Delaney mentioned is down there." I

point off in the distance, where the street dead-ends into a black fenced area filled with trees.

"Probably. We can check that out later. Come on." King jumps out, then walks around to open the truck door for me. I take a quick glimpse at my reflection in the mirror, smoothing down a stray curl before hopping out.

"We looking for anything in particular here? I mean— besides Lacey?" I whisper as we approach the store.

"Snacks. Water. I don't care, whatever you want. Then we can try to strike up a conversation with the cashier. With any luck, it'll be another McCauliffe."

"Good plan."

The door chimes as we enter, the space the epitome of a small-town general store. Seems like they have just about anything one could possibly need, from paper towels to mac and cheese, all neatly lined up on wooden shelves that have to be original.

"Morning, y'all."

A tall man with dark hair and stylish glasses waves, welcoming us in.

"Looking for anything in particular?" He cocks a brow, leaning his lithe frame against the front register, which also appears to be vintage. This isn't the Super Wal-Mart, that's for sure.

"Just picking up some snacks," I say in a singsong voice, smiling over at him.

"Great, that's down the middle there." He points us in the right direction, then turns his attention back to the thick ledger on the desk, brow furrowed in concentration.

"Cool, thanks," King grumbles before ducking into the center aisle.

Trailing my hand over the packaged foods, I pluck a

bag of salt-and-vinegar chips from the shelf. King adds some cheese puffs and a package of beef jerky; then we move to the next row.

Household goods. Nothing we need here. We march up and down every aisle systematically, killing time, picking up things here and there.

"Damn, maybe we should have gotten a basket." An apple escapes, bouncing on the wood floor and tumbling down the aisle. The thump echoes through the quiet store, and the cashier appears at the end of the row, holding a green basket.

"Thought y'all could use this." He holds the basket out to me, and I drop everything in, then take the basket from him.

"Thanks." I shoot him a grateful smile. King squares his shoulders next to me, scooting in closer and taking the basket from me.

"No problem. You staying through Peach Fest? That's a big haul there." He eyes the overflowing basket.

"No, don't think so. We got into town late last night, though. Kind of a last-minute trip." King shoves a hand in his pocket.

"Too bad. It's always a good time. Where y'all visiting from?"

"Seaglass Beach." I try to sound bright and friendly—the opposite of King.

"Where's that? Florida?"

Interesting. Probably not a sibling of Lacey's then. Chances are she would have told her brother about reaching out to her birth mother.

"East Coast, north of Daytona. Kinda sleepy, but a nice spot." I drag my finger through the air like I'm drawing a straight line from north to south on an invisible map.

"I'll have to check it out. I'm Liam, by the way. Liam McCauliffe. If you need anything else, give me a shout." He walks away, and King's shoulders slump.

"Now what?" I whisper as soon as Liam's out of earshot.

King shrugs. "No idea. I should've sent Rome up here. He's a lot better at this shit than I am."

I squeeze his forearm, his muscles as strong as steel beneath the skin. "Hey, I think we're doing great. We at least talked to her extended family. They all have to be related somehow."

He presses his lips together in a tight line. "I suppose. Seems like we should have more info by now."

"We've been here less than twenty-four hours. This has been buried for how many years? Give yourself some grace."

Sighing, he doesn't say anything, and I'm not sure my pep talk was all that effective.

"We better check out before Liam gets suspicious." I jerk my head in the direction of the register.

"Fine."

We head to the register with our bounty, setting the basket down on the counter. King unpacks the groceries, Liam ringing up each item. Then King slides his credit card through the reader.

"Here's the receipt. Y'all have a great trip, and if you need anything, we'll be here!"

"Thanks." I shoot him another wide smile, and we walk out of the store, carrying all the groceries to the truck.

"That wasn't particularly fruitful," King grumbles, shoving the paper bags into the back seat.

"At least we have enough snacks for the next few weeks."

"That's true. I won't have to shop for a while."

"Let's walk up and down Main Street, see what we can see."

King and I explore Main Street all morning and well into the afternoon, popping into shop after shop. Everyone's so friendly, introducing themselves, asking about our travel plans, where we're from. After several hours, I feel like we've met everyone in town.

Everyone but Lacey.

"I'm beat. Tired of talking to people, and we know nothing more about Lacey than we did this morning."

I check my watch. It's almost two p.m.

"Let's have a snack and then head over to the school. The website said dismissal's at two thirty."

We walk hand in hand back to the truck, then sit with the windows rolled down and enjoy our makeshift lunch. I devour a bag of chips and an apple, and King eats the jerky before rolling out of the parking spot and heading toward the school.

He slows as we turn off Main Street, heading into a residential area. Bright-yellow school-zone signs alert us to the presence of young pedestrians, and I expect to see a bus or two, a carline of SUVs and minivans winding down the street.

But the street near the school is practically empty.

"Huh. I swore it was two thirty. I hope we didn't miss it." I tap into my phone, scrolling down and double-checking the time.

"Shit."

King points to the bulletin board in front of the building.

Enjoy Your Spring Break!

"School's out. Lacey might not even be in town." He shakes his head and puffs his lip out, exasperated. "I can't fucking believe this. Of all the luck . . ."

I run a hand over my face, deflated. "Well. This is a kink in the plan. Let's go back to the B and B and regroup."

We drive back in silence, King stewing behind the wheel. I peer out the window, hoping to spot Lacey, but no such luck. Finally, we roll into the driveway, and King slumps against the seat.

"This was a bad idea. I should have checked the dates better, I guess."

"Not your fault. What were the odds that this would be spring break?"

"One in fifty-two, I suppose." King scrubs a hand over the back of his neck.

"We could always just ask after her, King. You know—directly. Instead of trying to be covert."

"Hard pass. I don't need everyone in town knowing our family business."

"New plan then."

"I'm all ears."

"We'll go to the Rowdy Tractor tonight. People talk when they're liquored up. And maybe Lacey will be there. It's spring break, after all."

King scratches his head, his lips screwed up. "Good a plan as any, I suppose."

"Trust me on this—I've waitressed forever. I know what I'm talking about."

22

KING

The Rowdy Tractor's crowded, the lot almost full when we pull in and park. Music pumps from inside, the thump of bass disrupting the otherwise quiet night.

"Ready?" Juliet smooths her hair down, soft light from the full moon a spotlight on her high cheekbones.

"As I'll ever be."

We cross the lot, pushing through the door into the dim space, a loud eighties guitar riff assaulting my ears. The floor's sticky as we make our way to the bar, shoving through the crowd. I keep a tight hold on Juliet's hand, nerves firing through me, my chest tight.

I don't love crowds, especially in a strange place. Juliet squeezes my hand, and I run my thumb over hers, trying to relax a little.

It'll be fine. Just focus on Juliet, not everyone else.

Finally, we make it to the bar, a blue neon glow reflecting off the shiny metal surface. One barstool's available, and I pull it out, offering it to Juliet. She takes a seat, leans against the bar, and considers her options. A busty redhead spots us, heading over to take our order.

"What'll it be?"

"I'll have tequila on the rocks," Juliet says.

"And you?" The waitress tips her head at me.

"I'll take a draft beer. Whatever seasonal beer you have on tap."

"Coming right up." She sidles away, in no kind of rush.

"Busy place." Juliet glances around at the packed space. The television screens flash behind the bar, the light reflecting in the golden flecks of Juliet's eyes. "You okay?"

She rests her hand on my arm, and I relax a little.

"Yeah. I'm good." Her fingers feather over my skin, and my lower body tightens. I'd much rather be in bed with Juliet right now, instead of standing around with a bunch of strangers. But the sooner we track Lacey down, the sooner we can get out of here.

"Here y'all go." The redhead returns, drinks in hand. She slides Juliet's drink across the bar, then hands me a frosty mug topped with foamy beer. "Y'all starting a tab?"

"Might as well." I plunk my credit card down on the bar, and she picks it up, slides it into her apron pocket.

"I'll check on you in a bit. You here for karaoke?"

Juliet shakes her head vehemently.

"No. No way."

"Aww, come on." I squeeze her knee. "You have a great voice."

"I don't."

"She does," I assure the bartender.

"Don't worry, competition's not all that stiff here."

A siren pierces the air, and the ground shakes, the bar

rumbling, beer bottles and wineglasses rattling against the metal surface.

"What the—" I wrap my arm around Juliet's shoulders, vaguely worried about an earthquake.

The bartender doesn't even flinch, swiping up stray droplets with a dishrag.

"That's the fire department next door. Y'all must not be from here. Happens all the time."

No one around us seems particularly bothered, carrying on about their business, chatting and drinking.

"Oh, right. The fire alarm. And no, we're just passing through." Juliet takes a sip of her drink, her cheeks flushing pink from the alcohol.

"There are pool tables in the back. Darts too." The bartender tips her head to the right, and I notice another room full of people.

"Nice. Wanna play pool?" Juliet's eyes slide to mine, and I nod.

"Sure."

Snaking my arm around Juliet's waist, I hold her tight against me as we push through the crowd. A Journey tune comes on, and several people cheer, rushing to the dance floor. We dodge them, working our way across the bar.

Finally, we make it to the back room. Several pool tables stand side by side, each illuminated by a single bright light. Five dartboards hang on the back wall, groups of people gathered at high-tops dotted around the space. A waitress circulates, taking drink orders. Juliet and I weave through the people, trying to find an empty table.

"There's Delaney," Juliet hisses, nodding at the table in the corner.

Sure enough, the baker is leaning on a pool cue, waiting

her turn. A broad-shouldered man's next to her, sipping beer from a bottle. Next to him is a tall, muscular guy I vaguely recognize.

"And I think that's the football player." Juliet's voice rises, her cheeks flushing with excitement.

Another woman's standing with them, a tallish blonde. They're all playing pool, and it's the football player's turn.

"Should we go say hi?" Juliet cuts her eyes at me, and I shake my head.

"No."

"We totally should. Come on." She grips my arm, dragging me in their direction. I try to hang back, but she's determined.

Putting on a bright smile, she waves at Delaney as we approach the table.

"Oh, hey!" Delaney waves at us. "These folks are staying at the Grove. Visiting from Florida."

Thwack. Pool balls fly across the green felt, one falling into the left pocket.

"Florida? That's nice this time of year I bet." The football player rises from his shooting position.

"Real nice," Juliet says before taking a sip of her drink.

My gut churns, and I push down the urge to bolt—from these people, this crowd, the whole damn scene. I've never wanted to be back home, working in the barn with the animals, more than I do right now. Hell, I'd rather be mucking stalls.

"What brings you to our neck of the woods? Peachtree Grove's not exactly a vacation destination. Not like Florida." The man next to Delaney furrows his brow as he stares at us.

"Geez, Quinn. No need to interrogate them." Delaney slaps his arm, and his scowl deepens.

"What? I'm not."

"You kind of are," the blonde points out. "But that's on brand for you. I'm Bree." She offers her hand to Juliet, then to me. "That's Ryder." She motions at the football player, and he waves his large hand in our direction. "And the grumpy one's Quinn." She lowers her voice, leaning over closer to Juliet. "He's harmless. It's mostly for show."

The guy named Quinn rolls his eyes at Bree, but she only smiles angelically across the pool table at him. Ryder laughs, and Delaney takes her turn at the table before coming back to chat.

"What did you think of the peach danish this morning? I've been tweaking that recipe for a while now. Too much cinnamon? Not enough?" She bites at the side of her lip, waits for our response.

"It was great," Juliet says, reassuring her. "I wouldn't change a thing."

"Whew." Delaney swipes at her brow. "Glad to hear you liked it."

"Excuse me." Quinn slides between us and Delaney, smacking her playfully on the ass as he walks by.

"Stop!" Delaney giggles, bright-pink spots staining her cheeks. The two of them are obviously a couple, and I'd bet money the football player's with the blonde. Must be date night at the Rowdy Tractor.

Quinn doesn't say anything, instead eyeing the pool table and assessing his next move.

"Purple stripe, right pocket." He lines up the pool cue and smacks at the balls, sinking the purple striped one.

"Nice shot, babe." Delaney blows an air-kiss at Quinn as he stalks around the table, calculating his next shot.

"What do you all think of Peachtree Grove so far?" Bree asks, fixing her gaze on me. She seems friendly enough, her eyes warm. Like someone you could talk to.

"It's real cute," Juliet says, swirling her glass in a tight circle.

"Where do y'all live in Florida?" Bree smooths her shiny golden hair over her shoulder, white teeth glinting in the overhead light.

"Seaglass Beach." Juliet's voice rings out over the hum of noise in the room.

Ryder moves to Bree's side, winding his arm around her waist.

"Isn't that where Lacey went on vacation this summer?" Bree lifts her chin at Ryder, and I freeze, the ambient noise fading away as blood whooshes loudly through my ears.

Lacey.

My entire body tenses as I lock eyes with Juliet. She stares back at me, unblinking, as we wait for Ryder's response. My mind kicks into overdrive as I try to figure out what to say, how to keep them talking about Lacey.

"Yeah, I think so. She stayed at a historic inn. She and Opal had a really good time. Said they were right on the ocean."

I suck in a breath, and I'm grateful for the loud music drowning out the hammering in my chest.

Lacey stayed at the Seaglass Inn? Was she looking for our mom that whole time? She had to see Poppy and probably Parker too.

"Wow, small world." Juliet takes a sip of her drink and tries to act normal, make polite conversation. "Is Lacey your sister?"

Ryder shakes his head. "No. Cousin on my dad's side. He has a bunch of brothers, all born and raised here. She belongs to Uncle Paul and Aunt Missy. They both passed now, though. She was their only child."

"Well, good thing she has lots of cousins, right?" Juliet says, and a wave of nausea washes over me.

Lacey has more than cousins. She has three half brothers and a half sister.

I get why she'd reach out, now that her adoptive parents are gone. It's too bad that our mom's gone too.

"Half this town is McCauliffes," Bree says, laughing. "At least every other person you meet is related somehow."

"That's why I had to import a wife." Ryder kisses Bree on the lips, and she blushes, patting his chest.

"You're so ridiculous. There are plenty of women in town who were ready and willing to date you when I showed up. Who *aren't* your cousins."

"None of them were you, though." Ryder gazes down at Bree, and I shove my hand in my pocket, look away. I feel like I'm intruding on their private conversation.

"Yo, Ryder. It's your turn," Quinn shouts from across the table, leaning on his pool cue. "Winner takes all."

"Y'all want another round?" I hold my empty bottle up.

"Sure. That'd be great," Delaney says. "But drinks are on us. You're visitors. What kind of hospitality would that be? Tell the bartender to put it on the McCauliffe tab."

"No, I got it." No way can I accept drinks from strangers.

"We insist. You need help? I can come with." Delaney moves toward us, but I shake my head.

"I can get it. No problem." I set my empty bottle on the nearby table, and Juliet follows close behind.

"I'll come with you," Juliet volunteers, threading her fingers through mine. We head out of the pool room, sliding through the crowd back toward the bar. The main room's packed now, and a DJ's setting up the microphone and projection screen for karaoke.

Juliet moves in close to me, her mouth at my ear. "So you found her cousins. That's good, right?"

I roll my shoulders, trying to shake the tension between the blades. Seems like it's been sitting there, constant, for the last few months. Since I got the blasted letter in the mail.

"I guess."

There's a line at the bar now, and Juliet and I take our place behind a group of middle-aged women. Probably enjoying a moms' night out, from the looks of it.

"You okay?" Juliet tips her head, eyeing me up and down, reading me.

"I don't know." I scrub a hand over my jaw, try to ease the tension.

"What do you think about calling her? Taking the direct approach? She comes from good people—they seem nice as hell. Highly unlikely she's a scammer. Take it from someone who knows scammers. She's probably just lonely."

Juliet squeezes my hand, and my chest loosens a tiny bit. She's probably right. Still, a part of me wants to jump back in my truck and head home. Mission failed and leave it at that.

"King?" She gazes up at me, the golden flecks in her eyes shimmering in the neon glow of the bar.

"Any chance you want to head home?" I throw the question out there. I can guess her response, but I throw it out there anyway.

"King Montgomery. No, absolutely not." She steps forward, rests her tiny hands on my chest, hovering over my heart.

"You've got this. *We've* got this. We're so close—let's finish the job."

I know she's right. I feel it deep in my gut. Doesn't make it any easier, though.

"Let's have another drink, hang with our new friends. Really enjoy a night out together, not worrying about the past or the future. We'll tackle those things again in the morning."

"Deal."

She rises on tiptoe, kissing me softly, and in that moment the world melts away. The stress, the uncertainty, all the negative bullshit. Gone, vanished with her touch.

"Thanks for coming with me," I murmur against her lips. The corners of her mouth tip into a smile, her arms winding around me.

"I'm happy to be your ride or die, King. Always."

My chest warms, surging with something I never thought I'd feel again.

Love.

This is exactly how I felt the last time we were together, before shit went south.

And I know I don't deserve her, but I can't help wanting her anyway.

Forever this time.

23

———

JULIET

King's freaking out about this Lacey thing, I can tell. He's been quieter than usual all night, which puts him at practically silent.

Not a great trait when we're trying to gather info about his half sister. I'm attempting to chat up our new friends, but he's not making it easy.

So I'm actually relieved when karaoke starts and Bree and Delaney drag the group away from the pool tables, claiming a table in the main bar area.

"Are you going to sing tonight, Delaney?" Bree flips through the paper songbook, studying the list of song choices as if they're fine wine.

"I don't know, maybe. Depends on how many drinks I have." Delaney throws her head back, laughing, then takes another sip of her beer.

"What about you?" Bree swivels to face me, and my face flames.

"No. No, I couldn't." I stare past her at the stage, the

DJ adjusting the microphone stand. Static feedback screeches through the room as he taps on the mic.

"Testing, testing." His voice booms through the bar, and everyone claps.

Eager crowd.

"All right, y'all. First up we have"—he glances at his clipboard—"Frank singing 'Friends in Low Places.' Let's give it up for Frank!"

Another round of applause, and an older man stands. He's in jeans and a gray hoodie sweatshirt repping the local 4-H group. After moseying up to the stage, he climbs the steps and raises the microphone to mouth level.

"Howdy. What's up?" Frank waves at the bar, and a group of ladies in the corner whoops and hollers for him. He's clearly a regular.

The familiar tune rings out from the speakers on either side of the stage, and Frank breaks out into song. He's a decent singer—on key, and he even has a few dance moves. The crowd gets into it, clapping along and stomping their feet, and when the song ends, everyone cheers.

"Great job, Frank. Way to kick us off right. Up next is Sylvie."

One of the women from the moms' night out sashays up, loosening her hair as she climbs the steps. A curtain of jet-black hair falls around her shoulders, and she flips it once before lifting the mic from the stand.

Another karaoke regular.

"Sylvie's back, and she's performing Aretha Franklin's 'A Natural Woman.'"

Sylvie's friends clap and cheer, the spotlight beaming down on her as she starts to sing. She has a great voice, hitting all the right notes, and I'm relieved I didn't sign up. No way do I want to follow her performance.

As I sip my tequila, King's hand rests on my upper thigh. His thumb rubs up and down over the denim, shooting pulses of excitement through me. I glance over at him, taking in the strong line of his jaw, the fine lines around his eyes and mouth. My heart squeezes when his gaze slides to mine, his lips curving up in a slight smile.

A smile meant just for me.

I've lived almost half my life waiting for this. Wanting this.

Wanting him.

Even more, wanting us.

His hand inches higher up my leg, and I'm on fire for this man, my core aching. I peek at my watch, wondering if it's too early to cut out. I desperately want to be alone with King.

"Next up to the stage is Juliet!"

I freeze, the heat in my body turning icy real quick.

"What?" My eyes widen as I stare at King, a smirk on his stupid handsome face. "You didn't!"

"I did." He tips his beer back, taking a long, slow sip.

"No. I'm not going."

"C'mon, Juliet!" Delaney grabs my hand. "It'll be fun. King told us you love to sing."

"I can't." I shake my head no, resist the strong urge to cover my face with my hands.

"You totally can! We'll go with you." Delaney drags me out of my seat, along with an equally protesting Bree.

"Delaney, I cannot sing. Not like these other people."

"Pshaw. I'm sure you're amazing." She pushes us both toward the stage. My legs are like lead pipes buried in concrete—the only way she gets me up there is sheer brute force.

Delaney's stronger than she looks.

Now the three of us stand in the hot beam of the spotlight. Tequila's churning in my gut, and I push down a wave of nauseous panic.

"Ladies, are we still good with 'Girls Just Want to Have Fun'?" The DJ directs his question to Delaney, the unofficial leader, I guess.

Delaney nods, but I grip her elbow and lean in toward her, away from the microphone.

"Delaney—mind if we switch songs? That one's harder than you think."

She raises her brow. "Sure. What are you thinking?"

"Let's do 'Like a Prayer' by Madonna."

"Excellent choice." The DJ gives his nod of approval, shuffling through his phone to cue up the music.

Everyone in the Rowdy Tractor's staring at us, and I could absolutely kill King right now. I try to find his face in the crowd so I can scowl at him, but the light's too blinding. Bree gives my arm a reassuring squeeze, and the music starts, purple text scrolling on the screen in front of us.

With a pounding heart, I sing the iconic words. Not needing the teleprompter but reading it anyway. Anything to keep my mind off the fact that I'm up onstage, singing to a packed house.

We start off a little shaky but quickly find our groove. Delaney throws her arm around both of us, swaying to the beat, and after the first chorus I'm much more relaxed. Almost enjoying myself.

The audience gets into it, clapping along, and Bree and

Delaney start dancing. I stay focused on the song and on hitting the right notes.

Both of them fall back, and now I'm singing solo. But I don't care at this point. Everything fades away, and I'm floating up here, drifting on the melody, carried by the beat of the music.

I nail the last note, and the crowd breaks into applause. Cheeks flushed, I smile, my chest lighter than it's been in a long damn time.

"Juliet! You were awesome!" Bree throws her arms around me, and so does Delaney, wrapping me up tight in a group hug.

"Well done, ladies." The DJ smiles, then ushers us off the stage so the next singer can perform.

King's waiting for me at the bottom of the steps.

"I knew you'd be great." He gazes at me with those dark-navy eyes, and I've never felt more seen.

"Thanks. Although I didn't love the strong-arm tactics." I chuck him on his biceps, my hand bouncing off the swell of his muscles.

"You ready to head out?" He tips his head toward the door, and excitement flutters low in my belly, heat racing to my core.

"Mm-hmm. We should say our goodbyes, though."

King rests his hand on my lower back, guiding me over to the table, and we say goodbye.

"It was great meeting all of you." I give Bree a quick squeeze, then Delaney.

"Oh my gosh, you all too! When are you heading back home?" Delaney asks.

"Soon. Maybe tomorrow, maybe the next day," King says.

"Well, I hope we see each other again before then. If not, have a safe trip home!" Delaney smiles at us.

The next singer starts wailing about Margaritaville, and that's our cue to dip.

"Bye!" We wave at the McCauliffes one more time before cutting across the room toward the exit.

Shoving through the door, we spill out into the night. The air's chilly on my skin after being in the warmth of the Rowdy Tractor, and I shiver.

King pulls me into his body, slinging his arm around my shoulders, and I've never felt more content than I do right now.

"Mmm," I murmur, leaning my head against his strong frame.

He smooths my hair from my face, glancing over at me.

"You really were something up there. They were okay, but you were amazing." His eyes lock on mine, and my stomach swoops.

"Thank you."

We're at the truck, and he presses me up against the door, stretching his arms over my shoulders so we're face-to-face, our breath syncing. Running his thumb down my jaw, he traces the outline of my face. I tip my head up, lick along the seam of my lips.

"I love you." His eyes lock directly on mine, pupils dark and wide.

My breath hitches, my pulse racing.

We stare at each other, the music from the Rowdy Tractor bumping behind us.

I've waited for this moment—this man—for years.

"I love you too." The words fall from my lips, emotions

I've kept locked up for over a decade bubbling to the surface.

King leans forward, touching his lips lightly to mine. So soft, so gentle, it almost feels like a dream. I melt into him, opening my mouth to his, and he slips his tongue in. Tasting me, claiming me.

"I want you," I whisper, my voice almost swallowed by our hungry kisses.

"I want you too. I've always wanted you." He inches his face away from mine, tipping my chin up. "I want only you."

My heart stutters, hot tears pricking at the corners of my eyes.

I never thought I'd hear those words again. And it's better than I even imagined.

Winding my hands around his waist, I gaze up at him through lowered lashes.

"Take me, I'm yours."

24

JULIET

King wastes no time ushering me into the truck and driving us back to the Grove. We take the stairs as quickly as we can, the bedroom door creaking as we enter our room.

"Damn, that thing still needs more WD-40," King grumbles, kicking the door shut behind us. He's already backing us up to the bed, undressing me as he goes. By the time we make it across the room, my shirt is off and my jeans are halfway down my legs. He pushes me gently onto the bed, pulling the denim fully off before dropping onto his knees and sucking at my clit through the thin silk of my panties.

Twining my fingers in his hair, I bite down on my lip to stifle a moan. I'm not sure how soundproof these old walls are, and I don't want Liz and Murphy to hear us. King applies more pressure, then hooks his thumbs in the sides of my panties and eases the fabric down. He kisses up and down my thighs, shivers of pleasure skittering over my heated skin, before sliding his tongue inside me.

"You taste so fucking good, Jules." The vibrations from his voice send me into overdrive, and my lower body clenches and tightens.

I keep biting my lip, my hands moving from his head down to his shoulders. Kneading his tight muscles, trying to release the knotty tension there. I tease his shirt from his jeans, pulling him up so we're face-to-face. He undoes his jeans, both of us eager. We're naked in under a minute, his body hovering over mine. Heat shimmers between us, the air charged with want.

Moonlight filters through the window, catching the few strands of silver in his hair. The man is gorgeous, even more so now that he's older, every muscle in his torso chiseled.

"What?" King peers down at me, a brow raised.

"You're the same." My fingers trace over his broad chest, tiptoe over his abs. "But better."

"I don't know about that—"

"Shh." I put my finger over his lips, then lean up and kiss him. "You are. So strong, so capable. But not a boy anymore."

"Definitely not a boy." He presses against me, his thick cock rock hard on my thigh.

"You're so beautiful."

King caresses my face, tracing over my cheekbone, my jaw, the bow of my lips. I suck his thumb into my mouth, swirl my tongue over the rough callus, never breaking eye contact. Watching as his pupils darken with desire. Groaning, he hardens further as I suck him in deeper.

He surprises me, depressing my tongue and forcing my mouth open before slamming his lips to mine. Instinctively,

I wrap my legs around his waist and pull him into me as he claims my mouth.

Hungry. Greedy. Like he'll never get enough of me.

He ravages my mouth, and I taste myself on his tongue as he slides in and out. Licking, sucking, nipping down the column of my neck. Pleasure skitters through me, my nipples diamond sharp against his chest. Palming my breasts, King caresses the smooth skin, moving round and round in circles until I'm panting with need. Pinching the rosy points until I squirm beneath him, then releasing, blood rushing back to the surface.

I'm so wet, the throbbing between my legs almost painful.

King slaps the side of my breast lightly—once, twice—and I suck in a breath. Every inch of me is on fire, nerves zinging at every touch. He reaches down, cupping my sex, and a soft moan sounds low in my throat.

"You liked that, didn't you?" The side of his mouth inches up in a smirk.

He knows damn well I did—he knew it before he even touched me.

I nod as he fingers me, trailing through my wetness. Circling the entrance, teasing me.

"Tell me what you want me to do to you, Juliet." His voice is deep, commanding, and I search for the right words. It's difficult to think in my aroused state, my tongue thick and swollen from kissing and sucking and biting.

He dips his head between my breasts, his tongue tracing along my curves. Goose bumps pebble my skin, and this isn't helping me think.

"Mmm," I groan.

His teeth graze my nipple as he sucks the tight bud

into his mouth, then bites down lightly. I wriggle my hips against him, spread my legs, aching for contact.

"No. Not until you tell me what you want." He reaches up, strokes my face. "Say the words, Juliet."

"Please." My voice comes out desperate, needy.

He chuckles. "Please what, baby?"

Shifting his body, he stares down at me, a look of amusement dancing across his face.

"Please fuck me."

A low growl vibrates his neck, rumbling his chest as he pushes three fingers inside me. Fast and deep, scissoring and stretching me. Preparing my body to take him in.

"Are you ready, baby girl? Because this isn't going to be gentle." He slides another finger in, and my breath catches in my throat. I nod.

"Yes, I'm ready. Take me."

After a few more deep thrusts, he pulls his hand out, and my pussy clenches. Already missing him, his body, the feeling of being filled up by this man.

I reach for his cock, run my palm over the swollen crown, and he groans.

"Fuck, baby. I'm so hard for you already." His pupils dilate as I move up and down his shaft, watch as he twitches and pulsates in my hand. He unwinds my fingers from his dick and lifts my hands above my head, clutching my wrists and forcing my back to arch slightly.

"Beautiful." His tongue darts out, circling my nipple, and a rush of heat washes over me.

Another moan falls from my lips, and I spread my thighs, granting him full access, permission to do whatever he wants with my body.

King doesn't make me wait any longer, pushing his cock

inside me. There's the initial shock, followed quickly by fullness and sparkly heat pricking my skin. Our bodies join together, and we find a rhythm, a dance only the two of us know.

A dance we've done many times before, but not like this.

Never like this.

Hands braced above my head, I bite into my lip as he drives into me, his navy eyes locked onto mine. He's in full control, has absolute possession of my body. All I can do is feel.

Every touch, every whisper of breath, every flex of his tight muscles as he thrusts into me.

Over and over again, pushing me closer and closer to the edge.

I want to fall, tumble straight into his arms.

Arms that will never let me go again.

"Oh my. King—"

The bed shakes and creaks beneath us, the headboard thumping against the wall as we rocket toward our release. I know I should care about the noise, but all I can do right now is chase the climax, the high that comes from fucking King.

"Come for me, Juliet. Come for me, baby." He murmurs the words, soft and sweet, his lips fluttering over my cheeks.

One last thrust and I shatter around him, crying out. He lets go of my hands, smashing his mouth onto mine to drown out my screams as my body bucks beneath him.

Never losing momentum, he drives harder and harder. Possessing me with a wild ferocity, sweat beading on his brow.

Finally, he spills his hot release inside me. Only then does he still, the room quiet again except for our panting breaths.

"Fuck, Jules." He collapses next to me, snaking his arm around my shoulders. Trailing the rough pads of his fingertips over my sensitive skin, every inch of my body lighting up with his touch.

I sigh, snuggling against his broad frame, soaking in his goodness, his strength.

Wishing we could stay here forever, snuggled up in our safe cocoon. Away from all the drama, all the bullshit. Just me and King, together.

Like we were meant to be.

"I love you." He strokes my hair, my chest light, filled with bubbly happiness.

I wind my leg around his, press even closer to him.

"I love you too." I trail my fingers up and down his abs, running over each strong ridge. "You think we woke anyone up?"

"I hope not. That'll be real awkward in the morning." He kisses the top of my head, and I melt into him, a heaviness creeping into my muscles.

We drift off to sleep wrapped in each other's arms.

I'M LYING ON A TILE FLOOR. SHARP PAIN SEARS MY GUT, AND I can't move. Arms and legs frozen, I'm paralyzed.

King's there, staring down at me, and I try to scream, to cry out and get his attention. But his navy eyes glaze over, and he says nothing, his face impassive.

A warm gush of blood oozes from between my legs; then the head of a baby crowns.

Our baby. But the skin is blue, and I need to get help. I try to move, crawl, anything. But I can't.

Trapped, immobile. Stuck to the floor in this horrible, familiar moment I've lived over and over again.

I want King to open his mouth, to speak, say something comforting. Take me into his strong arms and carry me away.

But nothing happens, and we're locked here together. So near to each other, yet worlds apart.

I wake with a start in a cold sweat. A sticky film covers my skin, even though the room's chilly. A crushing sadness pushes down on my chest in the darkness.

The nightmare.

I've had it for years now. But this time it's different.

Worse.

Before, King always walked away.

This time, he stayed but did nothing to help me, help our baby.

A heavy arm pulls me closer, his naked body pressed against mine. One hand rests on my belly, warm breath tickling my neck as he snores lightly.

What if I can never have a baby?

King would be a great dad. He deserves the chance to hold his own child in his arms.

What if I can't give that to him?

Tears prick at my eyes, and I stifle a sob, choking it down. King stirs behind me, his fingers rubbing over my bare skin.

"Jules? You okay?" His voice, gravelly with sleep, startles me. I only nod, not trusting my voice.

A tear leaks down my cheek, splashing onto the pillow.

"Hey, what's wrong?"

"Nothing." I whisper the lie and try to hold back the wave of tears threatening.

"Tell me. It's okay." He caresses my arm, stroking it slowly, gently, breaking down my defenses.

"What if I can never have a baby?" My voice cracks as I contemplate the reality of our situation, and more tears fall.

"Shh, don't talk like that. The doctor said it probably wouldn't happen again."

"But I might not be able to give you a baby."

"And that'd be fine. I only need you."

His words somehow make me cry harder, and now I'm full-on sobbing.

"Hey." He spins me around, pulling me up against his broad chest. "Hey, don't cry. We're good."

I bawl into his shoulder, long, racking sobs, until I'm all cried out. He holds me to him the entire time, wrapping me up in a tight embrace.

This. This is what I needed from him all those years ago.

And for the first time the jagged edges of the wound start to come together, the rough pieces of my heart healing.

"Thank you." I say the words so softly I'm not even sure he hears. He rubs my back in light circles, rocking me oh so slightly. Comforting me.

Pressing a kiss to my forehead, he smooths the damp hair from my face.

"Jules, I love you. You're enough for me. You always were."

I gaze up at him, a lone streak of moonlight illuminating his face, and my heart stutters.

"You don't know how much I needed to hear that."

"I should have told you sooner."

I cup his cheek, running my thumb over the stubble peppering his jaw. "You said it now. That's all that matters."

"I don't deserve you, Jules. I never did."

"Shh." Now it's my turn to press a finger to his lips, quiet his doubts. "You always deserved more than me."

"I never stopped loving you. Even when you were thousands of miles away. I lay in bed at night and thought of you, dreamed about you. Prayed you were safe and happy."

"The happiest times of my life were with you, King."

He trails his finger over my cheekbone, down my neck, across my collarbone. Melancholy stretches between us, a dull, pulsing ache in my chest from all the moments we've lost.

I meet his gaze. "I tried to stay away. But I couldn't do it anymore. I needed to be home." I take a shaky breath, my insides churning. "I needed you."

He doesn't say anything.

Instead, he takes my face in his hands and kisses me with a force so strong, so deep, it steals my breath away.

I love this man.

Deep down, I never stopped loving him. Even when every breath, every beat of my heart, physically hurt because we were apart.

It's always been him. And now we both know it.

King pulls away from my lips, locks his gaze on mine.

"I needed you too, Jules. More than you'll ever know."

Warmth blooms in my chest as he holds me in his strong arms, my head resting on his chest. Snuggling in, I drift off to sleep, happier than I've ever been.

THE BUZZ OF MY PHONE JOLTS ME AWAKE. I FLING MY arm out from beneath the sheet and grab the cool metal, hitting the button to silence the dang thing.

"Shit."

I stare at the string of missed messages, delivered last night while we were otherwise preoccupied.

> Sabby: Your brothers are here looking for you. I'm sticking to the plan

Heart pounding, I keep scrolling.

> Sabby: Cash keeps pushing. But I'm acting like I don't know anything

Another text, thirty minutes later:

> Sabby: Where are you? Call me

Then another one, thirty minutes after that.

> Sabby: SOS

Ten minutes later, she sends a photo. I tap the pic and zoom in.

"Oh my god." My stomach rolls, acid rising up my throat. "Those bastards."

Sabby's arm is black and blue, handprints visible on her

pale skin. *My brothers' hands.* Those pigs laid hands on my friend, all because I asked her to cover for me.

I immediately text her back.

> Juliet: Sabby, I'm so, so sorry. I can't believe they hurt you. I never would have asked if I thought they would touch you. Call the police and file a report. They deserve it

Guilt washes over me, and I fight back the urge to scream, instead clenching my fists so hard my knuckles ache. The movement wakes King. He runs his palm down my arm, soothing me.

"Babe. What's the matter?"

"This." I thrust my phone at him, and he holds it away from his face, squinting at the screen.

"Is that your friend at the Tipsy?"

"Yeah, Sabby. I asked her to cover for me if my brothers came in. You know—because they were sniffing around and love to cause trouble. Well, guess they didn't believe her and got rough to get their point across."

King's jaw tenses, his muscles flexing behind me. Readying for battle.

"I'll handle them, Jules."

Not a question. Not a warning.

A statement.

"No, King. For starters, it's two against one."

"I can handle your thug brothers."

"I know. You probably could."

"No *probably* about it." His nostrils flare, chest puffed.

"I know you could, babe. But it's not your fight. It's

mine." I trail my fingers over his pecs. "I'm the one who put Sabby in this situation in the first place."

"No, I did. When I asked you to come with me. It's not your fault. You don't control your brothers or their bad decisions. Besides, they should never put their hands on a woman."

"And they wouldn't have if it weren't for me."

"Stop." His voice is firm, eyes flashing with fire. "This isn't your fault. And I'm going to handle them. If you're really worried, I'll take Rome with me."

"Oh, great, get your brother involved. That will make our relationship super smooth." I roll my eyes, and King grabs my chin, forcing me to look at him.

"This. Isn't. Your. Fault." He says each word crisply, slowly, making sure every single syllable sinks in.

"And I don't need backup, I have full confidence I can handle your idiot brothers."

I swallow hard over the lump in my throat, tears pricking behind my gummy eyelids.

"I've got you, Jules. You don't ever need to worry." He lets go of my face, and I take a shaky breath, trying to think.

I want to believe him, but loud alarm bells clang in my head. Warning me not to let my guard down, to be prepared.

My phone trills beside us, the sound muffled by the sheets. I reach for it at the same time King does, but he's closer and gets to it first. Cash's name flashes on the screen, and King answers before I can stop him.

"Hello?" he growls into the speaker.

"Hello? Who the fuck is this? Where's my sister?"

Cash's voice goes from surprised to angry in a quarter second.

"You don't have very good phone etiquette, Cash." King scowls down at the phone, taunting my brother. My gut twists.

"Shut the fuck up. I know who this is. It's the little prince. Where's my sister? I need to talk to her."

"Too bad. She's busy."

"Busy screwing a Montgomery? That's low, even for her."

"Don't talk about your sister like that, Cash."

"I can talk about her however I want. She's my sister."

King brushes past this argument, deep lines furrowing his brow. "You have anything important to say, Cash? Or should I just hang up right now?"

"I don't have anything to say to you, dickhead. I wanna talk to my little tramp of a sister."

"Sorry, I told you she's not available."

I grab for the phone, but King pulls it away.

"Maybe if you find some manners, I'll put her on."

"What are you, her fucking keeper or something?"

"Okay, guess you didn't find them. Buh-bye." He goes to disconnect, but Cash pipes up.

"Fine. Could I please talk to my darling little sister?"

King holds the phone out to me, and I wrap a shaking hand around the cool metal.

"What do you want?" Anger seeps into my voice, and I wish I'd let King handle this like he wanted to.

"Your stupid friend Sabby lied to us. Unless you're straddling the porcelain pony right now. But seems like you're more interested in straddling the prince instead."

"Shut the fuck up, Cash," I snarl into the phone. "And if

you ever touch Sabby again, I will let King beat you bloody. Got me?"

"Oh, now you're a tough little bitch, threatening to send your boy toy over to teach me a lesson."

"Unless you have something important to say, I'm hanging up."

"I came by the Tipsy Taco to tell you the good news."

A gaping pit yawns open in my stomach—Cash and I have very different ideas of good news.

"And what's that?"

"Jags is getting out early, on account of good behavior."

The pit sinks like a rock, hot panic rushing through me. I haven't missed Jagger one little bit. And having him on the outside, roaming free when King and I are just getting started again, is less than ideal.

"Little sis? You still there?"

"When?" I try to tamp down the panic rising in my voice.

"Soon. They said the next day or two. You baking him a cake? Maybe making a 'Welcome Home' sign?"

"Fuck off, Cash."

"I'll be sure to tell him how excited you are. And that you're sleeping with the enemy. He's going to be real interested in that."

A cold slither of fear winds through my chest, snaking into my gut. Cash and Damon are one thing—Jagger's a whole different beast.

The line goes dead, a dial tone cutting through the silence. King lifts the cell from my hand, smooths my hair from my face.

"Don't worry, Jules. I've got you. Jagger won't be able to touch you, I promise you that."

I huff out a shaky breath, tears welling in my eyes.

"He won't do anything, really. It's just—" I shut my eyes, pinch the bridge of my nose to stop the tears from falling.

Why is everything so damn complicated all the time?

"What, baby?" King pulls me to him, stroking my hair, and I inhale his clean, woodsy scent.

"He knows." I whisper the words into his chest, feel the steady thudding of his heart against my cheek.

"About the trial? How you helped us?"

I nod, my hair rustling on his bare skin. His muscles tighten and flex beneath me, his heart racing.

"Last time I went to see him at the jail—he knows, King. I don't know how, but he does."

"I knew I should have stayed away from you." His voice is quiet, filled with regret.

Lifting my eyes to his, hot panic grips me. I hate the fear I feel in this moment, shaking me to my core, my heart pounding like I ran a damn marathon. The past comes rushing back—the desperation, the anxiety, the overwhelming sadness—and my chest is tight, so tight I'm afraid I might pass out.

I need King—like I need air to breathe—and I hate it.

"No. Not this time. Not again." My voice breaks on a plea, a tear spilling onto my cheek.

"Baby . . ." King swipes it away, cupping my cheek. "Don't cry. Please don't cry."

"I'll handle my brothers. Just please don't give up on us."

25

———————

KING

I CAN'T STAND THOSE MOTHERFUCKERS.

Seeing her cry, knowing all of this is happening because of me, is a sucker punch to the damn gut.

I brush those tears away, but my gut's tight and knotty, twisted up with dread.

She should be out living a good life, have a baby or two, a cute little house with a front-porch swing. A stable job that uses her smarts. She was in college, for fuck's sake.

Until me.

I ruined that for her. Her chance to get out. Be free. Far away from her asshole brothers.

Free from me and all the bullshit of our small-minded town.

This is why I pushed her away the first time.

You tried.

I should have stayed away from her, kept my distance. Stuck to the plan.

But no. I let my cock lead the way, and look what's happening. Her friend's being threatened. She's getting grilled by Cash. And now Jagger's going to come looking for trouble.

And I'm in fucking deep with her all over again.

Leaving her might actually break me this time.

Even if I don't deserve her, I can't walk away again, make that kind of sacrifice.

It's too much to ask.

Because you're in love with her.

"I'm gonna take a shower." I unwind myself from her, already missing her warm curves, the smooth skin, the light floral scent of her shampoo. "We should get going."

"What? Where?" Juliet's brow creases in confusion.

"Home."

"But you didn't find Lacey."

I shrug. "I know. But that'll have to wait. I need to get you back."

Her hand darts out, grabbing my forearm, and I stop moving.

"Wait. We can't leave without seeing her, King. That was the whole point of this trip. And I'm not letting you down again."

The word *again* cuts through me, a dagger straight to the heart, shock waves of pain rippling through my chest.

"Jules, you've never let me down." I cup her cheek, gazing into her eyes.

Beguiling.

She blinks, her long dark lashes fluttering, but says nothing. She still doesn't believe me.

"You should call her, King." She brushes past my declaration, focusing on the task instead. I freeze, chest tight with panic.

"What? No, I couldn't. What would I say?"

"I'd lead with the truth. That you're the son of her birth mother and you received her letter. You could meet up with her."

I huff out a breath. The concept of being forthright in this situation doesn't sit well with me. I wanted to check her out, get a quick look, and then report back to my siblings. Having an actual conversation with this Lacey woman—my half sister—is too, I don't know, real.

I close my eyes, pinch the bridge of my nose hard.

"I'll think about it in the shower. We should pack up, though. Head home today."

Juliet untangles herself from the white sheets and stands, twining her arms around my neck.

"We can head home. But let's meet Lacey. I'll call her if you want."

I cut my eyes and gaze out the window, at the clear blue sky, the golden rays of sunlight filtering through and streaking the wooden planks.

"I'll do it."

Reaching around her, I unplug my cell, then root through my wallet and find the now-well-worn sheet of aqua stationery. Scrawled at the bottom of the note is her phone number. I'm assuming a cell phone, but who knows? I know nothing about this woman and her life.

Damn, this is gonna be awkward.

Juliet stares at me, but I back away toward the bathroom. I love her, but this is a call I need to make in private. Alone.

Shutting the door behind me, I sink down onto the toilet seat and stare at my phone.

What the fuck am I going to say to this woman?

Hey, I'm King, your half brother. Our mom is dead.

Shit. That's terrible.

I stare at the tiny floral pattern in the wallpaper, delicate pink roses climbing up toward the ceiling. With a deep breath, I dial the number on the paper, praying she doesn't pick up.

One ring, two rings.

So far, so good.

Three rings.

"Hello?"

Dammit.

"Uh, hey. Um, hi. I'm trying to reach Lacey McCauliffe?"

There's a half-second pause, then a muffled sound, like the speaker's being covered.

"Mom! Someone's on the phone for you!"

Wow. That's probably Lacey's kid.

My half niece.

My heart hammers, toe tapping on the tile, knee bouncing up and down like I'm on speed or something.

Finally, more noise, the phone being handed over or picked up.

"Hello?" Her voice is calm but slightly suspicious.

"Yeah, hi. Hello—"

"I'm not interested in extending my car warranty right now. Or ever, for that matter—"

"Good to know. But I'm not calling about your car warranty."

"Oh. Well, I already donated to the police department. And I'm not interested in upgrading my cell phone plan either."

"Okay."

"Goodbye."

"Wait!" I shout into the phone, trying to keep her on the line. She didn't even give me a chance to say my piece. "I'm not a salesperson. I'm your half brother."

There's a long silence, punctuated only by our breathing.

"Excuse me? Who are you?"

"King. King Montgomery. My mom—our mother—was your birth mother, I believe. I got your letter. And I'm sorry to tell you this over the phone, but she passed away. Three years ago. I didn't want you to think, you know—" My voice hitches, a swell of emotion I'd been pressing down rising up from my chest to my throat. "That she didn't care or something. I'm sure she would have loved to meet you."

I wipe my sweaty palm on my boxers, the cotton absorbing my liquefied anxiety. This is so much harder than I thought it would be.

"Oh." Disappointment seeps through the line, and overwhelming sadness crushes down on my chest. "I guess you live in Seaglass Beach, then?"

"Yeah, I do. I have two brothers and a sister. We all live there."

"Nice."

Awkward silence fills the space between us, and I wish Roman were here right now. Or Parker. Or Poppy. They're all good at talking to people, better than me.

"I'd love to meet you."

Her statement catches me off guard.

"Um, ah—"

"But I understand if you don't want to. It's fine—"

"No, no, it's okay. We can meet. I'm actually here in town."

"In Peachtree Grove?"

"Yeah."

"Let's meet at the Five-to-Niner at eleven then. If you don't know where that is, just ask around. Everyone in town knows it."

"I'm good. I know where it is."

"Okay, I'll see you then. Bye."

"Bye."

The line goes dead, and I set the phone down on the edge of the vanity. My head's pounding, mouth dry as toast.

I'm going to meet my half sister. A total stranger who shares half of my DNA.

The very thought makes me queasy, bile rising in my throat. Shoving the acid down, I text Roman.

> King: I'm meeting Lacey at 11

> Roman: Wow. How? What went down?

> King: I called her. She's on spring break. Also related to half the town, which is kinda weird

> Roman: You nervous?

> King: Hell yeah I am

> Roman: Just be yourself. It'll be fine

> King: Because I'm so charming?

> Roman: Something like that

> King: You checked on the ranch since I left?

Roman: Once. Beau's got it. That rascal Oreo hopped the fence, though. Beau called me for backup. Spent an hour chasing that little asshole

King: Beau or Oreo?

Roman: Haha, very funny. I won't tell Beau you said that

Roman: Good luck today. Try to get a pic. And if you need me, I'll be around

King: Thanks

King: One more thing—Jagger's getting out of jail early. Lock your doors. Don't imagine he'll be too happy with any of us

Roman: Shit, really? Why?

King: Good behavior. Cash called to harass Juliet and dropped the news on her

Roman: I'll warn the others

King: Thanks. Talk to you later

Roman: Bye

JULIET AND I CHECK OUT OF THE GROVE, SAYING goodbye to Liz and Murphy. They send us on our way with

a doggy bag of Delaney's pastries and a stack of business cards to share with our friends.

We kill time walking up and down Main Street, checking out the shops we didn't hit yesterday. The mood's shifted, though, the adventure vibe gone, replaced by anxiety and apprehension. Neither of us talk much, too wrapped up in our own feelings. I want to know what she's thinking, but I can't deal with our relationship right now. I need to focus on Lacey and what the hell I'm going to say to her.

I guess the hard part's out of the way, telling her that Mom's gone.

But what will she look like? Will she want to hang out, be part of the family? Get to know us? Send holiday cards and call on our birthdays? What does she expect?

I have way more questions than answers. And I don't like it one little bit.

Finally, it's almost eleven. Time to meet Lacey.

Parking my truck near the diner, Juliet and I walk up the sidewalk hand in hand. I'm happy she's here with me, even if all our shit's complicated. I squeeze her fingers, silently telling her how I feel.

She gives me a sad smile, and my chest aches. I want to talk about what's going on between us, but I don't have time to get into all that right now. We push into the restaurant and my heart's hammering so hard I can barely hear anything, what with the whoosh of blood pumping in my ears.

Glancing around, I take note of the few people around the diner. An older waitress stands behind the counter. The same two police officers are sitting, chatting with her and sipping coffee from white ceramic mugs. There's a table full of kids, probably middle schoolers, near the back. And an elderly couple sits in a booth by the window.

No one who could possibly be Lacey. .

"Where do you want to sit?" Juliet surveys the diner, scouting out all the possibilities.

"At the counter?"

"That will probably be awkward. You'll have to strain your neck to talk. Plus, no privacy."

"Good point. How about that table over there?" I wave my hand at a corner booth overlooking the street.

"That works."

We make our way over, sliding into the pleather seats. Juliet plucks a menu from behind the metal napkin dispenser, studies it. I'm zero percent hungry, nerves strung out and hopping like live wires.

"Hey, kids. What're you having this morning?" The waitress from behind the counter appears. Her name tag reads "Milly," and judging by the yellowed corners, it appears to be an original, back when the Five-to-Niner first opened.

"I'll take a glass of OJ and the silver dollar pancakes." Juliet slides the menu back behind the dispenser.

"Good choice. And you?" Milly peers over at me, pen poised over her notepad.

"I'll just have a cup of coffee. Black, please."

"That's it?"

I nod, my stomach gurgling. No way am I putting any food down there right now.

"Yes, thank you."

"You want sugar, sugar? Room for cream?"

"Sure."

Right now I could give a shit, but she seems intent on

making me happy. Satisfied with our responses, Milly bustles away, assuring us the food will be out shortly.

I lean back against the booth, knee bouncing double time beneath the table.

"Calm down." Juliet reaches across the Formica table and pats my hand.

"I am calm."

"King, you're shaking the entire table with your fidgeting."

Water sloshes out of the plastic cup in front of her, and my cheeks flame. She does have a point. I take a deep breath and wipe my palms down my thighs to quiet my legs.

The door opens, and a woman about my age walks in. Her light-brown hair's swept up in a ponytail, and she's wearing a casual dress and sneakers. She glances around the diner, and Milly waves to her.

"Hey, Lacey. Morning. Sit anywhere you'd like."

So that's Lacey.

A man comes in just behind her, and I recognize him as the guy from the general store, Liam.

"And hello, Liam! How's Macy? She with you?" Milly cranes her neck, presumably searching for this Macy person.

"Hey, Milly. No, just me and Lacey today. Macy's at the store."

"Of course she is. Tell her I say hi."

"Will do." Liam shoots her a grin as Lacey shuffles from foot to foot, looking every bit as nervous as I feel.

"Are you going to wave her over?" Juliet whispers, lowering her head.

I shoot my hand into the air, and Lacey's face visibly

relaxes. Juliet stands and slides out of the booth, joining me on my side to give Lacey and Liam space.

A few seconds later, they're standing at the table. I rise, sticking my right hand out.

"Hey. I'm King."

"I'm Lacey." She takes my hand, and I'm struck by her eyes. They're the exact same color as Poppy's—and our mom's.

"I'm Liam. But you already know that." Liam looks from me to Juliet, recognizing us from yesterday.

"I'm Juliet." She waves up at both of them, then motions at the empty side of the booth. "Y'all can have a seat if you want."

Liam folds his tall, lanky frame into the booth, and Lacey follows his lead, sitting across from Juliet. Milly sets two fresh glasses of water, Juliet's OJ, and the cup of coffee on the table, then hustles away. The four of us shift around in the booth, trying to get comfortable in the world's most uncomfortable situation.

Good fucking luck.

"So—what do you want to know?" I peel the lid off the tiny plastic creamer, dump the white stream of liquid into my coffee.

Figure I might as well cut to the chase, get this over with.

Lacey fiddles with the napkin sitting beneath her water glass, avoiding eye contact.

"I don't know. Anything. Everything."

"Well, that's going to take some time." I pick up the coffee, take a tentative sip, scorching my tongue. *So long to those taste buds . . .*

"Did you know about me?" She raises her eyes, sliding them up to meet mine.

I shake my head. "No."

Two rosy spots bloom on her cheeks.

"Oh." She plays with a charm necklace sitting at the notch of her neck, swinging it left, then right, then left again. "I'm sorry about, you know—your mom."

"Yeah. Me too."

Liam pats Lacey's arm, and Milly appears, pancakes in hand.

"Syrup's on the table, love." She points at the syrup sitting next to the napkins. "You two gonna order anything else?" She peers down her nose at Liam and Lacey, and they both shake their heads no.

"Alrighty, then. Holler if you need me."

Juliet unrolls her napkin, pulling out the knife and fork. She starts cutting the pancakes systematically, and I pass her the syrup before she can ask.

"Liam, how do you fit in?" I ask, my thumb ringing the edge of the coffee mug. There's a tiny chip in the lip, and I wonder if the mug's an original too.

"We're cousins. Lacey's dad—adoptive father—was my dad's brother."

"Gotcha."

"Can I see a picture of her?" Lacey meets my gaze across the table, and I nod, flipping my cell over and clicking it to life. I scroll through the camera roll, trying to find a good photo of my mother.

Finally, I find one. A picture of her and Dad on the beach, a few Memorial Days ago. The sky's a brilliant shade of blue, and they look so damn happy, his arm slung around her shoulders. She's not looking at the camera. Instead, she's gazing up at him with a smile bright as the Florida sun.

A deep ache throbs in my chest as I hold the photo out to her.

"Wow. She's stunning."

"She was, yeah. That's my dad. They were college sweethearts."

I study Lacey's face—the straight line of her nose, the curve of her lips, the high cheekbones. She definitely bears a strong resemblance to our family, especially our mom. Her coloring is a little different, less fair, and she has darker hair than Poppy or Parker, but lighter than me and Rome. But in a lineup, you could tell we're related.

It's a weird feeling, staring at a stranger who looks so much like you.

"Have you always lived in Peachtree Grove?" I ask.

She nods. "Yep. Far as I knew, I was born and raised here. My parents had baby photos of me in our house. I just assumed I was from here. Until I found the birth certificate last year. They always told me I was adopted but never went into any of the details. And I never asked because it was a, um, delicate subject."

I clear my throat, the question burning in my brain. I open my mouth to ask, but no sound comes out. Swallowing hard over the gigantic lump, I try again.

"Any idea who your birth dad was?"

26

———

KING

"Nope. Not a clue. The only name listed on the birth certificate is your mother."

"Really? That's odd." Juliet takes a bite of pancake and chews, her jaw moving up and down slowly. "Seems like they'd list the father too."

"Not if he wasn't there and your mom didn't give his name," Liam says, stabbing with his straw at the ice cubes in his glass.

Great. Another dead end.

"I can maybe petition the court and get the record unsealed. But thought I'd start with the easy path first." Lacey fingers her silver chain, biting down on her lip.

An awkward silence falls over the table, and Juliet's fork scraping against the plate is suddenly deafening. I take another sip of coffee, shift in the booth. I'm stiff from the bed at the Grove, and I want to be back home. Not sitting in a sticky seat at a diner, shooting the shit with a long-lost relative.

"What was she like?" Lacey's soft voice cuts through the quiet, and my heart squeezes.

How can I sum up my mom in one or two sentences?

I stare at the dark liquid in the mug, trying to figure what to say.

Finally, I lift my head and meet her gaze.

"She was the best person I know. She loved with all her heart. Had the most infectious laugh. Was the life of every party. My sister Poppy's a lot like her."

Lacey sighs, sadness flashing in her bright-blue eyes.

"She sounds wonderful."

"She was."

Juliet squeezes my leg under the table, and I fight hard against the wave of grief threatening to engulf me.

I'm glad Juliet got to meet my mom.

"Here's your check, kids." Milly plops the paper slip on the table in a metal basket. "Stay as long as you like."

"Thanks." I grab the basket, pop my credit card in, and hand it right back to her. She pivots on her heel and goes to run the card.

Lacey takes a sip of water and swallows. Swirls the ice in her glass, her brow creased with faint lines.

"Do you think I could come meet your siblings?" She holds her breath, waiting for my reply.

I want to say "thanks, but no thanks" or maybe "hard pass," but the desperation on her face stops me.

"Uh, I guess."

Juliet kicks my foot under the table, and I struggle to keep my balance.

"I mean, sure. That would be fine."

The corners of her mouth tip up into a smile, and her shoulders relax.

"I can probably come down over the summer break. Except I'll have Opal with me."

"Oh, right, your daughter. You mentioned her in the letter."

"Yes. She's eight, so I can't leave her alone. I could maybe get a friend to watch her."

"Macy and I could keep her for you, Lacey," Liam says, rubbing his hand across his jaw.

"She might like to visit the beach, though. It could be our summer trip." Lacey's eyes light up at the prospect of a beach vacation. I don't mention the fact that I know they've visited before—and stayed at our family's inn.

"King lives on a ranch. He has horses and goats." Juliet crosses her fork and knife over the last few bites of pancake. "She'll love it out there."

I bite my tongue, hold my eye roll in check. The last thing I want to do is entertain some kid all summer out at the ranch, but I figure now's not the time to dive into logistics.

"Great. You have my number, and now I have yours. Text me some good dates, and we'll work something out. I don't want to inconvenience you any."

I hold off on telling her that having a half sister I never knew about is damn inconvenient. Wouldn't be polite.

Instead, I agree to the plan. Milly brings the check, and we say awkward goodbyes. Juliet and I let Lacey and Liam leave first; then we follow a few minutes behind.

"She seems nice," Juliet says, climbing into the truck.

I slam the door behind her, circle round to the driver's side, and hop in. Pull up the GPS and prepare for the long drive back home.

"She was all right."

"Not a ringing endorsement, King."

I fire up the truck, slowly backing out of the spot. A million things run through my mind, none of them positive.

"Didn't know I needed to endorse her. It's not like she needs my vote to visit Seaglass Beach or meet the rest of the family."

"It kind of is like that."

I expel a heavy breath, every bone in my body already tired. Tired of this saga, tired of the drama—and it seems like it's only just beginning.

"Whatever you say. My siblings can make their own choice. I'm not going to sway them one way or the other."

"Right—"

Hot anger flares through me, from my gut up to my breastbone.

"What's that supposed to mean?" Frowning, I glance over at her.

"It means that you're the leader of the crew. Sure, they'll have their own opinions. But without your blessing, none of them will let her in, accept her."

"Bullshit." I grip the steering wheel hard, knuckles turning white from the force as I ease onto the interstate.

"Not bullshit. Facts."

Juliet kicks back, propping her bare feet up on the dash, and we fall into a strained silence. The radio hums, hit after country hit, but Juliet doesn't sing along. Tension's thick in the truck, too many raw emotions running fast and hard below the surface.

Happy as I was to have Juliet with me earlier, right now I wish I was alone. I need time and space to think, to process all of this.

By myself.

We drive all afternoon, Juliet scrolling through social media on her phone, frown lines creasing her pretty brow. I'm almost certain she's pissed at me, but I'm not sure why. And I don't have the bandwidth to deal with it anyway, so I leave it alone.

I can't stop thinking about Lacey. Our mom and Lacey's father. A mystery man we may never identify. Who was he? A man worthy of my mother? How come I never heard anything about him? Do I know him? Does he live in Seaglass Beach still? Or was he passing through? Maybe a random guy from school?

It shouldn't matter—he's nothing to me—but for some reason it does. It feels like a betrayal of our dad, even though there's no proof of this.

My mom loved someone before my dad.

The very idea has me off-kilter, like I'm on a boat in choppy water. I feel seasick, and I'm on dry fucking land.

"I have to go to the bathroom." Juliet interrupts my twisted-up thoughts.

Pressing my lips together, I pull off at the next exit and make a sharp right into the first gas station I see. May as well fill up. One less stop to make, and we'll get home sooner.

She laces up her shoes and darts from the truck without saying a word.

Fine by me.

I'm too wrapped up in my own crap to worry about making conversation.

Five minutes later, Juliet's back at the truck and we're all gassed up.

"Listen. I get that you're dealing with a lot right now,

what with meeting your half sister and all"—Juliet takes a deep breath, her chest rising, falling—"but I hate when you block me out like this."

I tense, a headache brewing behind my eyes. Last thing I want to do right now is chitchat about my feelings.

"I need space, Juliet." I pull out of the station, heading back to the interstate, my eyes fixed on the road.

"I hear you, I do. But this feels like before—"

Out of the corner of my eye, I notice her lip quivering, and a part of me wants to pull over and make everything better. But another part of me—a bigger part of me—wants to keep driving, drop her off at home, and be alone.

"This has nothing to do with you. Or us. I just need time is all."

She turns away from me, her shoulders squared toward the window. I don't have anything more to say, so I crank up the radio. A drum solo fills the cab, and I retreat.

Back into myself, my thoughts, and away from her.

She stares out the window the rest of the way home.

27

____

JULIET

IT'S TRUE WHAT THEY SAY. *THE MORE THINGS CHANGE, THE more they stay the same.*

Even after all this time—and everything that's happened between us—King's still the same old guy.

Grumpy.

Broody.

Closed off.

Silent.

And I fucking hate silence.

It's the worst, sitting here with all this noise running through my mind, loud incessant chatter. I want to talk things out, hear what he's thinking, how he's feeling. How I can help.

Instead, he shuts down and locks me out.

I'm all alone again.

Just like before.

Like always.

And it fucking sucks.

King takes the Seaglass Beach exit, and we drive down

Main Street, the familiar sights and sounds of our quaint beach town comforting me a little. A seagull squawks overhead, a shrill reminder that we're near the ocean again. I roll down the window, balmy air hitting my hot cheeks.

Home.

Peachtree Grove was nice and all, but the beach will always be home.

At the stoplight, King hits his blinker, then hangs a left.

"You're taking me to my apartment?"

He nods, his square jaw tense. "Yep."

"I don't work until tonight. I could come to the ranch, help you get caught up on the chores."

"No need. Beau's there. I'm sure it's all good."

I press my lips together so hard they're probably turning white from loss of blood flow. Anger bubbles in my stomach, and I crack my knuckles one by one to release tension. Anything to distract myself from this terrible sinking feeling.

We pull into the apartment parking lot, and King slides his truck up next to my Toyota, cuts the engine. But he still doesn't say anything. Doesn't even turn to look at me, kiss me, nothing.

Just sits there staring straight ahead at the ugly gray stucco building, lost in his thoughts.

"I can't do this with you." I shrink back against the seat, my insides quivering.

"What?" He squints over at me, confused.

At least I got his attention.

"This—" I wave my hand between us, careful not to touch him.

Touching him could ignite something, some feeling I'm not interested in chasing at the moment.

"What are you talking about, Juliet?"

"This, King!" My voice tips up in exasperation, and his expression matches my tone, his brow creasing.

"What the fuck is *this*? What do you mean? What are you talking about?"

"You. Me. And the silent treatment. This is exactly what happened last time. After the baby. You always shut me out. And I can't do it again."

Tears sting my eyes, my throat thick, and I will myself not to cry. I need to get out of his truck, away from him. Being with him like this is too much—it's too painful.

I depress the handle of the door, try to get out, but King's hand grips my shoulder.

"Wait."

"No. I'm going now. This is too much for me." I shove the door open and scramble out of the truck. I want to dart up the stairs, away from him, but I have to get all my shit first.

Reaching behind the seat, I wrestle with my suitcase, trying to slide it out. Naturally, it won't budge.

"Here, let me help." King hops out, coming around and easily maneuvering the luggage out like a damn valet at a fine hotel. Our fingers brush as he hands the bag to me.

Sparks fly up my arm, and I hate him a little more for it.

Asshole.

He stares at me, hurt swimming in his deep-blue eyes. I will him to speak—to say something, anything that makes sense—but he doesn't.

His Adam's apple bobs. The breeze blows, my hair flying around my face. He reaches out, tucks a stray lock behind my ear. His touch gentle, yet still leaving fire in its wake.

We're fire and water, me and King.

This is never going to work.

I should have listened to him when he said to stay away.

He warned me, but I didn't want to hear it. I wanted to believe in him—in us—so badly. So damn badly.

With a shaky breath, I say the word I know I should have said a long time ago.

"Goodbye."

Then I turn and head toward the stairs.

"Juliet—" King's hand darts out, his fingers wrapping around my wrist.

I try to shake him off, but his grip is too tight. Sadness morphs into madness, and I struggle away from him, breaking free.

"Don't, King. You'll only make this harder. You were right, and I should have listened when you said we can't work. You told me who you were. I just didn't want to believe it."

Pain, raw and wild, flashes over his face, quickly replaced by anger.

"So this is it? After one hard afternoon, you're gonna quit on us?" He flings his arms out, dark brows raised.

"I'm not quitting, King. I'm walking away. Two very different things. I love you. But I need to save myself."

"What are you talking about?"

"I need to save myself from the heartache that is you. You know how many nights I cried myself to sleep, wishing you were with me? That you gave a shit?"

"That's not fair, Juliet. You had no idea what I was feeling."

"Exactly my point, King. I had no idea because you never let me in. You shut me out. When things get hard, you stonewall me. And I'm tired, King. I'm so fucking tired. Tired of being alone, even when we're together. I deserve more than that."

His jaw tics, and he scrubs a hand over the back of his neck, shuffling his boots against the pavement.

"You're right."

His quiet admission stuns me.

"What?"

"You're right. You do deserve more than that. More than me."

I stare at him, wait for him to man up. Say he'll do better, try harder. At the very least, open up a little.

Thunder rumbles off in the distance, and the wind picks up. I gnaw at my lip and wait. He stands rooted to the spot like a damn fence post.

Finally, he shoves a hand in his pocket.

"See you around."

He retreats to his truck, leaving me speechless on the sidewalk. Turning the engine over, he throws an arm over the passenger seat, glances over his shoulder, and backs out.

Away from me.

The truck guns out of the parking lot, and only then do I let the tears spill, fast and hard, coursing down my cheeks. A heavy sob racks my chest, and I can't breathe, choking on salty tears.

Fifteen years ago, the pain hurt. Physically, mentally,

emotionally. A crushing ache bearing down on my body and my soul. My dreams shattered in a split second.

But this?

This is fucking worse.

Because I knew it. I knew the players, the stakes. Worse—I knew the outcome before I even started the damn game.

And, like the idiot I am, I went for it anyway.

Dammit, Juliet. Why?

Because you thought you'd finally get your happy ending.

But life's not the fucking movies, and I'm no Cinderella.

And King sure as hell isn't Prince Charming.

No. We're just two fucked-up people locked in a never-ending pattern of hurting each other. Passionate fuckery, that's what this is.

I sink down on the concrete, head in hands, and cry until my voice goes hoarse and there are no tears left to shed.

The only thing I know for certain is I'm done with King Montgomery, for real this time.

28

KING

WHAT IN THE ACTUAL FUCK JUST HAPPENED BACK THERE?

One minute we're all good. Happy, holding hands, and kissing. Going on a road trip, making love.

The next minute Juliet goes all bananas on me, and we're done. Over. Splitsville.

In one motherfucking second, she throws everything we have together away.

What the fuck?

I speed out of town, more relieved than ever to be heading home. Back to the horses, the goats, shit that makes sense. Feeding schedules and training patterns, dawn and dusk. Reliable, predictable, safe.

Stuff you can count on.

I knew I should have stayed away from her. I fucking knew it. And I still went back, drawn to her like a moth to a flame.

I'm a damn fool.

Why couldn't I have just left her alone? Trusted my instincts, like I usually do.

Because she's the best thing that's ever happened to you. And you know it.

Trees whiz by, a green blur out the window, dark storm clouds building on the horizon. The road gets bumpier, and I'm close to home.

Far away from town.

Far away from her.

Pain stabs me in the center of my chest, so sharp it steals my breath. I clutch the steering wheel and focus on the path I've driven so many times before it's second nature. There's no traffic, no one out here but me and mine. My muscles relax, and I suck in air, try to shut down my brain and keep moving.

Not think about her.

A fucking impossible task.

Those eyes dance in front of me, and I'm blinded. By the golden flecks, the sparkle of desire glinting there.

Beguiling.

I cut the wheel and turn down the gravel drive, dust clouds puffing up around the truck. Must have been dry here while I was gone.

Beau's truck sits in the distance, parked close to the barn. I kill the engine and take a second to regroup, my mind still swirling from the fight with Juliet.

Let her go. It's for the best.

But every heartbeat hurts. Actually fucking hurts.

I don't know if I can do it again.

Let the thing between us die, wither on the vine like a rotting, shrunken grape. The world's duller, blunted, without her in it.

Cutting my eyes to the empty passenger seat, I run my palm over the indent in the leather where she sat only a short while ago. Fingers tracing the soft outline of her ass, her familiar floral scent winding around me like a silk cloth. Then tightening around my neck like a noose until I can't breathe. The familiar tingle behind my eyes, a hot prick I squash down immediately.

Get your shit together, King.

I've cried more tears than I'd like to admit over that girl.

No. I've got to move on, get over her.

But how can I do that when all I can think about is getting her under me, her chest flushing a pretty shade of pink as she gazes up through those dark lashes? Her lips slightly open, a breathy exhale begging me to come in.

To fuck her and make her mine.

All the blood in my body rushes south, and I have a giant hard-on, a fucking weird response to the crushing sadness sitting like a lead pipe across my chest. I shift in the seat, adjusting my jeans, but there's no getting comfortable.

I close my eyes and count to ten, real slow, trying to calm myself. I need to go in and relieve Beau, but all I can think about is relieving myself. Putting my dick out of his throbbing misery.

Tap, tap, tap.

I jump off the seat, eyes flying open, heart pounding.

"You okay, boss?" Beau mouths through the closed truck window, his shaggy hair sticking out of his backward baseball cap.

So much for dick relief. Guess I'm going to have to try to adjust myself and get straight to work instead.

"Yeah. I'm fine."

"The goats missed you." He grins, lopsided and goofy, and I shake my head.

"Uh-huh."

I climb out of the truck, stretching and shifting in my pants, trying to conceal the stiffy situation.

"How was the trip?"

"Long, but fine. Everything good here?"

"Mostly. Oreo's a little dickhead, though. He hopped the fence, and Roman had to come help me chase him back home. We added another level of fencing, and the rascal escaped that too. I've been watching him real close, but I still can't figure how he's getting out. Unless he has ups like LeBron."

I snicker in spite of myself. "I could tell that one was gonna be trouble from the get-go. I'll scour the perimeter, make sure nothing's out there, helping him escape. I'd hate for a coyote to get him."

"I know, me too. The little guy's kinda growing on me. Even if he is a dickhead."

"Any word on the pony?" I glance over the fence toward the barn.

"Nothing yet. I can follow up if you want."

"Nah. The owner will call when he's ready."

I head toward the barn, and Beau follows right behind, keeping up with my quick pace. Tension seeps out of my shoulders, my chest, my abs as we cross the lawn and cut through the paddock. Being home always does that for me.

"Trip was good. Does that mean you found her?" Beau doesn't name names or mention her title, which I appreciate. He's pretty astute for being as young as he is. Well, guess he's not so much young as I am old.

Another depressing thought.

I shove that one away, too, and answer his question. "Yes, we found her."

"We? Did Poppy or Parker go with you?"

Well, shit. Guess he didn't know about Juliet, and now I have to explain myself.

I scrub my jaw. "Juliet went with me."

"Juliet? Capelli?" He tilts his head to one side, very much resembling a confused golden retriever. Same floppy hair and everything.

"Yeah."

"Huh. I didn't realize—" His voice tapers off, waiting for more details.

"Nothing to realize."

His head bobs, real slow, as if he's trying to work out the calculations on some complicated math problem. He doesn't question me further, though. Another reason the kid has the job.

"And I found Lacey. So at least I did what I set out to do."

"Nice. Good for you." He screws up his lips, and I feel a question floating in the air, but he holds back.

"Well, thanks for covering for me and staying out here. You can get on now, head on home. You've worked more than your fair share of hours." I wave my hand, shooing him away.

"You sure? You look pretty drained. I'm happy to stay and help with the dinner feed."

"Nah. I've got it. Get on home."

"Okay. Thank you, boss. Get some shut-eye."

"Will do. See you tomorrow."

Beau shoots me a two-finger salute, then strides toward his truck, his carefree whistle trailing behind him. Thunder rumbles, and the horses neigh loudly, stomping their hooves. They always know when a storm's approaching, the vibrations trembling up through the earth and alerting them.

I hurry into the barn, anxious to finish the dinner service before it starts pouring. Mercifully, the task keeps my mind off Juliet, at least for the moment. Moving from stall to stall, I feed and water, saying my hellos to the horses as I go.

Done with that, I gather the food pellets for the goats and hand-feed the mama before chasing after the kids. Beau wasn't joking when he said Oreo's an asshole. Every time I get close to him, he dashes away, and that son of a bitch got even quicker while I was gone.

Eventually, I give up the chase and collapse in the corner, winded. Only then does Oreo trot over, settling down next to me on the straw, nuzzling his soft fur against my hand for a pet.

Probably trying to get to the food pellets, but the gesture's still comforting. He cuddles up on my thigh, and I stroke his head. He lets out a soft whinny as I scratch behind his ears.

"Don't fall for a woman, Oreo. It will only stir up trouble."

He peers up at me with round, black eyes, like he's soaking up my advice.

"The second you let your guard down, that's when they get you. Crawling under your skin, working their way through your system like a damn drug. And let me tell you —you can't get enough. You want more and more and more. Even if it's bad for you."

Or for her.

Oreo blinks, the tip of his pink tongue sticking out of his mouth. The first few plops of rain hit the roof—one, two, three, four—and I should probably run up to the house right now if I have any chance of staying dry. But it's cozy out here in the barn, and I have a captive audience.

"It's stupid, the whole love thing. Easier to stay out here and be alone. Maybe not as nice, but definitely easier." I huff out a sigh, the kid bumping his head against my hand for more scratches as the rain picks up.

"I should have left her alone, like I said I would all those years ago. I'm no good for her—I only cause her trouble." I stare down at the pale straw covering the ground, my throat tight.

"She was right about me—I didn't man up before. It was easier to let her go than to face all the pain, the loss. I pushed her away, then pretended I was noble and saving her."

Squeezing my eyes shut, I take a shuddery breath, the ugly truth pounding in my brain. "Deep down, I knew I was really saving myself."

"Are you talking to a goat?" Roman interrupts my confession, the corner of his mouth tugging up. He runs his fingers through his hair, water droplets falling from the dark strands.

"Me? No, course not."

"It sure sounded like you were." He slides down to the ground, sitting beside me, Oreo tucked up between us. "He's a cute little guy. When he's not hopping fences."

I shake my head. "Seriously? You let a goat outrun you? Thought you were Marine Special Ops? You got beat by a kid?"

"I know. I couldn't believe it either. The little shit is

quick." Roman tousles Oreo's head, and I swear the goat shoots him a dirty look.

"Takes after the mama. She's quick on her feet too. Good thing Chip and Nilla Wafer are tamer. I should separate them so Oreo doesn't teach them his bad habits."

"Probably a good idea. How did the meeting with Lacey go? What was she like?"

I screw my mouth up, searching for the right words.

"The meeting went fine. It was—strange."

Rain slaps against the barn, but otherwise it's quiet. Roman sits perfectly still, waiting for more details.

"She looks like Poppy. And Mom."

Roman inhales sharply, his chest rising and falling, and my gut churns. Everything about today's been hard.

"She nice?"

"Yeah. Seems like good people. We met her extended adoptive family, and they're all super chill. Good folks. She wants to meet y'all."

"Really?"

"I think she may come down this summer. Check out the beach. Figured that'd be okay. But I can tell her to forget it."

"No. That's not right. She should come."

Rome and I sit in the quiet for another minute, listening to the soothing sounds of the rain, the light breathing of the animals.

"Where's Juliet?" Roman's gaze slides around the barn, presumably searching for her.

"Back home."

"Really?" He draws the word out, long and slow, but doesn't ask anything else.

"Yeah, really."

Oreo snores lightly, my hand thrumming with the soft exhalations.

"Road trip didn't go well?"

"The trip was fine. Drive back wasn't great."

"You hit traffic? Have road rage?"

"Nah. Apparently I don't talk enough."

"Huh. Never heard that one before." Roman shakes his head, a stray drop of water landing on my hand. I brush it away.

"Fuck off. I talk plenty."

"Do you?" He cocks his head, a dark brow raised high.

"Yeah. I'm very communicative."

"Did your eighth-grade lit teacher write that on your essay or something? Because I'm pretty sure I've never heard anyone describe you that way. Literally ever."

I exhale so loudly Oreo stirs. "Sorry, buddy." I scratch behind his ears, and he snuggles back into me. "We had a fight. She said I shut her out."

The rain beats down on the barn roof, a loud pounding as Roman sits with this intel.

"Ever consider maybe you did that?"

I run my tongue along the inside of my bottom lip, contemplating. "Maybe I did. But I just met Lacey—our half sister—and that's a helluva lot to process. What does she want me to do, make small talk about the damn weather?"

"I don't know exactly what she wanted. I wasn't there. But from my experience—take it for what it's worth— women like when you talk to them. Actually, you can probably generalize that out to most people like when you talk to them. You and me—we're more guarded than most. We have to work to let people in. But I'm here to tell you that when you do let your guard down, it's worth it."

I suck in a breath, holding the air deep in my lungs.

If anyone else said this to me, I'd tell them to get the fuck outa here. But coming from Roman, it feels different.

Better.

Like solid advice.

"You should talk to her, King. I see how you are with her. And how she is with you. I don't know the whole deal with you two—and you don't have to tell me or anything. But I can tell that whatever's going on between you is different. It feels—I don't know—deeper. Better than most things. Like it could work out for you. Don't throw that away over some stupid bullshit argument."

I let his words sink in, absorbing them.

Roman's like me. Neither of us talks that much, but when we do speak, it tends to be important.

"Just think about it. You deserve to be happy."

Roman pats Oreo on the head one more time, eliciting a lazy one-eye peep; then he rises and dusts himself off. A few pieces of straw fall to the ground before he walks out of the barn into the rain, leaving me sitting alone with all the animals and my regrets.

29

———

JULIET

AFTER BAWLING MY EYES OUT IN THE PARKING LOT, I haul my suitcase upstairs. Much as I'd like to call in to work, I missed the last few shifts and can't in good conscience ask Sabby to cover for me again. Especially after my brothers roughed her up.

I make it to my apartment, fumbling around in my bag for the key. Going for the knob, I notice the door's ajar. Cold fear slithers down my spine.

What the hell?

Someone broke into my apartment while I was gone. I hesitate, debating what to do. I should probably call the police and not go in. But if I do that, I'll definitely be late for work, and I can't afford to get fired from the Tipsy Taco.

I kick the door open, scanning the dark living room. Nothing's out of place, and the television's still up on the wall.

Odd.

That's about the only valuable item I own, and it's still here, in the apartment. If this was a burglary, it wasn't a very successful one.

"Hello?" I duck my head into the apartment, my thumb hovering over the emergency button on my cell.

Silence. And no one comes running out, bum-rushing me, either. Whoever was here is probably long gone by now.

Taking a deep breath, I shove inside, leaving the door wide open behind me. Just in case.

I flip the light on, and that's when I hear the creaking of a metal door.

"Ohmygod! Ohmygod, ohmygod, ohmygod!" I jump up and down, screaming, as I stare at the beady eyes of a large gray rat sitting on my kitchen counter. He hops down from his perch and scurries away, and now the little rat bastard's running around in my apartment.

Wonderful.

I hurry over to the counter. A note scrawled in black Sharpie is propped up next to a metal cage.

Welcome home, little sis! Jags wanted you to have a new friend. Birds of a feather flock together, he said.

—Damon

You've got to be kidding me. My asshole brothers planted a rat in my apartment to send me a message. And now he's on the loose, darting around all over my stuff. Probably taking rat shits everywhere.

A shudder rolls through me as I think about all the possible hiding spots. The pantry, the closet, curled up in my shoes. Under my bed, where he could jump out and crawl all over me with his little rat feet.

The idea's too awful to even contemplate. He could eat my eyes out while I sleep.

I stare down at my cell, my gut instinct telling me to call King. He'd know what to do, how to get rid of the rat.

But I can't do that. We're over.

No, I need to handle this on my own.

Jogging back to my bedroom, I yank a Tipsy Taco shirt and a clean pair of jeans out of my dresser. There's no rat in sight, but he could be hiding, waiting to pounce and give me rabies.

I hustle out of the apartment with my suitcase, slamming the door shut behind me. Leaning against the cool wall of the building, I wrap my arms around myself and shiver. I can't believe my own brothers would do this to me. They're raging assholes, totally out of control.

Eyes squeezed shut, I pinch the bridge of my nose and try to regroup.

First things first—I need to call an exterminator and get the rat out of my apartment. After a quick search, I dial the first company on the list.

"Seaglass Pest Control, what can I do for ya?"

"Uh, yeah, hi. I have a rat in my apartment and need an exterminator."

"How do you know it's a rat? Not a mouse or insects?"

"I saw it sitting on my counter. In the kitchen."

"Oh. Okay, then. You think you only have one rat? Usually where there's one, there are many."

Another terrifying thought.

"Pretty sure it's just one. Long story."

"Well, that's an easy job then. We could make it out to you by Friday."

"Friday! That's three whole days from now!" I shriek, every muscle in my body trembling.

"Sorry, lady. We're busy. Termites are swarming, and we're pretty backed up. Every exterminator in town's busy. You want to book or not?"

I bite down on my lip, debating. I may be able to find someone else sooner, but right now I have to get to work.

"Sure, I guess."

"Great. We can do nine a.m. Friday."

"Um—quick question. How much is this gonna cost?" I'm already hearing cha-ching, cha-ching sounds clanging in my head.

"Two fifty. Since you're a new customer, we'll waive the consult fee."

"Two hundred and fifty dollars?" My voice tips up into hysteria. "For catching one rat?"

"You can try to catch the little bugger on your own, if you'd prefer."

I shake my head at the phone, even though he can't see me. "No. No, thanks. Fine, two fifty, Friday, nine a.m. Got it. I'm at the Seaglass Shore apartments, unit 236."

"Got it. See you then." He disconnects, and I shove my cell into my bag, the fear turning into hot anger. My stupid brothers are costing me money—and I have no idea where I'm sleeping tonight.

FML.

Defeated, I trudge to my SUV and head to work,

uniform in hand. I'll change in the bathroom at the Tipsy. There's no way I'm going back inside the rat den.

NEEDLESS TO SAY, I'M NOT IN THE FRIENDLIEST OF moods. Finding a rat in your apartment and breaking up with your boyfriend in one afternoon will do that to a girl, I suppose.

My shift drags, and the tips are meager, probably due to my less-than-stellar disposition. I alternate between being depressed about King and being furious with Jagger, Cash, and Damon. I'm not sure which feels worse, but by nine p.m. I have a pounding headache and desperately want to go home to my bed. But, of course, I can't. One, because I still have another hour left in my shift, and two, because I have a fucking rat squatting in my apartment.

"You okay?" Sabby elbows me hard, the margarita on my tray sloshing out onto the paper napkin.

"Yeah. Fine."

"For someone just back from vacation with her man, you're in a pretty shitty mood."

"He's not my man. We broke up."

"Already? That's, like, record pace." She scrunches up her nose at my news, popping the lid on a beer bottle. "What the hell happened?"

"We had a fight, and I can't do it anymore, okay?" I snap at her, and she holds one hand up like a shield.

"Whoa—okay. Fine. Doesn't hurt my feelings any."

"Sorry. I'm having a bad day is all."

"Understandable. He was a fine piece of ass. I get it. Must suck to have to let that go."

I flash back to King's ass. The skin pale compared to the rest of his tanned body, those perfectly round cheeks. The broad plane of muscle stretching across his back, the sharp cut of his triceps.

A pain stabs me deep in the chest, spreading into a dull, thudding ache.

"Thanks, Sabby."

"Anytime, girl." She bobs her head, not picking up on the sarcasm.

"Hey, I'm really sorry about my brothers coming in and hurting you."

She brushes me off, shrugging, the bright blue tips of her hair moving up and down over her shoulders. "Family. What can you do?"

"They're complete dickheads."

"Aww, sis. Such a nice compliment, coming from you."

Gritting my teeth so hard my jaw aches, I spin toward the familiar voice.

"Get the hell out of here, Cash," I hiss across the bar, keeping my volume low so as not to make a scene.

"What? No, why? I came in for some chips and salsa and an ice-cold cerveza." He draws the word out in a terrible Spanish accent.

"Go somewhere—anywhere—else. I don't give a shit where, just get the hell out of my face." Anger bubbles up inside me, my empty fist balling at my side. I grab the rest of the drink order, hurrying before I lose my cool.

I slide around the bar with the heavy, loaded tray, and Damon appears out of nowhere, blocking me.

"Did you give your new friend a name yet?" His thin

lips curl up into a sneer, and Cash chuckles at the stupid joke.

"I hate you. Move." I try to get around him, but now Cash is blocking me on the other side, and I'm boxed in.

"Did you like him? We thought he was pretty cute. Thoughtful of Jagger, wasn't it?" Cash says.

"Get the fuck outa here. I'm working." I turn sideways, attempting to shimmy out from between them, but Cash grips my waist and holds me in place.

"Get your hands off me, Cash. Right now."

"Bet you don't say that to the prince. Where is he, by the way? Thought for sure he'd be here." Cash peers around the Tipsy, trying to spot King.

"He's not here, okay? Now bounce. The ice is melting in these drinks." I squirm in his grip, his thumbs pressing into my hip bones so hard I'm sure I'll have a bruise.

"You heard what she said. Get off her. Now." King's deep voice rumbles behind me, low and menacing.

"You're such a lying bitch, Juliet," Cash hisses, spittle flying from his lips. But he drops his hand from my waist, edging away from me.

King takes a long stride forward, standing toe to toe with Cash, their chests inches away from each other.

"Don't talk to her like that. And if you touch her again —or her friend—I will personally break every one of your fucking fingers, one at a time. Got me?"

Anger flashes in Cash's eyes, but he's not a total moron. After living with Jagger for so long, he knows when he's about to get his ass kicked. Wisely, he takes another step back, moving to stand beside Damon. A brotherly united front.

"Whatever, Prince. You can have the little tramp. She's

a fucking traitor anyway. Good riddance." Cash brushes his hands together, wiping himself clean of me.

"Yeah, she's stupid anyway. You can have her. And her little rat pet," Damon chimes in.

"Scram, assholes." King waves his hand toward the door, and my brothers puff out their chests and swagger away.

I exhale, cool relief rushing through me, quickly replaced by aggravation.

Why's King showing up at my job, after I told him we were through? He's only making this harder on both of us.

With a huff, I stomp off and deliver the drinks to the waiting customers, grabbing another table's order while I'm at it.

King's waiting at the bar when I return.

"Go home, King." I shovel ice into plastic cups with way more force than necessary, sharp jolts racing up my arm with every scoop.

"I came to talk. That's what you wanted, right?" He shoves a hand in his pocket, shifting his weight to his left, then his right.

"Before. Not now. It's too late." *Scoop, scoop, scoop.* I hack at a block of ice, the cubes frozen into an icy mass.

"Dammit, Jules. I'm trying here." His tone's strained, lips pressed together in a tight pink line.

I fill each plastic cup with water, breaking eye contact. Because I can't bear the look in his eyes, the pain etched on his face.

"I can't do this with you, King. I told you that. You won't change. You never have."

"Give us a chance, Jules. Please." His voice breaks and

my chest squeezes, aching with sadness. Of what we lost, what could have been.

I should stick to my guns. Not go back for more heartache. Like my mama used to say, a leopard doesn't change his spots.

Shaking my head, I sigh. "I'm done in fifteen minutes. Have a beer."

Then I hustle back to the table full of thirsty customers, seriously questioning my sanity.

30

KING

I HAVE A BEER WHILE I WAIT ON JULIET TO FINISH HER shift, letting the chilled liquid cool me down. I haven't been this nervous since high school, when I asked Mary Beth Evans to prom. And that went horrible, so . . .

Shoving that memory out of my mind, I kick around all the things I need to say to Juliet.

I'm sorry for shutting you out.

I need time to process things in my head.

I made a mistake.

I'm sorry for abandoning you.

I love you.

That last thought has me choking on my drink, bubbly fizz stinging my nostrils.

For fuck's sake, King. You're forty years old. It's time to man up.

The lights go up, the music cuts off, and the last few customers pay their tabs and shuffle out of the restaurant. Juliet, Sabby, and one other guy move through the dining area, wiping down tables and stacking chairs. I polish off the last sip of my drink and stand up, stretching. Juliet unties her apron, tossing it on the bar.

"Sabby, we good?" she calls across the room.

"Sure, babe. Get some sleep. See you tomorrow." Sabby waves, and I follow Juliet out of the Tipsy Taco.

The air's cooler after the rain, and she shivers. "It rained?"

She toes at a puddle on the sidewalk, glancing up at the sky. The storm's cleared, and the darkness is interrupted by the occasional glittering star.

"Yeah. Couple hours ago. Big storm out at the ranch."

"How's Oreo?"

"A horrible troublemaker. But he's a cute little dude."

Her mouth tips up into a smile, and my heart pounds double time. I shove a hand in my pocket as we shuffle over to her SUV, itching to touch her but biding my time. Waves pound the shore off in the distance, the rest of the town quiet.

"What did you come all the way out here to say, King?" She purses her lips, arms folded across her chest.

"Uh," I stammer, heat rushing over me. "I'm sorry."

"Good start."

"That's the whole thing."

"You drove thirty minutes to say you're sorry?" She arches a brow high, staring at me.

"Yeah." I kick my boot at the puddle, watch as a ripple echoes out from the center.

"Not super compelling."

"C'mon, Jules. I'm not good with apologies, okay?"

She starts to walk away and panic grips me. I reach out, grabbing her arm to stop her.

"Dammit, Juliet. What more do you want from me?"

She whirls around, her eyes blazing. "I need you to actually change. To do better."

"Yes."

"Yes what?"

"Yes to both. I'll change and do better. Swear."

"I don't know . . ." She stares across the parking lot toward the beach, even though it sits on the other side of the building.

I stand there like an idiot, practically hyperventilating as she gnaws her bottom lip. I want to say more, but the words dry up in my throat.

"You can't keep shutting me out, King. You have to be able to talk to me. I get that you're a private person, and that's fine. So am I. But for fuck's sake—you act like a teenage boy, scared to talk about your feelings. If we're going to have a shot at a relationship—a real relationship— you have to at least try to make an effort."

My jaw clenches. "I am making an effort, Juliet. This is what trying looks like."

"Well, fuck. If this is effort, I hate to see not trying."

Her voice drips with sarcasm, and anger flashes through me. I take a deep breath, work to stay calm. I know what I need to say, I just need to muster the courage.

"Look, I shouldn't have left you. Today—or fifteen years ago. I never admitted it, even to myself, but I was scared." My voice wavers, but I forge ahead. "I wanted to do the right thing, by you and the baby. And then when we lost the baby, I couldn't deal with all of it."

I run my palm over my neck, my skin hot as the painful memories come rushing back. "Everything hurt too much. It was easier to shut you out than to face you, face the grief."

Juliet sucks in a sharp breath. "What?"

"I'm sorry, Jules. I did want you to have a better life, away from here. But I also couldn't bear the pain in your eyes, the sadness. I should have been stronger—for you, for us. Instead, I was a coward and I pushed you away." I drop my head, ashamed. "You were right, what you said in the alley. When I pushed you away, I saved myself too."

Her lower lip trembles, and she wrings her hands, my entire life hanging in the balance.

"I appreciate you saying this, King. But words aren't enough. Not now."

I grab her wrist, pulling her toward me. The scent of tortilla chips mixes with her shampoo, her warm body pressing against mine. I wrap my arms around her hips, my lower body tensing.

"I want us to work, Jules. I'll do better. You want me to talk, I'll talk. Hell, I'll fucking yodel for you if that's what you want. Just come home with me tonight."

Her lips part, and I long to run my tongue along that sweet mouth, to taste her, nip at the graceful column of her neck until she moans. Begs me to fuck her.

I want to bury myself balls-deep inside her until she cries out my name.

I want her to take me back.

"King." Her voice is a breathy whisper, a gentle exhalation.

Heart pounding, cock throbbing, I stare into her eyes.

I need her like I need food, water, air.

"Please, Jules." I'm desperate, every part of me blazing for the woman standing in front of me.

She shakes her head, and my stomach sinks. She's going to turn me down, and then what?

"I shouldn't be doing this." Scooting away from me, she presses her key fob, and the Toyota beeps to life. She pops the trunk and grabs her suitcase.

"Let's go."

She said yes.

I resist the urge to punch my fist up toward the sky and cheer.

Instead, I take the bag and slide my arm around her waist, dropping my lips to hers. She's minty and sweet, and everything inside me swells with pure joy. My heart belongs to this woman, and I'm going to spend the rest of my life proving it to her.

Wasting no time, I guide her to my truck and load the luggage, then help her into the cab.

I turn the engine over and ease out of the lot. "You didn't unpack yet?"

She shakes her head. "No. It's a long story."

"We've got time." I rest my hand on her upper thigh, fingers itching to touch her, stroke her, watch her come undone.

"My brothers are dicks. They let a rat—I think it's just one; god, I hope it's just one—loose in my apartment."

"They did what?" I almost slam on my brakes in shock. I can't imagine doing something that awful to Poppy.

She'd probably kill me with her bare hands, for starters.

"Yep. Damon got a rat, broke into my apartment, and released him from his cage. Ratigan's probably eating through my dried goods as we speak."

"Those fuckers—"

"It's under control. I called the exterminator. He's coming out on Friday."

"That's not until the end of the week."

"Best he could do. Apparently it's termite season."

"Yeah, it is. Where were you going to sleep tonight? I'm assuming not at your apartment with the rat."

"Definitely not. Maybe in my car."

"Juliet. That's totally unsafe."

Her shoulders inch toward her ears, then back down again. "I didn't have anywhere else to go."

I glance over at her. "You should have called me. I can handle the rat tomorrow. And you're always welcome at the ranch."

"I know. But we broke up, remember?"

Of course I remember. It's all I've thought about since I left her.

"Plus, you're busy. You can't be swooping in and rescuing me all the time."

I huff out a breath. "I can, actually. Swoop in and rescue you. That's what I'm here for."

Her cheeks flush, pink staining her skin, and I squeeze her thigh, reassuring her.

"Thanks, King. I'm a big girl, though. I can handle my bonehead brothers. Been doing it my whole life."

Unease creeps into my happiness, dulling the joy. Juliet's brothers wouldn't be bothering her if it weren't for me. She only helped with the trial because I asked her to.

I shove the thought away, instead focusing on her curves, the way her smile lights up her entire face when she's happy.

The way she feels when I'm driving into her, pushing her higher and higher toward release.

The way she quivers on my cock right before she unravels and cries out.

Every muscle in my body's tight, ready to spring into action, and I can't get us home quick enough. The radio fills the cab, Dustin Lynch warbling about being a small-town boy.

You should probably talk. Say something, anything. That's what the whole damn argument was about.

"I missed you."

She lets out a laugh, a low, throaty sound, sending more blood pumping south.

"We were apart a few hours."

"A few hours too long."

"I never thought I'd hear you say something like that. Where's this romantic side coming from?"

"I can do romantic. And I can definitely do romantic-plus." I inch my hand toward the V of her jeans, seeking her heat. A tiny moan escapes her lips as I slide my hand between her thighs. She presses against my palm slightly, and now I'm at full mast, straining the denim.

I run my thumb along her zipper, and she squirms in the seat.

"Are we there yet?" She shimmies against my hand.

"Almost." The road turns bumpy, and I keep stroking her, not wanting to lose our connection.

She reaches across the console and rubs my stiff cock, eliciting a groan.

"You really did miss me."

"Told ya." I glance over at her as we turn down the driveway, the front-porch light glowing in the darkness.

After throwing the truck into park, I scramble out, then rush around to open her door. I lift her into my arms, and she giggles, beaming up at me.

"Welcome back to the rat-free ranch. Well, there's

probably rats out by the barn, but they're outdoors at least."

She shakes her head, patting my chest, and I wonder if she can feel the banging of my heart through my shirt. I climb the steps, carrying her over the threshold.

"King . . ." Her eyes glisten as she stares up at me, pupils dark and wide.

All I can think about in this moment is her. Not our past, not the feud between the two families, not the aftermath that may rain down now that we're back home and really doing this.

Just her and the way she makes me feel. Whole, complete.

"I love you," I murmur, and tears sparkle in her eyes.

"I love you too."

Smashing my mouth to hers, I kiss her hard and fierce. Wanting her to know how I feel about her. That she's the only girl for me.

Lips soft and sweet, she tastes like forever.

In too big of a rush to make it all the way upstairs, I set her ass down on the kitchen island instead.

"I need you, Juliet. Right now."

We lock eyes; then she reaches up and loosens her ponytail, tousled waves spilling over her shoulders as she shakes her hair free. The soft white glow from the refrigerator highlights her high cheekbones, her full pink lips.

"You're so gorgeous." I run my thumb over the smooth skin of her jaw, trace down the length of her neck, skim my hand over the side of her breasts. She spreads her legs, and I unbutton her jeans, untuck her T-shirt and lift it over her head. She's a fucking vision, sitting on the granite in her black bra, nipples already hard and poking through the lace.

I drop my mouth to her breasts, sucking at the peaks through the thin fabric. Her head falls back, a soft moan vibrating her exposed neck. I reach up and stroke the delicate skin, up and down the long column, then encircle her throat with my hand. Squeezing slightly, testing her limits as she arches her body toward me. Releasing, allowing her to breathe in deeply as I nip at her skin, then squeeze again. Her nipples diamond sharp as I suck a rosy point into my mouth.

I need her naked. Need to see every glorious inch of her beautiful body.

I yank the lace down, and her pale breast spills out. I take as much of her flesh into my mouth as I can. Sucking her hard, squeezing her throat at the same time as she writhes against me.

"You like me to take charge of your body, don't you?" I tease her nipple, flicking my tongue against the bud. She nods, eyes closed as I rub the notch at the base of her neck. "Such a good fucking girl."

I ease away from her cleavage, unhooking her bra and tossing it aside. Stroking her bare tits, rolling her nipples in my fingers until her skin's rosy and flushed. Running my hands over her belly down to the waistband of her jeans.

"Lift up your ass now."

She does as she's told, and I ease the denim down her legs, letting the pants fall to the floor.

"Panties too."

She eases out of the tiny scrap of lace, now completely nude, sitting bare-assed on my counter.

I cup her face in my hands. "You're magnificent."

She smiles up at me, and my chest expands. I want to spend the rest of my life making this woman happy, giving her pleasure.

"I'm going to lay you down on this counter now and feast on you. Scoot your ass all the way to the edge and spread your legs. That's right, baby."

I press her back down on the smooth surface, guiding her legs over my shoulders as I drop my face to her warm pussy.

"Absolutely perfect," I murmur, sliding my tongue through her wetness. "Best thing I've ever eaten in this kitchen."

She giggles, the sweet sound echoing off the high wooden beams. I lap and suck at her, savoring her juices. I swirl my tongue around her clit, her body quivering with the promise of release. Her fingers twine through my hair, her small hand fanning over my neck, pulling me to her.

"Oh god, I'm so close." She groans, arching her hips up. I flatten my tongue, licking her harder. Her thighs quake as I thrust my tongue into her tight hole.

"Yes," she hisses, her juices exploding on my tongue as she comes on my face. She tries to pull away as her body spasms beneath me, but I pin her down, sucking her clit into my mouth. She cries out as she climaxes, and I grin, my cock throbbing and ready.

"Such a good fucking girl." I stroke her belly, watch as she trembles at my touch. "But that was only the appetizer."

Another giggle as her muscles relax beneath me.

"Very delicious."

I rise up, wiping my hand across my mouth before stripping off my shirt. Her pupils widen as she watches me undress, her tongue darting out and licking her lips. I kick off my shoes, then undo my pants and drop them to the ground, followed by my briefs.

"So sexy." Her voice is a low purr, and my cock twitches in response.

"Come here." I lift her off the island, spinning her around and pressing her belly up against the granite. Running my hand over her perfect peach of an ass, I smack lightly at her soft flesh. She gasps, then wriggles her cheek, rubbing against my palm.

"You want more of that, baby?" I murmur against the shell of her ear, and she nods, her hair tickling my nose.

"Yes, please."

"Such a dirty girl." I smack her ass, harder this time, pink blooming over her pale skin. Smooth my palm over the warm spot as she relaxes into me. My dick twitches, so hard it's almost painful.

Smack. I hit the other cheek, and she groans, squirming and rubbing against me. Rub, smack, rub, smack, until both of her ass cheeks turn rosy.

Grabbing her hips, I pull her up against me, her back pressed to my chest. My fingers move from her hip to the cleft between her legs.

"You're fucking dripping wet for me."

"Yes."

I suck her earlobe into my mouth, and she inhales sharply as my teeth graze the flesh. Pressing my thumb hard against her clit, I shove three fingers into her wet heat. Fast and rough. I want to possess her, claim her body.

"King," she moans, grinding down on my hand, seeking more. More force, more friction. More of me.

Gripping her hip, I piston in and out, scissoring and

stretching. Her muscles flex and release, tension already building.

"Are you ready to be fucked, baby girl?" I whisper into her ear. She nods slightly, panting as she rides my hand.

"Tell me how much you want me to fuck you." I slow my movement, stilling in her pussy, and she whimpers.

"Very much."

"And do you want it slow and sweet? Or fast and rough, baby?"

"Fast. Please." She rocks her hips back, her ass rubbing my hard cock. "Please, King. Fuck me now."

Pulling my hand away from her pussy, I bring it up to her mouth, slicking her juices across her lips. She opens for me, tentative, licking at my fingers.

"See how sweet you are, baby? So delicious." I slide my index finger between her lips, and she swirls her tongue on my calloused skin, tasting herself. My dick hardens as she sucks, throbbing, aching to be buried deep inside her.

"That's a good girl. Now I'm going to bend you over . . ." I press between her shoulder blades, pushing her chest down against the cool granite, her ass tipping up into the air.

My eyes trail over her smooth skin, the long line of her vertebrae dancing downward, the twin hollows at the small of her back. I run my hand along her spine, brushing her with only my fingertips. Goose bumps rise on her heated flesh as I caress her back, her ass, her breathing shallow. I lean down, body suspended over hers, my lips hovering at her ear.

"Gorgeous. Now breathe, baby. I'm going to make you feel so fucking good."

Then I drive my dick up into her. Hard, fast, decisive.

She gasps, her fingers splayed on the granite. I pound into her, over and over again, fucking away all our doubts and uncertainties. Skin slapping together, I'm buried balls-deep inside her. No space exists between us, nothing keeping us apart any longer.

This feels right.

It's always been her.

It's only been her.

"Juliet," I growl, pummeling hard against her ass. Her pussy clenches around me, milking my cock, as I plow into her. The familiar tingle at the base of my spine grows, pressure increasing, warning me I'm close, so fucking close.

"That's a good girl, letting me rail you on the kitchen island. So fucking beautiful, stretched out for me."

I stroke up her spine, wrapping my fingers around the delicate column of her throat, tightening my grip as I ram into her, squeezing her in my hand before letting go. She sucks in air, then cries out.

"Ohmygod, King . . ."

"Let go for me, baby." I caress her back, raining kisses over her skin. "Come for me."

The words push her over the edge, and she screams, unraveling beneath me. I keep going even as she bucks, pistoning hard inside her, chasing my release. I'm sweaty and panting with exertion as I pound against her.

"Fuck," I hiss, streams of hot cum exploding inside her.

With one hand on her hip, the other curled around the edge of the island, my cock pulses as I give her everything I have. After a long minute I slip out, spent from the effort.

Running my hand along her silky-smooth curves, I slide my palm over her pink ass cheeks, cupping her sex. She lies still on the counter, her breathing ragged as she comes down from the high, her chest rising and falling with every exhalation. I drag my fingers through her wetness, rub the sticky fluid over her skin. Liquid proof that she's mine.

I lean over, pressing my lips to her neck, kissing up to her ear. Sucking the tender lobe until she groans.

"You're so gorgeous like this, laid out for me, my hand on your soaking pussy."

She sighs, a quiet, happy sound, her muscles relaxing as I paint her skin with our release.

"Tell me you're mine, Jules," I murmur into her ear, nuzzling her velvety smooth skin.

"I'm yours, King. You know I'm yours."

31

JULIET

King's words catch me off guard, my face still pressed against the cool counter. "What?"

He smooths the hair from my neck, lifting me up and spinning me around to face him.

"Don't go back to your apartment. Move in here. With me."

"King—" I fan my fingers over his chiseled pec. "I—I don't know what to say."

"Say yes. We can pack everything up tomorrow when I take care of the rat. Come live here with me. We can be together, make up for lost time." He reaches down, lacing his fingers with mine. "Please stay, Jules."

He stares down at me, waiting. My mind tries to find a good reason—even a slightly decent reason—to say no, but nothing comes.

I take a deep breath, exhale.

"Okay."

"Okay?" His dark brow rises.

"Yes." I break into a smile. "Yes, I'll stay."

King smashes his mouth to mine, claiming my lips. Sliding his tongue in and devouring me, like he can't get enough, will never get enough. Of me, my body, my soul.

Every inch of me is on fire for this man, and I've never felt more complete.

Now everything's right between us.

Lifting me in his arms, he carries me upstairs to bed, both of us finally at peace.

DAWN BREAKS, AND I SLEEP RIGHT THROUGH IT. KING rustles around, getting dressed in the low light; then he comes over to the bed. Rubs my back and tells me it's early, that I should stay in bed.

I happily oblige, snuggling down into covers that smell like him. Crisp and woodsy, with a sweet hint of hay.

By the time I open my eyes again, bright sunlight streams through the window, and I figure I should probably get moving. I have an apartment to pack, a lease to terminate, and a rat to exterminate.

Climbing out of bed, I remember my suitcase is still downstairs from the night before. Not wanting to traipse around King's house in the nude—at least during daylight hours—I open the top drawer of his dresser in search of a T-shirt. Instead, I find a neat pile of boxer briefs and undershirts. Sticking my hand in, I rifle through the clothing, hoping to find at least one decent-size tee I can throw on. I grab at a gray T-shirt, pulling it from the bottom of the stack. A glossy square of paper clings to my finger, and I lift it up, hold it to the light.

The black-and-white image trembles before me. Stomach sinking, I can't catch my breath, my chest and throat tight. So damn tight. The skin on my arm prickles, darkness dancing at the edges of my vision.

The ultrasound picture of our baby. I have one exactly like it tucked away in a journal somewhere.

King kept it all this time.

I can't believe it.

He really did care. Was maybe even as heartbroken over the loss as me. He just didn't show it.

I back up to the edge of the bed and sink down onto the duvet, muscles quaking. Hot regret washes over me as I stare down at the grainy photo, the outline of the head, the tiny feet. We had the ultrasound a few days before I lost the baby, one of our last days together before everything came undone.

I blink back tears, all the memories flooding back. Memories I buried long ago so I could keep moving, keep living. Survive.

Otherwise I would have crumbled, a shattered mess of grief prostrate on the floor.

But life moved on—we moved on, both of us—and that chapter was over.

Still, he never forgot.

Something swells in my chest, a warmth spreading from the center all the way to my arms, my belly.

Throwing the T-shirt on, I head downstairs, ultrasound in hand. No more secrets, no more deception. Maybe if we talk things out together, we can finally put the past behind us and move on.

The kitchen's quiet, empty. King must be out in the barn still. A Seaglass Inn mug sits on the counter next to the coffeepot, along with a note. I set the ultrasound down on the island and sidle over to read the message.

Morning, sunshine. Out feeding the animals. Be back soon. Have a cup of coffee, then we'll head to town when I get back.

Love,
King

I smile down at the paper, his messy, scribbly handwriting inked at an early hour. Always thoughtful, considerate.

Pouring a steaming cup of coffee, I sweeten it up with a heaping teaspoon of sugar, then slide over to the island. I sip at the dark brew and stare out the window, over the lush green lawn, the huge canopy of oaks shading the grass.

I'm so lost in thought I don't even hear the front door open.

"Hello?"

A high-pitched voice startles me, and I jump, coffee sloshing onto my skin.

"Ouch! Dammit."

Setting the mug down, I hustle to the sink to rinse the burning liquid from my skin before it blisters.

"What are you doing here?"

I spin around. Poppy's mouth hangs open as she stares at me from across the island. It dawns on me that I'm wearing King's T-shirt and literally nothing else—no bra, no panties. She can probably see my nipples straight through the thin material.

Not exactly the best impression to make on his sister.

"Uh, hi . . . ," I stammer, cheeks flaming. Shifting my weight, I try to make the fabric hang lower on my upper thighs. I'm acutely aware of the cold air on my bare skin beneath the shirt, fanning my ass.

"Where's my brother?"

She cuts straight to the chase, her button nose scrunched up. No *hi*, no *good morning*, nothing.

"Out at the barn." I swallow down my nervousness as she scowls at me from across the room, the massive island physically separating us.

"I take it you're sleeping together then." She folds her arms over her chest, juts out her chin. It's not a question, more of a statement. My face burns, my mouth going instantly dry.

"Um . . ." I go to fiddle with the hem of the shirt, then think better of it due to the length—or lack thereof. The last thing I need to do is give Poppy an up-close view of my bare everything.

She frowns, shaking her honey-blonde head. "It's fine. You don't have to say it. In fact, I'd rather you not. It's kinda weird hearing about your brother's sex life, to be honest."

She takes a step, then another, inching closer to me, closing the distance. A sliver of tension releases from between my shoulder blades, and I can kind of sort of breathe.

Tilting her head, she narrows her bright-blue eyes. "Do you love him?"

I ignore the pitching of my stomach as I meet her gaze.

"Yes. I do."

"Good. Because if you didn't and you were just using him for his connections or whatever, we'd have a real problem."

We stare at each other, woman to woman, and I swear she's sizing me up. Gauging my sincerity or something. After what feels like an eternity, she tosses her hair back over her shoulder and starts to turn toward the door, presumably to go find King.

Then she freezes.

Her hand darts out, and she snatches up the ultrasound photo, staring at the image.

"Ohmygod—are you pregnant? That's why you're here?" Her eyes fly to my face, searching for answers.

"What? No!" My voice tips up in shock, sweat forming under my arms, slicking my palms.

I can't believe I left that sitting out there on the counter.

"Then explain this!" She waves the paper through the air, shaking her head in disbelief. "You're pregnant, and that's why the two of you are together!"

"No, it's not what you think." I try to explain, panic clawing at my chest. I don't want to get into my history with King. He obviously never told her about the baby for a reason, and it's not my place to do it.

"It's all making sense now. There's no other reason for King to be with a Capelli. Unless you're having his baby."

"Poppy. Enough."

King's voice bellows from the doorway, and I almost collapse onto the ground with relief.

Poppy whirls on her brother, flashing the ultrasound in his face. "Explain this, King!"

His face blanches, turning the same shade as the

kitchen cabinets, and I worry he might faint. But he calmly steps forward, takes the paper from his sister, and slides it into his back pocket.

"That's none of your damn business, Poppy."

"My brother's baby is most definitely my business. Unless it's not yours." She spins back on me, eyes narrowed. "Is it? Is it my brother's?"

"I told you, I'm not pregnant." I keep saying the words, but she's not believing them.

Poppy shakes her head, blonde hair swishing behind her. "Someone needs to start talking. Right now."

King straightens his shoulders, his lips a tight, thin line. "I don't need to tell you anything. But I'm certain that if I don't, you'll never stop hounding me about it. So sit down."

32

KING

Well, shit. I didn't want a showdown in the kitchen this morning, but here we are.

Poppy takes a huffy seat on a barstool at the island, and I pull Juliet to the side, dropping my voice.

"Are you all right if I tell her?" I scour her face for clues, any indication of what she wants me to do. Her cheeks and chest flush pink, and she gnaws at her bottom lip.

"I guess. It's as much your information as mine." Her eyes flick up, and something passes between us. A moment of shared loss, solidarity.

"Still. I want to make sure it's okay with you."

She nods, folding her arms tight across her chest. "It's fine."

I squeeze her arm, try to offer at least some comfort before dealing with my sister.

"I'll give you two a minute." Juliet tips her chin at Poppy, stewing at the island, her fingers thrumming a mile a minute on the granite. "I'm going to get dressed."

"You're welcome to stay."

"That's okay. Talk to your sister."

She dashes away, grabbing her suitcase as she heads upstairs, leaving me and Poppy alone in the kitchen.

"Juliet didn't want to stay for your little speech?" Poppy's voice leaks sarcasm, and I glower at her.

"Cut the crap, Poppy." I take a seat next to her, our elbows brushing.

"So what's the deal, King? What's really going on with Juliet? She's pregnant, isn't she? And that's why you're with her?" Her tone's accusatory, like I've been withholding top-secret information from her and she doesn't appreciate it one little bit.

"Stop. Just stop." I try to tamp down the irritation bubbling up in my gut. Poppy's always known how to push my buttons—everyone's buttons, really—and this time's no exception.

"You don't know what you're talking about. So be quiet before you make things worse." I cut my eyes at her, slightly satisfied to see her lips pressed shut.

Thank god for small favors.

"She was pregnant. A long time ago. But we lost the baby."

For once, Poppy's quiet, a yawning silence filling the kitchen. A part of me, deep down, still aches when I think about the baby. Saying the words out loud is even worse. I sit with the dull, aching pain, let it settle over me like a familiar blanket.

Finally, Poppy speaks.

"I'm sorry, King." Her hand finds mine on the counter.

I don't say anything, my throat tight and dry. I don't like being in this space, thinking about the past, what could have been.

We sit quietly for another long minute before Poppy breaks in.

"You don't have to answer if you don't want to. But when did this happen? How long ago?"

"I told you, it was a long time ago. Before Juliet moved away."

"Shit, like fifteen years ago? You guys were kids!"

"Yeah. We were going to make it work, though. But when she lost the baby, I took it as a sign. She deserves more than this town. More than me."

I hang my head, staring at the pattern in the island, painful memories swirling. All the negative feelings flooding back through me, weighing me down. The sadness, anger, inadequacy, the inability to help her. I did the best I could, but it still wasn't enough. To save the baby or her.

"King." Poppy turns to face me, her hand warm on my shoulder. "That's ridiculous. She deserves more than her brothers, that's for sure. But any girl would be lucky to have you. You're strong, loyal, kind. You put your family first, above all else. What woman wouldn't want those things?"

Heat rushes to my face, cheeks burning. It's weird hearing my sister say all these things about me. Mostly she runs around busting my chops, just like everyone else.

I swallow hard over the giant lump in my throat, unable to speak or make eye contact.

"Does everyone know about this but me?" Her voice wobbles, and I can practically feel the hurt radiating off her skin at the possibility of being left out.

"No. No one else knows. Just me and Juliet. And Mom. She knew." Another wave of sadness rolls over me. Mom was always the best person to turn to when you needed to talk something out. And she knew her children. She was the one who came to me, pried the news out of me like the lid off a swollen pickle jar.

"Oh. Of course Mom knew. She always knew." Poppy trails off, lost in her own memories of our mom.

Sometimes I feel her in this house, catch a hint of her perfume in the air, the echo of her tinkly laugh off the walls, and I swear she's still here with me. Standing right behind me, watching over my shoulder and guiding me to do the right thing, say the right thing.

"I miss her so much." Poppy sighs, her voice soft and filled with regret. At the things we'll never get to say to her, the time we'll never have together.

"Me too, Pops." I lick my dry lips, pat my sister's arm, so much smaller and more delicate than mine.

Poppy's such a strong force, such a big personality, that I sometimes forget how tiny she is.

"I take it you still love her then? Juliet?" She spins on the stool to look at me, locking her aquamarine gaze on mine.

Something unlocks in my chest, some of the tightness, the anxiety clearing, replaced with lightness.

"Yeah, I do."

My sister scrunches her lips together, frown lines creasing her brow as she digests this info. She laces her fingers together, then loosens them, then laces them again.

Finally, she straightens up her shoulders and smooths her hair down.

"As long as she's good to you, that's all that matters. If she does anything to hurt you, though, she's going to answer to me."

Juliet and Poppy going head-to-head would be a good matchup. Juliet's tough, but you should never underestimate Poppy, especially when family's involved.

I chuckle, my lips tipping up. "I'll be sure to give her fair warning."

Poppy leans over and hugs me, throwing her arms around my shoulders. Caught off guard, I stiffen, then relax as she wraps me in her embrace. Like a freaking ray of sunshine, warming me all the way up.

"You're a good guy, King. Like I said, she's lucky to have you."

Poppy pulls away, jumping down from the stool.

"How was Lacey? That's why I came over in the first place."

The mention of our half sister throws me off-kilter, and I scramble to get my bearings.

"She was fine. Good. She's probably making a visit this summer."

"Really?" Poppy scrunches up her nose.

"Yeah. She wants to meet all of you."

"What was she like?"

"We only chatted for a bit. But she seemed nice."

"Don't you find it strange that she wants to meet us?"

"Not really. Look at all those people doing the at-home DNA kits and shit. Same type of thing."

Poppy shrugs. "I guess. What'd she look like? Tall? Blonde?"

"No and no. She's taller than you, but not tall. And her hair's brown."

"Brown? Like dark? Or more chestnut?"

"Hell, I don't know, Pops. *Brown* brown. And she has blue eyes. Like you and Parker."

Poppy exhales a quiet breath. "And Mom."

I press my lips together and nod. "Yeah. And Mom."

"She's really our half sister then." She clasps her hands together, thumbs running over each other again and again.

"I believe so."

"Wow."

Juliet steps tentatively into the kitchen, one brow raised high. I give her a subtle nod, letting her know the coast is clear. Poppy follows my gaze, her head spinning to face Juliet. The two women stare at one another, and I'm half-worried Poppy might start something right here in the kitchen, despite what she just said about being okay with me and Juliet. I prepare to break up whatever Poppy might start with her.

She walks over to Juliet, straightening up to all five foot nothing, and squares her shoulders.

"Take good care of him. He's the backbone of this family. And one of the best men I know. You're lucky to have him."

"I know." Juliet says the words so matter-of-factly, like it's common knowledge or something, my heart stammers.

Then Poppy surprises me, reaching out and touching Juliet on the arm.

"I'm real sorry about the baby."

Juliet nods and murmurs a thanks; then Poppy's gone with a quick wave. Vanished as quickly as she appeared.

Both of us stare at the hallway, the kitchen still and quiet in Poppy's wake. Juliet walks over to me, her bare feet shuffling on the plank floor.

"I'm sorry about all that."

I reach out, taking her hands in mine. "Don't be. You couldn't have known Poppy would stop by this morning."

"I wasn't going through your things. I was trying to find a T-shirt because my clothes were all down here, and the paper stuck to me . . ."

Leaning over, I press my lips to hers, swallowing her explanation. "It's fine. I didn't think you were."

"I was surprised."

"You were?"

"Yeah. I didn't think you'd still have that, after all this time."

"Jules . . ." I run my thumb down her cheek, tipping her face up to meet my gaze. "I wanted that baby too. That was one of the worst days of my life. And when I pushed you away, it felt like I was ripping my heart out of my damn chest. I did want to save you. I wanted you to go to school, have a good life. Not get sucked down with all the bullshit of this town, your family. I only wanted you to be happy."

"King . . ." Her voice wobbles as she stares at me, the golden flecks in her eyes sparkling in the ray of sunlight slanting through the window. "I'm happy now."

She lifts up on tiptoe, brushing her soft lips against mine, and the entire world stops.

Everything is Juliet.

I know she's it for me. Always has been, always will be.

This time nothing's going to keep us apart.

"Let's go get your stuff and move you out of that rathole." I trace her bottom lip with my thumb. "It's time for you to come home."

33

JULIET

Not gonna lie, Poppy's blessing makes me feel a lot better about my relationship with King.

After our first encounter, I wasn't holding out hope. But now it feels like the two of us turned a corner. Like King and I may actually be able to make this thing between us work.

His strong hand rests on my thigh, and I haven't been this at peace in a long time. Everything between us is right, and I can breathe again, really breathe.

We turn into the apartment lot, and King backs the truck into a spot close to the stairs. Not that I'm bringing much with me. I don't have a ton of stuff to begin with, and I'll need to get boxes to properly move out. For now I plan on packing up my clothes and a few personal items. I'll come back and get the rest of it later, maybe sell some of the furniture online or something.

Climbing out of the truck, I'm careful not to ding the matte-black Porsche parked next to us. The car definitely costs more than my entire net worth, and in my experience, anyone driving something that flashy is always precious about dents and scratches.

King grabs the rat trap from the back seat, and together we climb the stairs to my apartment. I unlock the front door, push it open slightly, and step aside just in case the rodent squatter decides to make a quick exit. No gray furry flash runs by. I couldn't get that lucky.

Muffled sound drifts from the apartment, and a chill slithers up my spine. A tinny laugh track echoes down the hall, and I know for a fact I did not leave the television on.

Someone's in my apartment.

King holds his hand up to my chest, stopping me from entering. As if I was about to anyway. I'm beyond freaked out, between the rat and the possessed TV.

"Let's just go," I whisper, ready to hit the stairs. I don't have anything that valuable anyway.

"Come on in, little sis. I've been waiting for you."

Jagger.

His gravelly voice sends another shiver of fear racing through me.

King doesn't hesitate, shoving through the door, unde-terred by my asshole brother. I follow close behind, praying there's limited bloodshed.

"What the fuck are you doing in Juliet's apartment, asshole?" King shoots Jagger a withering glare, the light from the television giving my older brother a garish white glaze. He lost weight in jail, his cheekbones high, pronounced slashes.

"Well, hello to you too, Prince. We meet again." Jagger doesn't move from his spot on the couch, legs spread wide. Like he owns the place.

"Get the hell out of here, Jagger," King growls, fists

clenched. The rat trap swings in the air, rattling with King's barely contained rage.

"And miss all the excitement of the rat hunt? Never." Jagger's lips turn up in a sneer, and I've never wanted to punch my brother in his smug face as much as I do right now.

"You're an asshole, Jagger. Leave before I call the cops on you." I scowl at him, and he laughs. Actually throws his head back and laughs.

I hate him.

"Like I'm scared of cops. Please, little sis. I'm friends with half the force. We have a mutual understanding. A real symbiotic relationship."

Great. Now Jagger's got connections within law enforcement. Wonderful.

"I'm a little hurt that you don't like your new friend. I thought the two of you would get along well, seeing as you have so much in common." He steeples his fingers, every knuckle inked, and sneers at me.

"Fuck off." I spit the words at him, my gut quivering with anger.

"I'm gonna give you five seconds to get out of here, Jagger. After that, I'll make you leave." King drops the trap on the floor, his jaw tight, the vein in his temple throbbing.

Jagger leans back on the couch, kicking his feet up on the scratched coffee table, arms behind his head. Clearly *not* leaving.

"That's it, you little weasel." King lunges for my brother, jerking him up and off the couch by the shirt collar. But Jagger's not going down without a fight. He throws a punch at King, knuckles glancing off his cheekbone. King drops hold of Jagger, and the two of them are in a full-blown fight in my living room. Fists fly, each of them making contact with the other's face. King's bigger and stronger than my brother, but Jagger's fast, bouncing out of reach like a skilled boxer. He definitely honed his fighting skills in jail, his feet constantly moving and weaving.

Jagger takes another shot, missing King's face by an inch as he dodges to the right. King swings at Jagger and lands a punch directly to his left eye. There's a loud, sickening crunch, and Jagger staggers back, his hand covering his eye socket.

"You fucker! You're going to pay for this!" Jagger cries, mouth twisted in pain.

"Stay away from Juliet, Jagger. And the rest of my family too." King rolls his shoulders and rubs at his hand, the knuckles red and swollen.

"You can have the traitorous little bitch. She's dead to me." My brother stares straight at me, his left eye puffy, almost swollen shut. A thin line of blood trickles from his nose. Then he screws up his lips and spits on the floor.

King springs toward Jagger, but he bolts out the door. We follow right behind, watching his every move to make sure he's actually leaving and not planting a bomb or letting an entire rat colony loose.

"See you around, Prince!" Jagger mocks King as he jogs down the stairs, middle finger extended high in the air. He hops into the fancy Porsche, revving the engine so loudly it vibrates the entire building before he peels out of the lot.

"How'd Jagger get a Porsche?" King furrows his brow, staring at the trail of exhaust Jagger left behind.

I shrug. "Who the hell knows? Probably stole it on his way over here."

"I can't believe you're related to that scumbag." King shakes his hand, flexing and stretching his fingers.

"I know. Sorry." I gnaw my bottom lip, the familiar wave of hot shame rolling through me. Much as I try to distance myself from my brothers, I can't seem to break free of their toxic grip.

"Hey, I didn't mean it like that." King wraps his arms around my waist, his hands resting on my lower back.

I swallow hard over the lump in my throat, the adrenaline rush fading, replaced with sour, acidic regret. Regret over my last name and all the bullshit that comes with me.

"Jules . . ." King cups my jaw, tipping my head up to meet his serious gaze. "You don't have to worry about them anymore. I promise you that. I've got you. What's more, my entire family's got you."

Lightness fills my chest, tension seeping from my tight muscles as King holds me in his strong arms. I let his words sink in, penetrate the armor I've built up over the years as a Capelli.

"Thank you." The quiet, simple words don't feel like enough. Not big enough, strong enough, powerful enough to share the entirety of how I feel.

Protected. Safe. Wanted.

Loved.

King bends down, brushing his lips with mine, and I know this is right.

This is forever.

Nothing—and no one—is going to keep us apart this time.

A loud snap from the apartment shocks us back to reality. We sprint into the living room, high-pitched shrieks and squeals coming from the rat trap. Inside sits the furry gray rodent, his tiny pink paws raised, his beady little black eyes staring at us.

He bears a striking resemblance to Jagger.

"Well, we got one problem taken care of." King walks over to the trap and kneels, making sure the door's secure. "Don't worry, little guy. We'll let you loose. Just not in the apartment, okay?"

A shudder rips through me, followed by cool relief. I'm glad I don't have to worry about rat paws running over me as I pack up my stuff.

"Thanks for catching the rat. I'll get my clothes; then we can head out."

King glances up at me, nodding. "Let me know if you need help."

"No, just keep your eye on the intruder. I can handle the rest."

King chuckles, his face breaking into a smile that reaches all the way to his eyes.

A smile I haven't seen in forever, the same smile that melted my heart all those years ago.

I crouch down next to him, the rat right beside us. Our knees touching, I kiss King hard and fierce on the lips.

"I love you, King."

"And I love you." He tucks a stray hair behind my ear. "Now get going. We have a rat to set free."

34

KING

"You sure this shirt looks good? I could wear the light-blue one instead." I fiddle with the button on the sleeve, my big, clumsy fingers unable to slide the tiny plastic through the hole.

"Yes. It's great. Makes your eyes pop. Here, let me help you." Poppy grabs my arm, easily moving the button through the hole.

"And Liv's setting everything up?"

"Yes, King. Geez, relax. You know Liv plans events for a living. How hard could this be for her? Plus, we've gone over the details like five thousand times. Take a deep breath—everything's going to be spectacular. The absolute perfect night."

I try to follow her advice and calm down, but my heart's racing, pounding so damn hard I'm mildly concerned I might have a heart attack on my way to the lake.

Since Juliet moved out to the ranch, life's been amazing. Better than amazing. Everything's been fucking perfect, each day better than the last.

And I know without a shadow of a doubt that this is right. We're right.

She's the woman I want—need—to spend the rest of my life with.

Our family names be damned.

Besides, hopefully after tonight, she'll be changing her name to mine forever.

"You have the ring?" Poppy cocks her head, scrunching up her nose.

Like I'd forget the ring.

"Yeah, of course I have it." I pat my pocket, the velvet box tucked deep down in the denim. Snug up against my thigh, a reminder of all the things to come.

It's the same ring I've had for fifteen years, the one I was going to give Juliet the day we lost the baby. The diamond ring's been tucked away in my nightstand ever since. Waiting for her.

"You should be good to go then. Oh my god, King. I can't believe you're doing this. It's going to be so romantic. You sure I can't come and film the proposal? Take pictures? Please?"

I shake my head hard, adamant. "Hell no. I'm nervous enough as it is. Last thing I need is my kid sister spying on me."

"Spoilsport." She chucks me on the arm but smiles bright and wide. "You're going to do great. Just tell her how you feel. You know she's going to say yes."

I think she'll say yes, but I still want tonight to be perfect. Juliet deserves it, after all this time.

"You better get going. Only twenty minutes to sunset. And you want to get to the lake first."

"Got it, boss." I catch Poppy off guard, giving her a quick hug. She pats my back, her tiny body pressed against me.

"Go get 'em, tiger."

Smacking my hip, she shoos me out of my bedroom. I head to the truck, the sun already starting to drop lower in the sky. The lake's only a five-minute drive from here, so I have plenty of time. I bump down the drive, kicking up dust as I leave the safe confines of the ranch behind.

This is it.

The day I've dreamed about for years.

I didn't think this time would ever come, that this could happen for us, but here we are. And I know it's going to be wonderful. Better than wonderful.

What Juliet and I have is timeless. It reminds me of my parents' relationship, and they were beyond happy. Made for each other and in love until the day they died.

I know they would approve. All they ever wanted was for me to be happy.

And I am, with Juliet by my side.

Parking the truck near the woods, I make my way down the trail to the lake. The air's cool, but not cold, a slight breeze rustling the leaves overhead. A few stray branches snap under my boots, a bird cawing from above.

Finally, I spill out of the trees, moving across the empty field toward the lake. Sunset's in full force, pink streaking the sky. Liv's gone, but she worked her magic, turning our special place into the most incredibly romantic spot.

A white canopy strung with twinkly lights sits near the water's edge, a table set for two beneath it. A mason jar full of red and white roses decorates the table, a bottle of champagne chilling in a silver bucket next to it.

But the real stunner is the lake. Floating golden lanterns dot the entire glassy blue surface, glowing in the fading sunlight. The scene's straight out of a fairy tale, and it is downright breathtaking.

"King?" Juliet walks out of the woods, and she's never been more beautiful, the waves of her hair tumbling around her bare shoulders. She's wearing a gauzy green sundress that highlights every spectacular curve of her body, and I can't stop staring as she sashays over to me.

Finally, we're face-to-face, the last rays of sunlight catching the golden flecks in her eyes. I grasp her hands, lace her fingers with mine. My heart's hammering, my throat tight with so many emotions. I work on keeping my voice steady as I gaze into her eyes.

Beguiling.

"Juliet."

She smiles at me, and my stomach swoops, nerves thrumming on high. I swallow hard, take a quick breath, start over again.

"I've been under your spell from the moment I laid eyes on you, all those years ago."

The wind blows, her hair fluttering around her face, and all my muscles tense. This woman's so damn perfect, I can't even think straight.

"I love everything about you. Your smile, your laugh, the way you sing in the shower when you think no one's listening. How you make me feel. Most of all, your kind, caring heart. I never stopped loving you. I need you to know that." I trace my thumb over the smooth skin of her cheek, down her jaw.

"I need you, Juliet, more than anything in this whole world. What I'm trying to say is—"

Dropping down to one knee, I pull the velvet box from my pocket, fumble with the clasp, and finally get it to open. I hold the ring up for her to see. The diamond sparkles in the cobalt darkness, the twinkly lights reflecting off the precisely cut surface of the gem.

She takes a deep breath, her eyes filling with tears as she stares at the ring, then back at me.

"Juliet, will you marry me? Do me the honor of becoming my wife?"

Nodding, she bites down on her lip, then smiles.

"Yes, King. Of course, a thousand times yes."

She drops down to her knees in the grass, taking my face in her hands and kissing me hard and deep. Letting me know she's mine and I'm hers.

Forever.

"I love you, baby," I murmur into her open mouth, her lips tipping up in a smile.

"I love you too. So much."

Sliding her tongue against mine, her hands move from my face to my neck, twine in my hair. Every inch of me is alive, wrapped up in this magnificent woman.

We break away from each other's bodies, and I ease the ring from the cushion.

I take her delicate hand and slide the diamond onto her finger—a perfect fit.

"It's beautiful, King." She moves her hand from left to right, admiring the sparkly ring.

"My mom helped me pick it out."

Her eyes fly to my face, her lips a pink circle, realization dawning.

"Your mom?"

"Yeah. I bought it the day we found out you were pregnant."

She places her hand on my chest, her fingers resting right over my heart, and we sit in the silence for a long minute.

"She'll always be with us now." Juliet's quiet voice, almost a whisper, blends in with the lapping of the water along the shore.

Nodding, I breathe in all the goodness, the sweetness that is Juliet.

"She will. I know she'd be happy for us." I move my hand to my chest, covering her hand with mine.

We're rock solid. She's mine and I'm hers and nothing will come between us ever again, of that I am sure.

EPILOGUE: KING

FIFTEEN MONTHS LATER…

"You sure you're not too tired to stop? We can do this another time . . ." My voice trails off as I search Juliet's eyes for the truth. She's too strong to admit when she's exhausted, too caring to tell me to wait.

But she locks her eyes with mine, fierce determination etched on her face.

"I'm good, King. Swear."

The baby starts to cry, and Juliet rocks our little girl in her arms, shushing her. Even after a grueling twelve-hour night of labor, Juliet's a vision, her hair swept up in a messy ponytail, her skin glowing. This time around, pregnancy agreed with her. I loved watching her body swell with our baby, her curves rounding even more as she grew our child.

Our perfect baby.

Madeline Montgomery, named after my mom.

"Y'all ready to go?" The labor and delivery nurse bustles into the room, pushing a wheelchair. "You passed the car seat check—good job. At least half of new parents don't."

Pride blooms in my chest at the praise. I had spent a

solid hour checking and rechecking every latch, making sure each of them was tight and secure.

"Yes, we're ready." Juliet stands up, wobbling a bit, and I rush over and grip her elbow.

"Here, let me help." The nurse comes closer with the wheelchair, and Juliet eases down into the plastic seat. Madeline's sucking on a pacifier, her tiny eyes shut as she works the soft rubber.

"I'll get your bag, babe." I do a quick sweep of the room, grabbing her phone charger still plugged into the wall and stuffing it into her duffel. We'd been in the hospital for a week right at the end of the pregnancy, Madeline surprising us by making her grand entrance a few weeks early.

But everything turned out fine, and now we have an absolutely beautiful baby.

"All right, Dad, let's go." The nurse ushers us out of the room, and the title starts to sink in.

Dad.

I wasn't sure that would ever be me, and I was okay with that. I meant what I said, that Juliet was all I needed.

Being able to have a baby, though, really is the icing on the cake.

We're not young anymore—at least I'm not—but I'm still plenty able to care for a child. She's going to have the best time growing up on the ranch, running around with the horses and goats and the golden lab puppy I gave Juliet right after we got engaged. Plus her cousin Archer, Roman and Skye's baby boy.

The elevator slides down to the ground floor, and I hold the button while the nurse wheels Juliet and the baby out. Trailing behind, I hustle to jog ahead and open the truck door for Juliet.

I'm as nervous right now as I was the day I proposed to Juliet. Taking the baby home for the first time, being alone with a newborn.

"You okay?" Juliet frowns at me as I pluck Madeline from her arms.

"Yeah, I'm fine. Just excited is all."

I fasten the baby into the car seat—just like we practiced with Archer—and she settles into the carrier, falling back asleep. The nurse and I help Juliet up into the truck, and I gently fasten the seat belt around her belly.

"Thank you." Juliet gives the nurse a warm smile and waves.

"Sure thing. Good luck, you two. You're gonna be great!" She spins the wheelchair around and heads back inside as I ease away from the curb and drive away from the hospital.

Juliet's eyes close, and she leans back on the seat as we move down Main Street through the center of town. Taking the last right before the gravel road, I head toward the cemetery. The sky's a bright blue, the grass lush and green as we make our way through the iron gates.

I pull to a stop, parking the truck near our family plot. Taking a deep breath, I sit with my feelings. Joy mingles with sadness, the constant push and pull between the two emotions vying for my attention. Glancing in the rearview, I catch sight of the car seat and let joy win.

"We're here. Wait and I'll help you out." I rub Juliet's arm, and her eyes slide open, the corners of her full lips curving into a soft smile.

Coming around, I offer her my hand, and she climbs

down from the truck. I unbuckle Madeline, easing her tiny arms and legs from the straps, then lifting her into my arms. Her soft breath tickles my neck, the sweet scent of milk wafting up from her warm body.

We walk across the grass over to the Montgomery family plot at the far side of the cemetery. All my relatives are buried here, dating back over a century. But today I'm interested in only two.

I stand before the twin gray headstones etched with my parents' names. Juliet's hand finds mine, and she laces our fingers together. Letting me know I'm not doing this alone, that she's right here by my side.

After a long minute I take a shaky breath, hot tears pricking behind my eyes.

"Mom, Dad—we brought someone to meet you." I lift Madeline from my shoulder, cradle her in my arms, holding her out. As if they could somehow see her.

"This is our daughter, Madeline. Me and Juliet had a baby. And we named her after Mom." My voice cracks, my body flushing with hot grief. I wish my parents were here with me, cooing over the baby, holding her and loving on her.

Juliet squeezes my hand, giving me strength.

"She's beautiful and perfect, your first granddaughter."

The wind blows, and I catch the scent of my mom's perfume, a cool sense of peace wrapping around me, holding me still.

She's here.

Madeline's eyes pop open, and she stares up at me, blinking. Her eyes are dark blue, and the doctor said they'll probably keep getting darker. Maybe even turn hazel like her mom's.

The baby doesn't cry. She stays calm in my arms, peaceful.

"They'll look out for her, King," Juliet whispers, glancing over at me and Madeline. "Your parents. They'll watch over us and her now."

"I know they will."

I lean over, pressing a kiss to Juliet's smooth forehead. "Thank you for this. Now let's go home, Mrs. Montgomery."

We walk back to the truck, and I sling one arm around Juliet's waist protectively, our baby snuggled up tight in the crook of my other arm.

Even after all the tragedy of the past, I have everything I need, I want, in this moment.

Juliet.

A baby.

Forever love.

A forever family.

We'll never be undone.

Keep reading for a special bonus scene — the surprise gift King gets Juliet after the proposal!

BONUS SCENE: JULIET

TWO WEEKS LATER…

Moving in with King and living out here at the ranch is easy. The only bad part about the whole deal is driving into town to go to work. But to be able to spend every night with King is one-thousand percent worth the commute.

"Jules? You in here?" King pops his head into the bedroom, dusty and sweaty from working all day out in the barn. The new pony arrived last week and he and Beau are busy ground training him, which requires a lot of running apparently.

"Hey. I'm just getting ready for work. What's up?" I catch his eye in the mirror as I fasten my hair back in a high ponytail.

"Come here…" He grabs me by the waist and spins me around, dropping his lips to mine.

He's warm from the sun and tastes a little bit salty, the sweet scent of grass and hay rising from his shirt as his tongue slides against mine. Firm, possessive.

I love it.

"Mmm...I missed you too, babe. And I'd love to keep this going, but I need to get going or I'll be late for my shift."

One hand palming my rear, he pulls me closer, his strong chest pressed up against mine. He squeezes my ass, sending hot pulses of desire fluttering through me.

"You're not making this easy—" I complain, my fingers fanning over his neck.

"Ah, then my plan's working," he teases, smirking.

"Stop!" I smack him playfully on his pec and he grins down at me. "Seriously, I have something to show you out in the barn. It'll only take a minute, then you can get going." He grabs my hand, pulling me toward the door.

"Fine. But this has to be quick. I was already late once this week."

We take the stairs two at a time, jogging out of the house and cutting across the lawn toward the barn. A light wind rustles the leaves of the old oak tree, birds chirping from a nest tucked into the high-up branches.

Matching King's long strides, we cut across the paddock and I follow behind him to the barn.

"Beau's already gone?" I glance around, but there's no sign of his truck.

"Yeah. I let him go home early. He's worked a lot of extra hours with the pony. Okay—stop right there."

King throws his arm out, stopping me in my tracks so fast a puff of dust kicks up and swirls around us. I brush the front of my black shirt, trying to wipe off the fine layer of dirt.

"Geez, a little warning next time." I pretend to frown and he laughs.

"Sorry. Stay here for one second." He dashes into the

barn, then shouts over his shoulder. "Oh, and shut your eyes."

Even though I feel ridiculous closing my eyes out here in the middle of nowhere, I do as he asks. The sun heats my skin and I relax, the soothing sound of the breeze lulling me into a calm state.

Then King's large hand's on mine, easing me forward into the barn, horses neighing all around me.

"Can I open my eyes yet?"

"Nope, not yet. Keep going, that's it."

I shuffle my feet forward, King guiding me and making sure I don't stumble.

"Okay. You can open them now."

My eyes pop open, my heart pounding in anticipation. I have no idea what he has up his sleeve, but the man's been full of surprises lately.

I glance around the barn, but nothing's out of the ordinary. All the usual suspects are here, including the pony.

Then something plops on my shoe and I look down.

"Ohmygosh, what?" My hand flies to my mouth as I stare down at the golden fluffball lying at my feet. "A puppy?"

King grins. "Yep. For you."

"What? How did you keep this little guy a secret?" I bend down and pet the puppy's soft yellow fur, his cocoa brown eyes gazing up at me. He lets out a big yawn, his pink tongue stretching out ridiculously far, and it's the cutest thing I've ever seen in my whole life.

"We just got him this afternoon. Beau picked him up over in Ocala. They had a litter and needed to find this guy a home." King scratches behind the pup's ears and he snuggles up under King's palm.

"King—" My eyes fill with tears, my chest light. "I can't believe you got me a puppy. I always wanted a dog."

"I know." He reaches up, runs his thumb over my cheek, brushing away the tears. "And now you can have one. He has lots of space to run and play. Besides, I'm gonna train him to keep the goats in line. Especially Oreo."

I giggle as King shakes his head. He's constantly exasperated by that kid, although I think he secretly loves him.

"This is the nicest gift anyone has ever given me. Well, besides the ring." I hold my hand out, the diamond glittering in the light.

"You deserve a ring, a puppy, and a whole helluva lot more, Juliet. And I'm going to spend the rest of my life working to make sure you get everything your heart desires."

Cupping his face in my hand, I press my mouth to his in a soft kiss. A kiss that I hope says everything I can't express in this moment.

"I love you, baby." King's deep voice vibrates my lips and I sigh happily into him.

"I love you, too."

"Oh. And one more thing."

"What?" I inch away, studying his face, wondering what other surprise he could possibly have.

"I think you should quit your job."

"What? How?"

The puppy wiggles on my shoe, lifting his paw up to my leg. I lean down, scooping him into my arms, and he licks my arm with his wet little tongue.

"Beau and I have been working on a kinda-sorta business plan."

"A business plan?" I tip my head, one brow arched high. The puppy mimics me and we both stare at King.

"Don't look so shocked. My dad and I used to talk about expanding all the time, back when we thought we'd be working out here together." A shadow crosses his face, darkening his navy gaze and my chest aches for him.

Eager to change the subject, I nudge him. "So tell me. What's your big idea?"

"Your big idea, actually. Well, you and Poppy."

I furrow my brow, thinking over the last few conversations I've had with King's sister. I definitely do not recall kicking around any business plans with her.

"The goats. I was gonna sell them, but I'm kind of attached now. And you and Pops both think they're so adorable and all. So Beau and I were thinking you could figure out how to make goat soap. Or cheese or milk or something. Maybe down the line—if you're interested—we could open a petting zoo."

"Really? You'd let strangers come out here, onto your land?" I screw my mouth up, doubtful.

"Sure, if it makes you happy. And keeps you from having to drive back and forth to town every day. I want you home here, with me. Working opposite shifts stinks. I want to be able to eat dinner with you, go to bed with you, make love to you. Now, you're at the Tipsy until at least ten and not home until almost eleven. It's fine, if that's what you want. But I'd much rather have you here. With me."

He tucks a stray lock of hair behind my ears, gazing down into my eyes, and my heart stammers.

"Of course I'd rather be here with you. And this little guy." I cuddle up to the puppy and he snuffles, a contented sigh tickling my arm.

"Call in right now. Stay home tonight. The first night with our new puppy." He brushes his thumb along my cheek and a ripple of desire shoots straight through me, heat unfurling in my belly.

"Deal." I lean over, kissing him soft and slow. Telling him without any words that he's the best thing that's happened to me in my entire life.

"Now—what should we name this little guy?" King ruffles the puppy's fuzzy head and together we walk back up to the ranch, hand-in-hand, the puppy in my arms.

CHAPTER ONE

Bree

Pacing the terrazzo floor of Terminal Three at LAX, I scowled with annoyance at my silent phone.

Crickets.

Pax, my soon-to-be-ex-boyfriend, was ignoring my barrage of angry texts.

Two days ago I'd seen a suspicious tweet from a twit named Keely: *Had the best night w/ @PaxJones!* But my breaking point was an Instagram pic of Pax kissing a rando girl smack on the lips.

It could have been a scene from his upcoming movie, but I didn't think so. He'd told me he was in Montana, filming scenes for his next big film, a Western flick starring him as a gorgeous-but-lonely cowboy. But the background in the photo appeared to be the Pacific Ocean, and even though I'd never been to Montana, I was pretty certain that's NOT what it looked like.

I immediately did some digging and sure enough, that asshole was in Laguna Beach, staying at the Ritz. And he definitely wasn't alone, judging by the amount of Veuve and spa treatments charged to his room.

"Final boarding call for Flight 4356 to Atlanta, GA. All remaining passengers should board at this time."

I hesitated, took a deep breath. If I was going to flee LA and the paparazzi, I had to get on this plane. Any second now, the disastrous headlines could hit:

Relationship expert Bree Hart is no 'expert' when it comes to her own love life

Superstar Paxton Jones leaves so-called 'dating doctor' for B-list actress

Relationship guru Bree Hart left brokenhearted by actor Paxton Jones

Gah. I so did *not* want those headlines to hit. My dating podcast was finally trending, and I'd just made it into the Top 25 in the Relationship Category. This could devastate my career. Never mind my heart—Pax had already broken that several times.

I'd been trying (unsuccessfully) to dump Pax for the last 24 hours. Timing was everything and I wanted to break up with him before the media got wind of a cheating scandal. Then I'd disappear for a bit, under the guise of visiting my sister. Pax could step out with someone new, and I'd fade into the background, yester-day's news.

But, per the usual, Pax was even making breaking up difficult. He wasn't answering my texts or calls, probably because he was too busy with his new sidepiece.

"Seriously. This is the last and final boarding call." The ticketing agent shot me a pointed look. I was the only person still standing at the gate.

Taking the not-so-subtle hint, I wheeled my suitcase over to the kiosk and presented my ticket.

"Have a safe flight."

"Thanks," I said, juggling my shoulder bag and luggage.

As I made my way down the ramp, my shoulder vibrated. Crap. That could be Pax, finally calling me back. I rooted through my bag and managed to fish out my phone.

"Hello? Hello?"

Silence. I checked the screen. One missed call and it was from Pax.

"Damn it!" I immediately hit his name, calling him back. One ring, two rings, three, four. Pax's voice came on the line, "*You know what to do. Leave me a message.*"

"Hey, Pax, it's me, Bree. So, I saw your Instagram and it looks like you're with someone else. Not going to lie, I'm pretty upset and it's really uncool that you're not even answering my texts. But whatever. Obviously, you've moved on. I'm not going to stall here or anything, I'm just going to come right out and say it. We're—"

"*Good-bye.*"

Seriously? Even Pax's *voicemail* was too busy for me. I dialed him back. I needed to get this off my chest this instant, so I could move on with my life and avert career disaster.

Ring, ring, ring. *Beep.* "*Sorry, but the voicemail box is full. Call back later.*" And with that, I was automatically disconnected.

"Ugh!" I cried, shaking my phone. "All I want to do is dump you!"

I slammed my phone back into my purse and looked up. Two flight attendants flanked the doorway to the plane and they were both staring at me.

"Boyfriend problems," I explained, a hot blush creeping over my face. They both nodded knowingly.

"Girl, who doesn't?" The attendants whispered something to each other, then glanced back at me. The one on the right ushered me over and checked my ticket.

"You're in Seat 2B now," she said, winking as she took my ticket. "We ladies need to stick together. Enjoy your flight."

"Thanks," I said, smiling in gratitude. "I will."

Breaking up with Pax would have to wait until I landed. I intended to take full advantage of first class while I had the chance.

As soon as the plane touched down in Atlanta, I powered up my phone to a string of missed texts from Pax:

"Babe. It's not what you think w/ Keely. But if you want to pump the brakes, that's cool."

"Life is too short to be unhappy."

And my personal fave:

"Could you still pick my laundry up at the cleaners? Thx."

Asshole, I thought, collecting my rollaboard and deplaning. *What did I ever see in that jerk? He couldn't even bother to call, just left me a bunch of texts, like a freaking middle schooler.*

I sighed and shook my head, exasperated at my terrible choice in men. Like most of my clients, I blamed it on my parents. If my dad hadn't skipped out on us when I was only eight, maybe I'd be better at this relationship thing. Probably not, but maybe.

Making my way over to the rental car area, I signed my life away for the opportunity to motor around the greater Atlanta area in a mid-sized Chevy Malibu. I collected the keys, dashed off a quick text to my sister, Brooklyn, and hit I-85, happy to be away from the prying eyes of the paparazzi.

Three minutes after I arrived at my sister's, she tasked me with afternoon chauffeur duty for my niece. Destination: Pee Wee football practice. Fine by me—it kept me busy and, frankly, I didn't have much else to do.

"Alexa, do you have your mouthguard? Water bottle?" I asked, popping the car door open for her.

"Yes, Aunt Bee, see?" She held up her pink mouthguard and water bottle as proof.

"Great. Then let's go." I shoved her mouthguard into my handbag and clicked the lock button on my key fob, although I highly doubted anyone would steal my car.

After all, we *were* in Peachtree Grove, Georgia. AKA, Smalltown, USA, home of the Peach Cobbler Festival and approximately 10,000 people, most of whom were born and would die in Peachtree Grove. My sister and her husband were two of the few "newcomers," meaning they'd only lived here for the last five or so years. (They wouldn't be considered "locals" until Alexa had children, probably.) Brooks moved when Alexa was a baby so her husband, Dr. Craig Williams, could be closer to the hospital at Emory, where he was both a prominent doctor and a professor. When she'd first described Peachtree Grove to me, I thought she was exaggerating, but then I came to visit. It was definitely a shock to my jaded LA system. No flashy cars or movie stars here. Just high school football. Which, by the way, is an actual, legitimate season. Seriously. It's *printed on calendars*, like the 4th of July and Easter. In Peachtree Grove, Friday is for football, Saturday is for football, and Sunday is for church and football. Weekdays are for work and football practice. Rinse and repeat.

Which I guess is why my niece loves football. And why I now found myself standing on a plushy field with tons of other pee wee players and their parents, looking for the head coach of the—what did Brooks say the name of Alex's team was?—oh yes, the Lions.

Holding my hand to my forehead, I shielded my eyes from the sun. Even with sunglasses on, it was still too bright to see across the field. Ah, September in the South.

"Is that them, over there?" I pointed to a group of about ten kids on a big square marked with a #4 sign, two fields over on the right. "That might be the coach, wearing the blue shirt." His back was to us, but his jersey said "Coach." An excellent tipoff. I *so* had this aunt thing down.

"Yeah, that's my friend Cole." Alexa nodded, then took

off in a sprint towards the group, deftly dodging clumps of boys, all Alexa-sized.

"Wait up!" I called, doing my best fast walk across the fields. It was futile; she was already way ahead of me. *I should have worn sneakers. Oh well, at least I'm not wearing heels and I go to the gym.*

When I finally caught up to Alexa, I was a little out of breath and perspiration beaded on my brow. Flipping my hair over my shoulder, I fanned myself with one hand. I slid in with the group of moms hanging out on the sidelines, just behind the man in the blue Coach shirt. Alexa and all the other kids were in a big cluster, facing the coach.

"Okay, guys, it looks like everyone's here," the coach announced in a loud voice, doing a quick once-over of the Pee Wees.

"What's your name?" He pointed at Alexa.

"Alexa Williams," she said in a soft voice. The other kids chittered away, while Alexa stared down at her sneakers and kicked at a clump of grass.

"Hmmm, I don't see that name on my roster." The coach went down the names on his clipboard. "Oh, here. Alex Williams?"

She nodded up at him with wide blue eyes.

"I'm her aunt." I gave a little wave and stepped forward to clear up any misunderstanding.

The coach turned towards me and my breath caught in my throat.

Coach was drop-dead gorgeous.

He reached his hand out to me and I shook it, noting he had very large, strong hands. He was super tall, probably

6'3", and had deep marine eyes with long, dark lashes. Dark hair, cropped short, and he looked like he'd be ripped.

"Does she go by Alex or Alexa?"

"What?"

"Your niece. Does she prefer Alex or Alexa?" he asked, nodding in her direction.

"Oh. Um, Alex. Or Alexa. I think she likes Alexa." My voice trailed off as my cheeks burned. *Really, Bree? You don't even know which name your niece prefers?*

"I like Alex," Alexa piped up. "Call me Alex."

Coach grinned over at Alexa, showing off perfectly straight, white teeth. A dentist's dream.

"I'm Ryder, by the way. Ryder McCauliffe." He smiled at me and I noticed he had very cute dimples and a nice square jaw. This man was fine.

"I'm Bree. Bree Hart. Alexa's, er, Alex's aunt," I corrected myself, shoving my hands into my back pockets. *Super awkward.* "I'm gonna just stand over here," I motioned to the group of mingling parents, chatting with each other and ignoring me. "And watch."

"Sounds good, Bree." He grinned at me again as I backed away toward the sideline, torn between wanting to crawl into a hole and die or watch this beautiful man coach Pee Wee football.

Coach Ryder turned towards the Pee Wees. "Does everyone have their mouthguards?" Eleven kids nodded yes, while Alexa shot me a pointed look.

"Oh yes, I have that!" I fumbled in my bag, produced the mouthguard.

Running back out to the field, I handed it to my niece, willing myself not to trip or otherwise further embarrass myself. I felt Ryder's eyes on me. Swiveling back around, I wished fervently for the safety of the sidelines. I was clearly out of my league here.

"Okay, so guys, how many of you have played football before?" Coach Ryder asked the kids. All twelve hands shot up in excitement.

"Great! We're gonna be a great team then. And on my team—your team—we all have to follow a couple rules. My number one rule is be safe. How do you think we can do that?"

I filed that away; I'd have to tell my sister as soon as we got home. Safety first here at Pee Wee football!

Oh shoot, I never called her to tell her we got to the field. Grabbing my phone, I tapped out a quick text:

> Made it. We're all good. And Coach is HOT

I hit send and listened to Ryder talk about rule number two, be kind and show good sportsmanship.

> Brooklyn: What's coach's name?

> Bree: Ryder McCauliffe

> Brooklyn: THE Ryder McCauliffe?

> Bree: ????

> Brooklyn: You know. Former NFL Wide Receiver for the Dallas Cowboys. High school hotshot. Played at UGA, then drafted by Dallas. First round

Bree: Um, obvi I did NOT know or maybe would have taken more than like 10 secs to get ready

Brooklyn: You're definitely calling things off with Pax, right?

Bree: Yes. I mean, I tried. I *think* we're broken up

Brooklyn: He's single, you know. Wink-wink

Bree: I didn't ask

Brooklyn: You didn't have to. I'm your sister

Bree: Am I that transparent? Geez, I hope I have a better game face than that

Brooklyn: His kid is probably on the team

Bree: Wha-what?!?!

Brooklyn: Yeah, cute kid. Think his name is Charlie. Or something like that

Bree: So you're telling me this hot pro baller is a Single. Dad.?!?!

Brooklyn: Yep. Look around. How many very attractive women are attending football practice right now?

I glanced around and did a quick mental survey. There were several blondes in tight spandex leggings gathered together, another pretty brunette on her phone (snapping a photo or two?), and one intense dad with a clipboard, taking notes.

Bree: Yes, loads

Brooklyn: He's a local celeb. I'm sure women throw themselves at him. All. Day. Long.

Bree: I can see why

Inwardly, I groaned. Of course they would. And I'd embarrassed myself already, within the first two minutes of meeting the guy. Mental head smack.

"And our last team rule is to have fun. Because if we do all of those things, we'll be winners! Now I want you guys to put your hands in here, like this," Ryder demonstrated, dropping his hand into the middle of all the kids, "and on the count of three say 'Go Lions! Roar!' Ready? One, two, three!" All the kids yelled out "Go Lions" and did their best roar, which was adorable. Cue heart melt. I glanced around and noticed several of the moms videoing the speech. Oh brother. This guy was a freaking saint.

Ryder had the kids run some drills, so I took the opportunity to find my way to the bleachers and do a quick Google search. A few taps and I had the dude's (Wikipedia) life history:

Age: 32

Height: 6'4" (I shorted him an inch. Shame on me.)

Weight: 220 lbs

Position: Wide receiver

Stats: Football superstar at Peachtree Grove High School, helping lead the team to state victory with 18 touchdowns his senior year. Recruited by University of Georgia (2004-2008), where he played first string Wide Receiver all four years. Team went on to win Nationals. First round draft pick in 2008. Signed with Dallas, #18, where he continued to play wide receiver position. Five successful seasons as starter for Dallas, including one trip to Super Bowl. Shoulder injury in sixth season left him benched. Retired in 2014.

No mention of personal life, relationship, kid. A few more taps, though, and I had additional dirt.

Ryder McCauliffe and Dallas cheerleader Shayna Bowman tie the knot in lavish multimillion-dollar wedding

Ryder McCauliffe and Dallas cheerleader wife welcome son

Dallas Wide Receiver Ryder McCauliffe and cheerleader wife on the rocks

Dallas cheerleader Shayna McCauliffe files charges of domestic abuse against former pro player-husband Ryder McCauliffe

Former Dallas Wide Receiver McCauliffe calls it quits with cheerleader wife

Sounded like a train wreck. I clicked through the articles, taking in as much info as possible.

There were a few photos of Ryder when he was playing for the team, looking about the same as he did now.

An article about his shoulder injury, sustained during game eight of his sixth season with Dallas. Separated shoulder, requiring multiple surgeries. He sat the bench the rest of the season, then was cut from the team.

Then it looked like his life pretty much fell apart.

Domestic abuse charges filed, but he was later cleared of all charges. Divorce looming, nasty custody battle.

From what I read, it seemed like Ryder had full custody and the articles alleged possible substance abuse by Shayna. I zoomed in on every photo of her. She was pretty. Very cheerleader. Chesty. Dark, straight hair, wide smile, curvy in all the right places. Perfect abs. *Just like me*, I thought wryly. Dumb to even compare myself, we were nothing alike. She was taller than me, curvier than me, definitely bustier than me. I had long, blondish hair with a slight wave, her hair was stick straight, and in most photos she had bangs.

It seemed like she was in it for the money. As soon as Ryder got cut from the team, she started the separation proceedings, which led to the divorce. *Bad situation for his kid*, I thought.

Just for fun, I did a quick Google search on Shayna McCauliffe. The same articles popped up, plus her LinkedIn page, describing her as a Dallas Cheerleader/Lifestyle Expert. Interesting plot twist, considering the drug allegations. There was an article about her dating one of the League owners, as well as the Defensive Coordinator. The girl got around, and she definitely had a type. Rich, with athletic being a bonus.

There was only the one mention of their son, Charlie, in the article about his birth. None of the Shayna articles mentioned the child at all and there were zero photos of him. Seemed like Ryder did his best keeping his private life private. I respected that. It was one of my (many) issues with Pax.

"Aunt Bee! Aunt Bee!" Across the field, Alexa jumped up and down, waving me over.

"Coming!" I waved back to her and bounced off the bleachers, taking the steps as quickly as I could. Most of the other moms were already gathered around Ryder, hanging on his every word. I hoped whatever he was saying wasn't critical; I wanted to make sure I got all the information for Brooks. She'd get an email about it, though, right?

Just as I was closing in on our team's huddle, a sharp pain hit me in my left knee. Next thing I knew, I was flat on my back in the soft grass, staring up at the blue sky. *Hmmm, very few clouds today...*

"Are you alright?"

I blinked several times; I wasn't sure if the blurriness was from the sun beaming directly into my eyes or from the blow to the back of my head. Eventually, Ryder's eyes came into focus, tiny wrinkles of concern forming around them. *Cute...*

"Uh, yeah, I think so." I tried to sit up, but Ryder put his hand on my shoulder, gently keeping me still.

"Wait a few seconds. Trust me on this, lots of experience getting tackled." He winked and my cheeks flushed crimson.

"K," I murmured. "Um, what happened? Did I really get tackled?"

"Yeah. A nine-year-old laid you out. Not sure you're gonna make the first-round draft picks this year. You may need a little more work on your game," he chuckled, guiding me up by my elbow.

"How's that feel? Are you dizzy at all?" He gazed deep into my eyes, trying to gauge my concussion risk, I supposed.

"Aunt Bee, are you okay?" Alexa stood by my side, furrows creasing her brow.

"No, not dizzy. I'm fine. I'll be okay, Alexa." I waved my hands to brush off their concern and demonstrate my fineness. I bent my knees to try to stand and involuntarily let out a tiny whimper. "Ouch," I whispered under my breath.

"Let me take a look, I'm a physical therapist by day." He poked and prodded my knee, bending it this way and that. "You're going to need to ice that when you get home. That will minimize the swelling."

"Swelling?" I asked in a panicky voice.

"Yeah. That kid ran straight into your knee." He pointed to the side of my left kneecap. "You'll probably be okay, but it's going to bruise and you could have a microtear. Why don't you come into the clinic tomorrow and I'll take a closer look, reassess the situation?" Ryder tilted his head, waiting for my response.

"I'll be fine." I waved my hand again, brushing off his concern.

"I insist. Plus, I have a knee brace, or at the very least, a wrap to decrease swelling." He touched the side of my knee to demonstrate the wrapping motion and a tingle ran up my leg. That was a good sign, no numbness or loss of feeling. And clearly my libido hadn't sustained any injury.

"Okay, I'll come in," I said.

"Great. I'll give you my card and you can drop in around lunchtime. We're usually pretty slow then."

"Cool. I mean, great, thanks." I blushed, stumbling over my words. Maybe I did have a slight concussion.

Some of the other moms were shooting me dirty looks, like I'd ruined practice, and the kids were getting rowdy since the coach wasn't looking.

"You better get back." I nodded my head towards the group.

"Let me help you up." Deftly, Ryder leaned in and scooped me up, wrapping one of his arms around my waist and putting almost all my bodyweight onto his strong shoulders. The kids cheered; several of the blonde moms rolled their eyes. *So much for good sportsmanship*, I thought.

He gave them a wave with his right hand and together we limped to my rental car, Alexa trotting behind. My close proximity to Ryder helped block out the shooting pain in my knee. He smelled fantastic, crisp and clean, despite having run practice in eighty-five-degree weather. I'd been right about his hands—they were large and strong, supporting me at my waist. His pec muscles were straining underneath his shirt, yet he moved effortlessly through the parking lot, as if I weighed nothing. I tried not to swoon.

"This is it." I nodded at the white Malibu, fumbling in my purse for the keys. I had to lean into him to get to my purse and I fully appreciated his strong, muscled chest against my side. He gripped my waist tighter while I searched, so I wouldn't topple over.

"Here they are." I dangled the keys, unlocked the car.

"Are you alright to drive?" Ryder asked, concern clouding his eyes.

"Yep, perfectly fine," I nodded, stifling a wince. He opened Alex's door first, then mine, easing me down gently into the seat. His face was so close to mine, I saw his five-o-clock shadow. My breath hitched and we locked eyes for a moment. A frisson of heat shimmered down my body as I gazed at the darker navy flecks in his eyes.

"Sure you're okay?"

"Right as rain," I sing-songed in my most cheerful voice, nodding.

In reality, I could barely hear him over the thumping of my racing heartbeat. No, I was definitely *not* okay.

I was crushing hard on Peachtree Grove's most eligible bachelor, Ryder McCauliffe, former pro football player and hot-as-hell single dad.

Read RUSHING INTO LOVE now!

ALSO BY KARA KENDRICK

SEAGLASS BEACH SERIES

Unmistakable

Unstoppable

Unrivaled

Undone

PEACHTREE GROVE SERIES

Rushing Into Love

Turning Up the Heat

Chasing After Forever

WILD BROTHERS SERIES

Forever Wild

MAN OF THE MONTH CLUB: STARLIGHT BAY

New Year's Renovations

Love in Bloom

Stars & Sparks Forever

MAN OF THE MONTH CLUB: SYCAMORE MT.

Snowbody But You

MAN OF THE MONTH CLUB: CANDY CANE KEY

Reeling Him In

Lights, Camera, Christmas

MAN OF THE MONTH CLUB: MAGNOLIA PT.

Brides & Birdies

HOLIDAY NOVELLAS

Christmas in Cayman

Mr. Right Under the Mistletoe

My Charming Holidate

Snowed In With the Scrooge

BILLIONAIRE SERIES

Charming the CEO

Flirt Like a (Fake) Groom

HEART OF A WOUNDED HERO SERIES

Soldier On: Heart of a Wounded Hero

Find them all at www.karakendrick.com

ACKNOWLEDGMENTS

Deepest gratitude to all the people involved in helping me put this book out into the world:

My alpha readers, my sisters and mom; Valentine Grinstead and the entire Valentine PR team; James Gallagher, editor; Sarah Sentz at Enchanting Romance Designs; and my ARC team and all the bookstagrammers and bloggers who took a chance on me.

Last, but never least, thank you to my home team—Lance, Luke, and Kinsey. I love you all and am so grateful for the opportunity to pursue my passion. Xoxo.

ABOUT THE AUTHOR

Kara Kendrick writes fun and flirty small-town romance destined to give you all the feels. A reformed English major, she also has a master's in counseling and was an elementary school counselor in her pre-mom life.

She loves the beach, wine, and rock-hard abs, not necessarily in that order. When she's not dreaming up Happily Ever After's, you can find her chasing after her boy-girl twins, working out semi-hardish, or walking her adorable Shiba pups with her husband, who's not too bad himself.

Let's be friends! You can be the first to hear about upcoming releases, promos, and giveaways.

Find her at www.karakendrick.com